MUSIC
OF THE
Soul

SOULS OF CHICAGO #2

ANNABELLA
MICHAELS

Music of the Soul
Souls of Chicago Series #2

Copyright © 2016 Annabella Michaels

ISBN: 978-0-9989888-1-8

annabellamichaels.blogspot.com

Cover art provided by Jay Aheer of Simply Defined Art – www.jayscoversbydesign.com
Editing provided by Pam Ebeler of Undivided Editing – www.undividedediting.com

Proofreading provided by Judy Zweifel of Judy's Proofreading – www.judysproofreading.com

Interior Design and Formatting provided by Stacey Blake of Champagne Formats – www.champagneformats.com

Copyright and Trademark Acknowledgments

The author acknowledges the copyright and trademarked status and trademark owners of the following trademarks and copyrights mentioned in this work of fiction:

Boy Scouts of America
Silence of the Lambs: Orion Pictures
Chicago Fire Department
MTV: Viacom Media Networks
Andrew Christian Underwear: www.andrewchristian.com
Snuggie Blanket: Bright Eyes Blanket
GHOST: Paramount Pictures
Terms of Endearment: Paramount Pictures
Darth Vader "Star Wars": Lucasfilm LTD
Animal "The Muppets": Walt Disney Productions
People Magazine
Bruno Mars "The Lazy Song": Atlantic Records and Elektra Records
Charlie Puth (featuring Meghan Trainor) "Marvin Gaye": Atlantic Records
Charlie Puth "One Call Away": Atlantic Records
Nickelback "Satellite": Republic Records

OTHER BOOKS BY ANNABELLA MICHAELS

DEDICATION

To Aimee. For encouraging me to try new things, but mostly for your unwavering friendship. You get me in ways only an evil twin can.

PROLOGUE

Carter

I OPENED MY EYES AS I HEARD SOMEONE ENTER MY ROOM BUT quickly squeezed them shut again when the sunlight, that streamed through the large window, threatened to pierce my brain with its intensity. I hadn't gotten any sleep the night before, because the hospital nurses kept coming in and waking me up to check my vitals.

At first, my brain had been foggy about the details of the incident that had put me in the hospital, but the nurses explained that I had been injured in a fire at Romero's, the restaurant that my twin brother's boyfriend, Giovanni, owned and that I had required surgery on my arm. They wouldn't tell me anything else, insisting that the doctor would go over everything with me during his morning rounds.

I was exhausted, I didn't know what was wrong with my arm, I had a pounding headache, and my body hurt all over. If they hadn't reminded me about the fire, I would have assumed that I had been run over by a large truck. Needless to say, I was in a very foul mood by the time the older gentleman, wearing a white lab coat and a stethoscope around his neck, walked into my room.

"Hello, Carter. My name is Dr. White. How are you feeling this morning?" I looked at his gray hair and kind, brown eyes that crinkled at the corners as he smiled at me.

"I'm pretty sore and my head is killing me, but mostly I want to know what's going on with my arm." I tried to control the nervousness in my voice, but the compassionate way he looked at me, told me that I had failed.

Dr. White pulled a chair over next to my bed and sat, leaning forward with his arms resting on his knees as he looked at me seriously. "You were in bad shape when you got here last night. From what I was told by the emergency personnel who brought you in, a large beam fell on you, hitting your head and landing on your arm. You suffered from smoke inhalation and a concussion. The beam laying on your arm cut off the blood flow for an extended period of time, which resulted in some nerve damage to your lower arm and hand."

My eyes darted down to the splint on my arm. I couldn't see what damage had been done, because of the layers of bandages that covered me from my shoulder to the tips of my fingers. I felt my heartbeat speed up in my chest as I became more anxious. "How bad is it?"

Dr. White looked at me with a sympathetic expression on his face. I imagined working in a hospital emergency room had taught him how to deliver bad news to people in a gentle manner. Unfortunately, I didn't want gentle; I wanted answers. "We needed to do emergency surgery to try to keep the damage to the nerves from becoming permanent. We were able to successfully restore blood flow to the entire limb so the prognosis is good."

"Will I get the full use of my hand back?" I didn't recognize the sound of my own voice as panic began to set in.

"I can't say for sure, Carter. I'm sorry, I wish I could give you a more positive answer, but at this point you need physical therapy and time to heal. Those are your best options for regaining full mobility of your hand."

I felt a flash of anger. "You don't understand, I'm a musician. I have to be able to move my hand to play my instruments."

I watched as he stood and moved the chair back to its original position. "I know you're very disappointed that I don't have better news for you, but I really think that physical therapy will help you regain at least some of your mobility, if not all of it. You're very lucky to be alive, Carter. From what I understand, you were trapped in that fire for quite a while." I visibly flinched as his words brought back memories I wasn't prepared to deal with yet.

"Do you have any questions for me?" he asked kindly. I stared straight ahead, not trusting myself to speak. After a few moments of silence, he patted my shoulder. "Okay, well, I have to finish my rounds, but I'll stop by later to get you set up on a physical therapy schedule."

I didn't wait for him to leave the room before turning my back to him. I curled up into a fetal position on the bed as I tried to swallow down the panic building inside of me. I bit down on my uninjured fist as I fought against the scream that threatened to burst from my throat. Music was my life, my love, my passion. Being a musician was the only thing I had ever wanted to do with my life and I might have lost that dream. What the hell was I going to do if I couldn't use my hand? My head throbbed as the intensity of my headache surged forward once again with my building anxiety. I had never felt so angry and so utterly lost in my entire life.

I heard the door open again and glanced over my shoulder, hoping to see the nurse. I needed her to give me something for my head before it exploded. Instead, I saw a tall, gorgeous man with blond hair and broad shoulders. Something about him was familiar, but I couldn't place where I knew him from. Most likely I had seen him at the bar where my band played regularly. He stood nervously in the doorway, one hand gripping the door handle and the other holding a bouquet of flowers. A sudden wave of nausea rolled through my stomach as the pain in my head washed over me. I didn't have time to deal with a band groupie, no matter how gorgeous he was. My whole world had just imploded.

"Unless you're here to suck my cock, you can get the fuck out because I don't have any other use for you." I turned my back to the door, but not until I had seen him throw the flowers on the floor in disgust, a sneer marring his perfect features.

"It figures you'd be a total asshole."

I heard the door shut and breathed a sigh of relief. I had never treated anyone so terribly in my life, but I just couldn't make myself give two fucks. I had bigger problems at the moment than worrying about hurting the feelings of one of the many bar flies that circled around me and the other members of the band, just trying to get a taste of us so they could tell their friends all about it. We may not have been famous around the world, but we had acquired many fans in the Chicago area. Usually I loved meeting my fans, but not when I was lying in a hospital bed and certainly not when I was in the middle of a personal crisis.

An angel, disguised as a nurse, came in and injected something in my IV, which immediately began to take the edge off of the blinding pain in my head and downgraded it to a dull ache. "There you go, sweetie, that should help with your pain." I didn't respond, instead I curled up into myself as I tried to block out the rest of the world.

I closed my eyes and flashes of what happened the night of the fire danced behind my lids in jumbled pieces, as my mind tried to make sense of it all. The images became clearer and I was able to make out a wall of flames through the smoke filled room. I'm sure it was only the medicine that now ran through my veins that kept me from feeling the sheer terror I had experienced that night.

As I sifted through the memories, I recalled a man wearing a fire suit who lifted me in his strong, sure arms. I had felt the smoke burning my lungs and then I felt the gentle press of warm lips against my own. My eyes had fluttered open to see a man bent over me. He had beautiful bluish-gray eyes, soot smeared across his cheeks, and his blond hair was soaked with sweat.

My eyes popped open, horrified, as the memories came back in full force and I realized that the man I had just treated like a bar whore was the same man that had saved my life. I groaned loudly. *Fuck my life.*

CHAPTER
One

Carter

"OKAY, CARTER, STACEY WILL HELP YOU AS YOU FINISH your final reps of exercises and then I want to meet with you in my office. We need to discuss your progress and evaluate where we go from here."

I nodded at Trevor as I picked up the hand weight and sat down on the bench seat. "No problem, Trev, I'll just stay here and work hard while you hide in your office and eat bon bons, with your feet up on your desk."

He shook his head at me as he chuckled at my familiar teasing. "What will I ever do with myself when you're not around to give me crap any more, Carter?" I smiled at the 6'5" man who was built like a tank, with broad shoulders and huge biceps that threatened to rip the tight polo shirts that were his usual workplace uniform.

Trevor Sanders had been my physical therapist ever since I was released from the hospital and we had experienced many difficulties throughout our working relationship together, which I could honestly admit were my fault. I had come into his therapy center with a giant chip on my shoulder and a shitty attitude. All I had wanted was to return to my music as quickly as possible and I was pissed off at the entire world because no one could guarantee me that I would ever be able to play again.

Trevor was patient and understanding as he explained why it was important for me to take the time to not only build up my muscles, but to also meet with the onsite counselors to discuss what was going on in my head. He was sympathetic to what I had been through and understood that it was fear that caused me to lash out at him, but he never let me use any of that as an excuse to quit. Trevor had a great aversion to people who felt sorry for themselves and would push them harder and harder, until they remembered their own potential.

In the beginning of my therapy I hated him, but over time I began to see that he pushed me because he wanted to see me get my life back, almost as much as I did. Once I let go of my frustrations and started following his plan, I quickly began seeing improvement in my range of motion. Trevor was an incredible man and had become a close friend, but that didn't stop me from giving him shit every chance I got.

I finished my round of exercises and thanked Stacey for her help, then made my way through the large facility towards Trevor's office. I knocked on the door and heard his deep, rumbling voice. "It's open."

I poked my head in the door. "You wanted to talk to me?"

"Hey, Carter, come on in and have a seat."

He was looking intently through a file on his desk so I shut the door behind me and sat down across from him. His office was sparsely furnished, with a desk, two chairs, and a couple of filing cabinets. The only personal items were the pictures of Trevor and his husband, Greg, that hung on the walls and littered his desk. It was obvious how much the men loved each other and how happy they were together. The way they looked at each other reminded me of my brother and the man he had fallen in love with and I wondered, not for the first time lately, if there would ever be someone special for me. Trevor's voice shook me from my musings.

"I've been reviewing your file and I wanted to go over things with you." He looked at me, a slow smile spreading across his face. "Before I tell you what *I* think of your progress, I want to know how *you* think you're doing."

I leaned back in my chair and stared down at my injured hand, turning it palm up and then making it into a fist. I could feel the strength in my grip and my hand no longer shook with the stress of regular use. The constant burning sensation, that had plagued me when my therapy sessions had first started, was no longer present. "It feels much stronger. The tremors have stopped and I haven't felt any pain in it in over a month. I've already begun playing guitar again and it seems to be getting easier each day." I looked at him hopefully as I waited for him to give me his professional opinion.

I didn't have to wait long before I saw a smile spread across his face. "After your latest evaluation, I would have to agree. You've made an incredible recovery and I feel like at this point, your hand is back to its full mobility."

I stared at him silently for several seconds as emotions washed over me. There had been times when I thought that moment would never come. I worried every day that my life was changed forever and I would no longer be able to pursue my dream of having a career as a musician. My voice wavered when I tried to speak and I stopped to clear my throat. "So what does this mean? What happens now?"

Trevor gave me a fond look. "Now, you get out of here and start living your life any way you want. Now, anything is possible."

I nodded my head as we smiled at each other. "I can't ever thank you enough, Trevor. I don't think I would have gotten my life back on track if you hadn't been here to push me, even when I wanted to give up."

"You never really gave up, Carter, you just needed to move past your fears and remember what was worth fighting for. I was here to guide you, but the work you put in and the victory you have now is all yours. You should be very proud of yourself." Trevor came around the desk and reached his hand out to shake, but I slid my arms around him in a quick hug.

"Thank you," I whispered and then pulled away as I tried to discreetly wipe away the tears that had filled my eyes.

"If you ever need anything, you just call me, okay?" I smiled at him and turned to leave, but he stopped me before I could walk out. "Oh and, Carter, feel free to write a song about my amazing healing abilities when you're famous, alright?"

I laughed. "You've got it, Trev."

I walked down the hall and into the locker room, relief and a touch of pride making me smile widely. I grabbed a clean towel from the rack and headed into the showers, quickly washing away the sweat from my workout. I turned the water off and wrapped the towel around my waist as I made my way back out to my locker to get dressed.

A dark haired man was sitting on the bench near my locker and he looked up as I approached. He eyed me appreciatively, his gaze following the water that dripped from my hair and over the planes of my chest before getting trapped in the towel tied around my waist. He gave me a seductive smile and stood. He was very attractive, with dark, curly hair and hazel eyes. I felt a familiar stirring in my groin as he walked closer and stood next to me.

"You are gorgeous." He ran a finger down my chest until he stopped at my towel, which was beginning to tent. He looked up at me through his lashes and arched a brow at me questioningly. "You seem to have a problem developing. You want me to take care of it for you?"

My breath hitched as he covered my groin with his palm and pressed against it. My eyes fluttered closed and I leaned my head back against the locker as his lips began making their way down my neck. I could easily imagine him on his knees, the warm heat of his mouth engulfing my straining erection. I would fan my fingers through his blond hair and feed my cock into his mouth as he looked up at me, with lust clouding his bluish-gray eyes. My eyes popped open when I realized who I had been fantasizing about and I quickly stepped away from the man. "Sorry, I've got to go," I mumbled. He looked shocked, but I ignored him as I quickly threw my clothes on. I tossed my bag over my shoulder and raced out of the room, not bothering to look back at him.

I stepped outside and breathed in the cool night air, letting it fill my lungs and calm my racing heart. No matter what I did, I couldn't seem to get Ryan, the fireman who had saved me, out of my mind. I hadn't gotten laid since the fire and as much as I tried to tell myself it was because I was focusing all of my energy into healing my body, the truth was that I had become consumed with thoughts of Ryan. Every time I closed my eyes, I pictured his beautiful face, but it always ended up contorted in anger, much like the way he had looked at me in the hospital after I had spouted those vile words at him. Like each time before, I was filled with shame and regret. The man had risked his life to save mine and I had repaid him by treating him like he was trash.

My brother Caleb had told me how, out of a large group of firemen there that night, only Ryan was willing to risk going back into the fire to search for me; based solely on a feeling that Caleb had that I was in trouble. As identical twins we were often able to pick up on each other's feelings, particularly when they were strong emotions. When he had felt my fear and pain, he begged the firemen to search for me, but Ryan was the only one who would listen. He had saved my life that night.

Caleb had tried to convince me to call Ryan, if for no other reason than to thank him for saving me, but I was so ashamed of the way I had talked to him that I hadn't been able to bring myself to make the call yet. I blew out a long breath and climbed into my car.

It wasn't long before I pulled into the driveway of my parents' house. I had been the last one to leave the nest. My sisters each moved out when they got married, Landon had gotten his own place as soon as he graduated from college, and Caleb had left right after high school before heading off to Italy.

As a musician, I was always picking up odd jobs here and there so that I could concentrate on my band and be available whenever we were offered a gig. Without a steady income, my parents had insisted I stay with them so that I could build up some savings. After working as a waiter, construction worker, dog walker, and photographer - all while playing as many gigs as possible - I had finally saved enough money that I could afford a place of my own.

When Caleb offered to let me take over the lease of his apartment after he married Giovanni, I jumped at the chance. Of course, being the last one to move out meant I got the full brunt of Mom's empty nest syndrome, so I had been going out of my way to stop by as often as possible to help ease the transition.

I walked in the door and tossed my keys onto the small table in the entryway. I smiled as I saw my parents snuggled together on the couch while they watched TV. After thirty-two years of marriage, Rick and Kathy Greene still acted like newlyweds. They had never been shy about showing each other affection and they shared that demonstrative quality with their five children. I wasn't sure I had ever walked in the door of their house without receiving a hug from one of my family members.

They smiled when they saw me walk in and Dad muted the

television as Mom jumped up and wrapped her arms around me. "How was your day, baby? Are you hungry? I saved a plate for you in case you stopped by."

I hugged her back. "It was good and yeah, I'm starving. Thank you."

I followed her into the kitchen and slid onto a stool at the counter as she pulled a plate out of the refrigerator and began heating it up in the microwave. Dad squeezed my shoulder as he sat next to me. "How is your therapy going?"

I smiled widely at him. "I have some news to tell you guys." Mom turned to look at me, giving me her full attention. "Trevor called me into his office so he could go over my progress. He said I've regained full mobility in my hand and I don't need any more therapy. I can officially get back to my life." I suddenly found it difficult to breathe as I was engulfed in a tight hug from my dad. I soon felt Mom's arms wrap around us too and heard her gentle cries.

I laughed as I pulled back from them so that I could see their faces. "Are you okay, Mom?"

She laughed as she wiped at her tears. Dad slid his arms around her tiny waist. "I'm just so happy, Carter. I have prayed for this day ever since you got hurt and I can't believe it's finally happened. This is the best news ever."

Dad smiled at me. "I know what a struggle it was to fight your way back to where you are, but you did it. You knew what you wanted and you never gave up. That shows a lot of character and I'm very proud of you."

"Thanks. I couldn't have done it without all of the support everyone showed me. I'm lucky to have such a great family."

Mom set my dinner in front of me and I dug into the tender pork chop and warm baked potato as she poured me a glass of water. "We're just so grateful to still have you with us. It could have ended so differently if that wonderful man hadn't listened to Caleb." Guilt slammed into me once again and the food stuck in my throat as Ryan's angry face flashed into my mind with my mom's words. I pushed my plate away and took a long drink of water.

"Thanks for dinner, Mom, but I'm more tired than I realized. I think I'll just head on home for the night."

"Okay, sweetie, get some rest. I love you." I kissed her on the cheek and hugged my dad before grabbing my keys and heading out the door.

When I got home, I quickly brushed my teeth and washed my face before climbing into bed. I lay there for an hour, willing sleep to take over, but my mind swirled with thoughts of Ryan. With a sigh of frustration, I reached over to my bedside table and grabbed a pair of headphones. I plugged them into my phone and started my favorite playlist, then lay back on my pillow and closed my eyes. As the music filled my ears, I let it push out all other thoughts from my head. Music had always soothed me and I soon felt myself drifting off to sleep.

I hummed a song as I climbed down the steps of the cellar and stared at the racks filled with row after row of expensive bottles of wine. I ran my fingers over their smooth glass as I tried to find the ones that had been specifically requested by the customers. I had been working at Romero's for a couple of weeks and I really liked everyone I worked with.

I found one of the bottles I needed and cradled it gently in my arms while I searched for the next one. I'm sure those bottles cost a lot of money and I didn't want to risk dropping and breaking one.

I pulled another bottle out to check the label when something slammed into the back of my head and I fell to the floor. Pain burst through my skull as whatever had hit me rolled over my body and landed on my right arm, ripping my flesh as it slid. I was stunned and confused as I lay on the floor, trying to catch my breath.

I raised my head to look around, trying to make sense of what had happened and was shocked to find the room quickly filling with smoke. My head throbbed painfully as I attempted to lift myself up off of the floor, but something was holding me down. It felt like I was moving in slow motion as I looked at my right arm and saw a heavy wooden beam, laying across it. Blood dripped from the wound on my head, coating the back of my neck. My arm felt like it was on fire and I couldn't feel my fingers at all.

My eyes burned from the smoke that irritated them and panic began to take over as I heard screaming and what sounded like people running upstairs. I twisted my body and tried to push the beam off of me, but it refused to budge.

I struggled to breathe as my lungs filled with smoke and I felt my head swirling with pain and lack of oxygen. I called for help over and over, but the noises overhead and an unfamiliar roaring sound drowned out my cries.

I was quickly becoming dizzy and I knew I was running out of time before I lost consciousness. My muscles screamed in agony as I tried once again to free myself from the beam holding me down, but my efforts were futile and I slumped back against the floor in frustration. Tears of helplessness filled my eyes as I realized there was no way I was going to make it out of there alive.

I couldn't believe that was how my story was going to end. I had so many things that I had wanted to do in my life, but it seemed like I wasn't going to get that chance. Nobody knew I was down here and they obviously couldn't hear my cries because no one had come to look for me. Images of my family flashed through my mind and I fought back a sob at the thought of what my death would do to them. I prayed that Caleb and Giovanni had made it out safely.

The smoke was so thick that it choked me, cutting off my pleas for help. I pressed my face against the rough floor as I struggled to find clean air. The heat of the fire was unimaginable as flames began to lick at the walls around me. Terror shot through me at the sight of those *flames and I prayed that I would suffocate before they could singe my flesh. I couldn't imagine a worse death than burning alive.*

After a while, the screaming from upstairs stopped and I took comfort in the hope that everyone had found their way outside. My eyelids grew heavy and I had just started to drift off when I imagined I heard a faint noise.

I heard the noise once again, coming from my left. It reminded me of the raspy sound I had made as I breathed through my mask the time I went snorkeling with my family in the Bahamas. I idly wondered if Darth Vader was coming to rescue me and I started to laugh, but it came out sounding more like a whimper. I must have been very out of it if I was able to find anything humorous in that situation, maybe it was the lack of oxygen to my brain.

"Carter! Are you in here, Carter?" a muffled voice called out.

I turned my head slowly and saw a small beam of light sweeping across the room and I realized it wasn't my imagination, someone was really in there with me. I forced my eyes open all the way and tried to call out, but only managed to wheeze around the acrid smoke that filled my mouth.

"He's not here, man, we need to get out. This whole place could cave in any minute now." A second voice muffled through the darkness and I felt panic clawing at me as I realized they were going to leave. This was my last chance, I needed to get their attention and let them know I was here somehow. I moved my left hand, desperately searching the floor around me for anything I could make some noise with.

"No, he's in here somewhere, we have to find him. Just give me a few more seconds." I heard the first voice say and I swear it was the most beautiful sound I had ever heard. Whoever it was, he wasn't giving up on me and I wanted to weep with gratitude. I needed to help him find me before it was too late. My hand continued to sweep across the gritty floor until it hit upon something hard and smooth. I trailed my fingers along the object, recognizing the bottle of wine that I had been holding before I fell. It felt like it weighed a hundred pounds as I lifted

it with a shaky hand and slammed it with as much force as possible against the floor beside me. The sound of the shattering glass pierced through my aching head and I gasped in pain.

"He's over here and he's still alive." The flashlight beam hit my face and I squeezed my eyes shut against its brightness. A fireman dropped to his knees beside me as he quickly assessed the situation. "Where are you hurt, Carter?" I opened my mouth to answer him, but only managed to sputter as the darkness threatened to take over once again.

"Okay, just hang on. We're going to get you out of here. You are going to be just fine." My head dropped back down on the floor, too heavy for me to hold up any longer and my eyes fluttered shut in relief. I didn't know this man, but I instinctively trusted him to keep me safe.

I must have blacked out for a few minutes because the next thing I knew, I was free of the heavy beam and being lifted into a pair of strong arms and cradled against the man. "I've got him. You lead us out of here and I'll follow." He began climbing the steps with me in his arms as he bent his body over mine, shielding me from the fiery pieces of ceiling that rained down on us.

As he reached the top of the steps the whole building made a moaning, shuddering sound and a huge chunk of the floor fell away, taking out the steps we had just climbed. I looked up at him in shock and through the dirty mask on his face and the sweat dripping down his cheeks, I saw the most beautiful pair of bluish-gray eyes staring back at me and my heart tripped over itself.

"I've got you, I'll keep you safe." His deep voice soothed my frazzled nerves. I wanted to tell him thank you, but the blackness that had been threatening to pull me under, finally won and I felt myself plunging into unconsciousness.

I jerked wildly as I fell and then landed with a thud. I pulled the headphones from my ears and shook my head to clear it as I looked around at the familiar surroundings of my bedroom. I took a deep, shaky breath, relieved to be able to fill my lungs with fresh, clean air. I was drenched with sweat from the nightmare that continued to plague me several nights a week ever since the fire and I wondered for the hundredth time if I would ever have another peaceful night of sleep again. At least that one had ended well; most nights I dreamt that no one had come to rescue me and I could feel the flames as they licked over my skin. Those nights were the worst.

I sat on the floor and leaned tiredly against my bed as I waited for my pulse to slow and the remnants of the nightmare to clear completely from my mind. I looked at the sunlight streaming through my window and then glanced at the clock beside my bed, noticing the time. I grumbled to myself as I stood and made my way to the bathroom. I was going to need a lot of caffeine to make it through yet another day with hardly any sleep.

I fumbled with my keys as I attempted to unlock the door to the old building the band rented as a rehearsal studio. The door swung open and I grabbed onto the coffee that was slipping from my fingers. I stepped in, breathing in the familiar, musty smell of the building. I turned on the lights and a grin spread across my face at the sight of our instruments. I quickly set my things down on a nearby table and made my way over to the large piano in the corner of the room.

I slid onto the bench seat and ran my fingers over the smooth black and white keys. I pressed down on one, letting its gentle sound fill my ears. I had picked up my love of music at an early age. My grandparents had a piano at their house and I loved to play on it, making up silly songs about anything that interested me at the time. I had already learned to play the drums, so when I started on the piano, my parents, who wanted to encourage their "musical prodigy" as they called me, bought me a guitar to try out. I taught myself to play the guitar as easily as the other instruments. From the moment I touched each instrument, they simply felt like an extension of myself, almost like another appendage. I loved all instruments, but my favorite had always been the guitar.

I played a few songs and let the notes calm my frayed nerves, until I heard the door open behind me. I glanced over my shoulder and smiled as the other members of the band walked in, laughing at something. I had hand-picked each member of Carter's Creed, about five years ago, forming the best band possible. They were each extremely talented on their own, but when we played together, it was something akin to magic. It was an added bonus that we all genuinely liked each other, often choosing to spend time together outside of practices.

"Hey, man, what's up?" Steve grabbed me in a manly hug, slapping my back before making his way over to pick up his bass guitar.

Tyler and Kalia came in next and my eyebrows rose in surprise as I noticed they were holding hands. "This is new," I said with a smirk. We had all known for a long time that they were crazy about each other, but they had refused to admit it, insisting they were only friends.

"Just shut it, we've already heard enough out of these douchebags," Tyler said, but there was no heat behind his words. Kalia just smiled at me and shrugged her shoulders before she took her place behind her keyboard. I watched as Tyler placed a quick kiss on her lips and then walked over to his own guitar. Kalia sighed dreamily and her eyes followed Tyler as he moved across the stage. I smiled, happy for my friends that they had each other.

"I don't think I'm a douchebag, I just spoke the truth. I told him it was time he finally grew some hair on his balls and made a play for the woman he's been lusting after." Rocko smiled mischievously at me as Tyler threw something at him, barely missing his head. We all laughed, taking it for the teasing it was and Rocko went to the back of the stage and plopped himself down behind his drum set.

"Hey, guys, I've got something to tell you." I noticed they all looked at me with concern. "It's good news, so quit worrying. Trevor gave me the all clear yesterday; he says I'm back to normal." I laughed as they all cheered for me and Rocko gave out a loud whistle.

"That's awesome, man, but I'm not sure you've ever been what anyone would consider normal," Steve joked and I heard murmurs of agreement from my other bandmates.

"Fuck you, assholes." I laughed. It felt good to no longer have the dark cloud of uncertainty hanging over our heads. Finally, we could focus all of our attention on what we did best, creating music.

I picked up my guitar and began strumming a few notes, listening with a keen ear to make sure that everything was perfectly in tune. Satisfied, I nodded to Rocko who snapped out a count on his drum sticks and we began playing the new song that we had been working on the last time we practiced. I began to sing the words I had written and was soon lost in the music. That right there, was my heaven.

As the final notes played out, I opened my eyes and found my older brother, Landon, leaning against a wall with his arms crossed and a smile on his face. Landon had worked for a company that scouted out talented musicians, but he wasn't happy working for an agency, so two years ago he had started his own company that helped up and coming musicians and he had taken over the management of Carter's Creed. I was thrilled to know I had someone I could trust completely, watching my back and taking care of the business aspects so I could just focus on the music. Most musicians weren't that fortunate, especially at the beginning of their careers.

Landon clapped loudly as the last note ended. "Awesome song. You guys sound amazing."

I smiled at him widely. "Hey, what are you doing here?"

"I got a phone call today and I thought it would be best if I came here to talk to you guys in person."

"Is something wrong?" Kalia asked.

"Not at all," Landon assured her. "I got a call from Golden Entertainment Studios. Apparently, they had a scout come out and listen to one of your shows. He liked what he heard so much that he recommended you to his boss, Mr. Edwards, who called me to say that he'll be in Chicago next month and wants to hear you for himself. This could be your big break, guys."

I stood motionless as my bandmates went crazy around me. Golden Entertainment Studios held contracts with some of the biggest names in the music industry. The fact that they liked our sound enough to listen to us a second time was huge. I had waited so long for something like that to happen that I wasn't sure it was real. Landon came up and clasped the back of my neck. "Are you okay, Carter? I don't think I've ever seen you speechless before," he said, laughing at my shell shocked expression.

"Is this really happening, Landon?"

"It's real, bud. You've got a lot of work to do to get ready, but this is really happening." He hugged me tight and spoke quietly in my ear. "Mom told me the good news about your hand. Everything's coming together for you and I'm so proud of you, brat."

I hugged him back and clapped him on the back. "Thanks, Landon. For everything."

He smiled at me and then stepped back and smiled at everyone else. "Okay, you guys have a lot to do so I'm out of here. I'll let you know all the details once I have everything ironed out. Congratulations!"

When the door shut behind him, we all began to talk over each other in our excitement. Finally, we settled down and returned to our instruments to begin working again. I loved the fact that I didn't even need to remind them of what a big deal this was for us. They knew what the opportunity meant for us and they wanted it to work out just as much as I did.

Landon was right, it seemed like everything was falling into place for me and I was about to get everything I had ever dreamed of. So why did I have the nagging feeling that something was missing?

After an hour or so of practice, I hurried home to get ready for our gig that night. I jumped in the shower, letting the refreshing water revive my tired mind. As I soaped up my body, my thoughts once again returned to the night of the fire. I had been so sure that I was going to die down in that cellar; I would have never imagined getting saved from that situation. It had been a close call too, with the stairs collapsing as soon as we made it up them. Ryan not only saved me that night, but he also risked his own life to do it. He could have very easily become trapped in the cellar with me and died that night.

I leaned my forehead against the cool tiled wall of the shower as I let out a groan. Ryan was so brave and risked everything to help me and here I was behaving like too much of a coward to pick up the damn phone. Enough of this, I thought with determination. I turned off the water and wrapped a towel around my waist, not bothering to dry off. I hurried into my room, grabbed my wallet off of my dresser and sat on my bed with my legs crossed.

I flipped open my wallet and pulled out the card that was becoming worn from the many times I had held it in my hands. It had been in the flowers that Ryan had brought to the hospital. My fingers traced his masculine scrawl. *Hope you're feeling better. Ryan.* I stared at the phone number he had given me and took a deep breath, trying to push down my nerves. What was the worst that could happen? Most likely he would call me an asshole and tell me to never call him again, but hopefully, I would at least get the chance to thank him first.

I grabbed my phone and punched in his number. I hit send before I could change my mind and then held my breath as it rang several times. After five rings, I was about to hang up when a man answered. The voice sounded different to me, gruffer, with just a touch of a New York accent, but some of the details of that night were still a bit hazy. I cleared my throat nervously. "Um, hi. I was trying to get ahold of Ryan?"

"He's in the shower. Who is this?"

I felt flustered as I stumbled over my words. "This is Carter. Um, it wasn't important, I'm sorry to bother you." I hung up before he could respond and stared at my phone as I began pacing my room.

My heart was racing and I felt an unexplained sense of disappointment, as I realized that the man who had answered was most likely Ryan's boyfriend. I didn't know why I was letting it bother me. Ryan thought I was a jerk, so even if he was single, he most likely wouldn't ever want to speak to me again. Besides, he was probably just being nice when he brought me the flowers. Maybe he did that for everyone he rescued.

So why had he given me his number if he had a boyfriend? Was it just a friendly gesture since I had been through a traumatic event? Maybe he had just recently started dating the man and had been single when he gave me his number. I groaned at the thought that if I had treated him better when he came to see me, maybe he wouldn't have gotten together with this other guy. I felt the stirrings of jealousy and laughed at how ridiculous I was being. I had no claim on him and besides, I wasn't even sure Ryan was gay.

Convinced that I was being an idiot, I stood up and threw on a pair of jeans and an old band t-shirt. I combed my fingers through my mostly dry hair and grabbed a beanie to pull over my head before checking my reflection in the mirror. My green eyes had dark smudges under them from my restless night and my lips were tilted down in a frown. I shook my head and forced a smile on my face.

I should throw away Ryan's card and forget about him. I chuckled ruefully as I remembered that as a fireman, Ryan saved people all the time. It was egotistical to think that I could have made the same impact on his life, that he had made on mine. I was being ridiculous and it was time to move on. I had just gotten the all clear from Trevor and I needed to focus all of my energy on my music and getting ready for Mr. Edward's visit.

I slid my phone in my pocket and scooped up my wallet. My gaze landed on the card laying on my bed and I picked it up and held it over the trashcan. My hand hovered there for a moment, my eyes taking in each word before I slid it back into my wallet with a sigh and made my way downstairs.

CHAPTER
Two

Ryan

I CLIMBED IN THE SHOWER AND LET THE HOT WATER WASH AWAY the aches and pains of the day. As a full time fireman for the Chicago Fire Department, I made sure to keep myself physically fit at all times in order to keep up with the demands of the job, but the physical tests they had put us through that day still managed to kick my ass. Every fireman dreaded the renewal tests which included hauling 200 feet of hose over his shoulder for long distances and crawling through cramped spaces with very limited visibility. It was all part of the job though, so we gritted our teeth and pushed forward. I had passed with flying colors, but I would bear the bruises and muscle soreness for several days to come.

I stood there until the water turned cold then quickly rinsed the soap from my body and climbed out, reaching for a towel to dry off with. I wrapped the towel around my waist and stepped out from behind the wall that served as a privacy divider for the bathroom area of my loft home.

I had inherited the old two-story warehouse from my grandfather when he died. He bought the large building and had used it to make his fortune, running a textile company until the early eighties. That's when it had shut down in favor of overseas processing, along with most of the other businesses in the area, leaving this portion of the city a virtual ghost town.

We had lived in the house he had shared with my grandmother and so the place had sat empty until he left it to me when he died unexpectedly, right before my high school graduation. I had always loved the old building and had used a small portion of my inheritance as well as the money from the sale of the house to fix it up, turning it into my home.

The top floor was set up as my private living quarters and I had done most of the work myself, refinishing the original hardwood floors and restoring the old wooden beams that ran along the ceiling and stood as posts in the center of the room. I had chosen an open floor plan so that when you entered, you could see everything at once, from the fully equipped kitchen with high-end appliances and granite counter tops, to my bedroom area with the large California king bed. I had painted the walls in neutral colors and decorated my home with antiques that I found at the many flea markets and estate auctions I liked to visit on the weekends.

The first floor had been set up as a personal gym and game room, complete with pool table, poker table, dart board, and a well-stocked bar. I was thrilled to discover that the ancient elevator still worked, but it was very slow and so I had also installed a spiral staircase to move back and forth between floors more quickly.

I loved spending my free time working on new projects around my house. My latest home improvement plan was designing an outdoor kitchen and garden area on the roof of the building. It offered an incredible view of the Chicago skyline and I wanted to be able to sit up there after work and enjoy the fresh air.

I was very grateful that my grandpa had left me so much in his will, but I would have gladly traded it all for more time with him. He had been the most important person in the world to me, the only one to ever show me unconditional love and I missed him every single day. Shaking off the melancholy I felt when I thought of him, I made my way to the bedroom, dropped my towel on the bed, and stood naked while I rummaged through the closet for something to wear. A deep voice made me jump and I spun around to find Joe standing behind me. He waggled his brows at me suggestively. "I bet that ass brings all the boys to the yard."

"Jesus, Joe, you scared the shit out of me. What are you doing here? And quit staring at my ass or I'll tell Suzy you've decided to switch teams," I joked. Joe was my best friend and a fireman like me. We had met during training and immediately hit it off. We were thrilled when we were assigned to the same fire station and had been working together for the past six years. Even though he had taken me by surprise, we had keys to each other's houses and often stopped in unannounced so he knew I wasn't upset that he had let himself in.

Joe had married his high school girlfriend three years ago. Suzy was a nurse at a local nursing home and was the sweetest woman I had ever met. Lately however, she had decided that I shouldn't be alone anymore and had made it her mission to find a man for me. She had attempted to set me up on two disastrous blind dates until I threatened to quit speaking to her. She knew it was all bluster though, they were like family to me and I knew how fortunate I was to have them in my life.

"Suzy's working the night shift and you know I hate being at home alone, so I thought I'd see if you wanted to go out for a beer or something. You know, since you have no life."

I flipped my middle finger at him, making him laugh as I traded the worn shirt I was getting ready to pull on for a new gray t-shirt, since I was apparently going to be leaving the house. "I have a life, asshole."

"Spending your days off wandering around a home improvement warehouse, is *not* a life, my friend. You need to get out more, meet some really hot guys and have a lot of sweaty gay sex." I stared at him for several long moments, just blinking at him. "What? I'm a supportive friend," he said defensively. I continued to stare at him until he broke, which I had learned worked every time. "Okay, Suzy made me promise to help you find somebody while we're out tonight."

I looked at him with disbelief. "Suzy wanted you to help me find someone to have sweaty gay sex with?"

He cringed. "Hell no, she wants you to find someone to fall in love, get married, and have babies with. I thought it would sound better if I focused on the sex part of it."

I chuckled at his innocent expression. Joe was the only person I worked with who knew I was gay and I appreciated that he never treated me any differently. There were some people at the firehouse that would have a problem with finding out that one of their own was gay, which could lead to serious consequences when trying to work together in life or death situations. I had chosen to tell Joe the truth since he was my best friend, but it wasn't worth the risk to tell anyone else at work and honestly, it was no one's business.

"Thanks, but I don't need your help getting laid; or finding a boyfriend for that matter. Tell Suzy I love her for trying, but I'm fine being by myself until someone special comes along."

He eyed me suspiciously as I moved to the kitchen and grabbed my wallet off of the counter. "So, there's no one special in your life already?"

"If there was, you'd be the first one to meet him. Why?" I pulled a bottle of water out of the fridge and took a long drink.

"Because, your phone rang while you were in the shower. I answered in case it was someone from work, but it was some guy looking for you."

I raised a brow at him. "What did he say?"

"He asked for you, but when I told him you were in the shower he said it wasn't important and hung up."

"Did he give you a name?"

Joe's eyes widened. "Shit, Suzy always tells me to write stuff down so I don't forget. I swear, I feel like I'm seventy years old sometimes; I can't remember anything anymore. I think it's because I've got too much going on up here," he said, tapping his head.

I rolled my eyes at him. "Yeah, somehow I don't think that's the problem, Joe," I teased. "Now focus, what was his name?"

He shrugged at me apologetically. "Um, something with a C. Maybe it was Connor? Chris? Carter! That was it, Carter." He snapped his fingers as he remembered.

I choked as the water I had been drinking went down the wrong way. There was only one person I knew by that name. The man I hadn't been able to get out of my mind since I had pulled him from a fire.

I had met Carter's identical twin as well that night and while he was beautiful, I hadn't felt anything except complete focus on the job at hand. One look at Carter Greene however, had knocked me for a loop. I vividly recalled his bright green eyes shining at me as the light from my flashlight found him in the darkened room. Even covered in blood and soot, the man was stunning. I couldn't explain it, but I had thought I had felt some sort of connection to him that night; almost as if I had always known him.

I turned my back on Joe so he couldn't see the blush on my face as I remembered how I had stood stupidly, holding a bouquet of flowers in Carter's doorway at the hospital, only to have him yell at me to suck his cock or get out. The guy obviously wasn't interested in anything beyond one night if he would say that to a virtual stranger. Even though I didn't want praise for doing my job, I could admit to myself that it stung that he would act like I was completely meaningless to him. I still didn't understand how I could feel such disappointment in someone I barely knew.

"Must've been a wrong number."

"A wrong number that asked for you by name? Is that really what you're going to go with?" Joe smirked at me. "Come on, Ry. Who was he?"

"I honestly don't know. There's only one man I know of by that name and he would never call me. *Ever*." Joe levelled his stare at me and I knew he wasn't going to let this go. I sighed loudly. "Come on, let's get going; I'll tell you all about it on the way."

After I had filled Joe in on what had happened with Carter at the fire and later at the hospital, my mind was spinning, so I let him choose which bar to go to. I didn't really care as long as they served cold beer to help soothe my frazzled nerves. The day had been physically exhausting and my heart was racing at the possibility that Carter may have called me.

Why would he possibly want to talk to me? He had made it very clear at the hospital what he thought of me and I had made my feelings equally as clear when I walked out. So, why bother contacting me after so many months if all he wanted was a quick fuck? Besides, one look at his stunning body proved that he could get that anywhere.

How the hell did he even get my number? I had thrown the flowers on the floor, not even making it fully into the room to give them to him, so he wouldn't have seen my number on the back of the card. I gave myself a mental slap. What difference did it make? We were obviously looking for different things and for all I knew, it wasn't even him that had called. Joe wasn't positive he had gotten the name right, so it may not have even been someone named Carter.

Convinced that it had all been a mistake, I climbed from Joe's car as he parked in the lot behind a bar. I hadn't been to that place before, but had heard several of the guys at the station talking about the great live music that pulled in big crowds several nights a week.

It was much bigger and nicer inside than it appeared from the outside. The bar itself took up the entire left wall, while a dance floor stood off to the right. The large space in the middle of the room contained tables and chairs, which were currently filled with customers who were drinking and talking animatedly as they unwound from a long day of work. A stage stood empty at the front of the room, but I noticed the instruments already set up around it and wondered if there would be live music that night.

I followed Joe as he made his way through the crowd, to a table near the back. A waitress came and took our drink orders, before disappearing into the fray of people. "Wow, this place is really busy for a weeknight. I can't imagine what the weekends are like."

"Nah, it's always busiest whenever the band's playing. They get a lot of talent in here, but I've heard that the band that's here tonight is the best. Suzy's been dying to hear them play, she'll be disappointed she missed it."

I was going to ask him what the name of the band was, but the waitress brought our drinks and then the lights went out, except for over the stage, where spotlights streamed down over each instrument. An excited buzz filled the room as people started looking towards the stage. I sat up straighter in my chair, wanting to see what all of the fuss was about.

I took a long pull from my beer as a short, balding man took the stage and spoke into the microphone. He made some sort of introductory speech, but it was difficult to hear over the noise of the crowd. He exited the stage and the excited murmurs reached a fever pitch as the members of the band walked out and picked up their instruments. It was obvious with the crowd's reaction that the band had a huge fan base, at least in Chicago.

The drummer had lots of tattoos and jet black hair that reached down to his waist. One of the guitarists was tanned with curly brown hair, while the other had pale, freckled skin and shaggy red hair that flopped into his eyes. Standing behind the keyboard was a tiny woman with short, spiky black hair and lots of colorful tattoos, easily visible with the sleeveless sundress she wore. She smiled at the red-headed man in a way that made me think perhaps they were more than friends.

The crowd quieted down as the lights went off on the stage, plunging the room into complete darkness except for the emergency exit lights. Suddenly, a voice filled the room and the tiny hairs on the back of my neck stood up. Singing the first few notes of the song without any accompaniment, was the sexiest, most seductive voice I had ever heard and it sent a jolt of electricity straight to my dick.

I was shocked at my reaction; I had never gotten hard over the sound of a stranger's voice before, but this one held the perfect blend of smoothness and rasp. I strained my eyes, willing them to see through the darkness and find the owner of the mesmerizing voice. Soon the band joined in as lights flooded the stage and I had trouble catching my breath as I stared up at, none other than, Carter Greene.

"They're awesome, aren't they?" Joe said loudly, so I could hear him over the music. He did a double take at my wide-eyed expression. "What's wrong, are you sick?"

I reached across the table for the flyer that was stuck under the bowl of peanuts. *Carter's Creed* was the name of the band. Unable to form a coherent thought, I slid the paper over to Joe. He looked at it and then looked up at the band, then back down again before his eyes widened and he swung his gaze to mine. I simply nodded before turning back to watch Carter.

Carter could easily turn any head in the room, but on stage, he was magnetic. The entire crowd, women and men alike, were putty in his hands as he worked the stage like he owned it. His obvious talent left me speechless. He played the guitar as if it was a part of his soul and I stared, transfixed on his expert fingers as they smoothed over the strings; wondering what it would feel like to have them moving over my skin instead.

The song ended and I held my breath, waiting for them to start another. As he began to sing again, I studied the way he interacted with the crowd. Carter was even more beautiful than I remembered and he used his raw sex appeal on stage to draw in his fans. Grown women were giggling and fanning themselves like school girls and more than just a couple of men were making their way closer to the stage, trying to catch his attention for even a few moments.

My heart sunk as I confirmed for myself that there was no way that the phone call earlier had been from *that* Carter. That Carter could have the pick of nearly every person in the room and was probably fucking somebody different every night. He didn't have to go looking to get laid, people were practically lining up to give themselves to him. He probably had thought I was one of his many adoring fans when I showed up at the hospital. Feeling nauseous at the thought, I decided to call it a night and go home.

After a few minutes, I told Joe that I was going to head out and he insisted on going with me. As we stood to leave, the song ended and Carter's head turned in my direction. Our gazes connected and held as I tried to remember how to breathe. His eyes widened in surprise and then a slow grin swept over his face. I scowled and hurried out of the bar, not slowing down until I reached Joe's car. As much as I had hoped to see Carter again someday, I refused to be just another notch in his belt.

CHAPTER
Three

Carter

I PEEKED MY HEAD OUT FROM UNDER MY BLANKET AND SQUINTED my eyes at the clock by my bed. I had woken up later than usual, but I felt like I had barely slept for more than a couple of hours. Every time I closed my eyes, I would see Ryan's face, the way he looked at me that night, right before he stormed out of the bar. I had been surprised to see him there and I would have given anything to get a chance to talk to him, but the look of disgust on his face told me exactly what he thought of me. Besides, it wasn't like I could have jumped off of the stage, in the middle of a set, to chase him down.

He looked sexy as sin though, with his t-shirt stretched tightly across his well-defined chest and jeans that showcased his sculpted thighs. The man was a genuine hero, who could easily be a cover model for a men's fitness magazine, and I had zero chance of getting to know him. I rubbed my hands over my face in frustration. Why the hell was I so obsessed with the man? I was acting like I wanted to date him, but I didn't. *Did I?*

I had always been known for being kind of a playboy; always out looking for the next guy, not afraid to try new things both in and out of bed and basically never taking life too seriously. So what had changed? The answer to that was easy: watching my brother fall in love. Seeing how happy Caleb and Giovanni were together, the way they worked as partners in every aspect of their lives and the joy they found in simply being near one another, had me longing for something more meaningful in my own life. *What would it be like to have a man that I wanted to spend the entire night with once the sex was over?*

Unfortunately, the look Ryan shot me that night had made it abundantly clear that he wanted nothing to do with me and I had no one to blame but myself. If I was going to give being in a relationship a try, it was going to have to be with someone other than the sexy fireman.

With a loud sigh, I climbed from my bed and pulled on an old pair of sweatpants and a ratty t-shirt that was made up of more holes than actual material. I wandered down the hall to the kitchen and poured myself a bowl of cereal. My apartment was peacefully quiet and I took a few minutes to revel in the solitude. I loved performing my music and I appreciated all of the fans that came to our shows and cheered for us, but once in a while I just needed to take a step back and have a moment to myself.

I decided to eat my breakfast on the fire escape. It was a beautiful day and I tilted my head back, enjoying the hot sun as it beat down on me, warming my skin. My phone rang in my pocket, startling me. I smiled when I saw my mom's face pop up on the screen.

"Hey, Mom! What are you up to?"

"Hi, baby! I'm with your dad. Say hello, Rick."

"Hey, son! We're talking to you without holding a phone. I just had to say your name and the car called you all by itself. Isn't that cool?" I chuckled. My parents had finally sold the old beat up family van they had been driving since Caleb and I were born and purchased a brand new sports car. They were still getting used to all the bells and whistles that came with the newer cars, but were most excited about having Bluetooth for the first time.

"We were down at the market, getting some fresh fish. Will you be coming over for dinner, sweetie?" Mom asked.

"Probably not, I'm going to head over to Agape House as soon as I get a shower and then I'll probably go practice for a while. I have a new song I've been working on and I need to get the lyrics down."

"Oh, I almost forgot. Your father and I signed up for a couples pottery class, so we won't be home tomorrow night." I wondered for a minute if they were joking. Was couples pottery even a real thing? Neither one of them laughed though, so I assumed they were telling the truth.

"Maybe we can recreate the scene from "Ghost" later." I heard Dad whisper and Mom started giggling.

I decided to cut them off quickly before any more damage could be done to my psyche. "Okay, that's definitely my cue to hang up. I'm going to take a shower. If you hear screaming from wherever you are, don't become alarmed, it's just me, bleaching my brain to rid it of the mental image you just gave me."

I heard my parents' laughter as I ended the call and I shook my head. *So much for my peaceful morning.*

I pulled into a spot in the parking lot behind Agape House, a center for local LGBTQ teens, many of whom were diagnosed HIV positive, had been abused, or became homeless once they came out to their families. Agape House was a safe place for them to go and get the help they needed to start living the lives they were meant to. It was an outstanding place that offered unconditional love to those who had never experienced it before. My whole family had volunteered there at one time or another, either tutoring the kids with their schoolwork, teaching them how to cook, or simply cleaning and doing maintenance around the building.

For the past year, I had been going there to entertain them with my music and to teach whoever wanted to learn how to play various instruments. The interest in my class had been building and I had recently begun looking into the cost of purchasing some more instruments that I could donate to the center. Many of the teens who came to Agape House had endured more pain and trauma in their young lives than most people would in their entire time on earth and if I could give them just a small measure of joy by teaching them to play music, then I was more than happy to do that.

I saw Caleb as he walked up the front sidewalk and I decided to tease him. "What are you doing here, man? I figured it would be at least another week or two before you saw anything outside of your bedroom walls. Married life boring you already?" It had always been very easy to make my brother blush, especially when the topic centered around sex, and he did not disappoint as his face turned a nice shade of crimson.

He playfully punched my arm. "Shut up, asshole. There is absolutely nothing boring about my marriage or what happens in our bedroom." A dreamy look crossed over his face and I knew he was thinking about his gorgeous husband.

As happy as I was for my twin that he had found his soul mate, I couldn't help the twinge of jealousy I felt as I wondered if I would ever find a love like he had with his husband. I would never begrudge Caleb his happiness, but I wouldn't mind having just a piece of it for myself too.

"Are you working here today?"

"Yes. Today's my day off at the restaurant and the condo is too quiet without Gio there, so I decided to come in and see what I could do to help."

We walked in the front door and I took a minute to let my eyes adjust after being out in the bright sunshine. I heard the sounds of a group of kids playing basketball in the gymnasium, their laughter and playful teasing spilling out into the other rooms.

Isaac, the front desk manager, looked up at us with a frazzled expression. He was a gorgeous young man with a soft voice and a sweet smile. He always seemed nervous though and I often wondered what had happened to make him so skittish. The only thing I really knew about him was that he used to be one of the teens that needed the refuge the center provided.

"Hi, Isaac, is everything okay?" Caleb asked gently.

The phone on Isaac's desk rang before he could answer and he sent us an apologetic look. "Do you guys mind waiting over there for just a second? I have a bit of a crisis on my hands. I'll be right with you after I take this call."

"No problem, take your time." I walked with Caleb over to a set of chairs at the front of the building and sat down. "I wonder what that was all about?"

"I don't know. When he gets off the phone we'll see what we can do to help with his crisis." Caleb tilted his head as he looked at me. "What's wrong? You look tired and stressed about something and I'm feeling weird around you."

"Maybe that's because you *are* weird," I teased.

He jabbed his elbow into my ribs. "You know what I mean, butthead."

"I haven't been sleeping well so yes, I'm tired." He stared as he waited patiently for me to continue. Realizing it would be useless to try to keep anything from him, I continued. "I called Ryan."

It was almost comical the way Caleb's eyes bugged out of his head. "Do you mean hot fireman, Ryan?" He squealed excitedly. "I had almost given up hope on you ever calling him. What did he say?

Did you apologize for what happened at the hospital? Did you thank him for saving your life?"

I held up my hand to stop him before any more questions could spill out of his mouth. "I didn't get the chance. Some guy answered, probably his boyfriend because he mentioned that Ryan was in the shower." Just saying the words made a scowl appear on my face and Caleb put his arm around me. Caleb knew that my interest in Ryan ran a little further than just gratitude.

"I'm sorry. Did you at least ask him to call you back?"

"No, I chickened out and hung up. Then last night I was playing a gig at the bar and there he was, out in the audience. He was with some guy and as soon as he saw me he gave me a nasty look and walked out." I couldn't disguise the disappointment in my voice.

"That sucks, Carter. I know how bad you feel about what you said to him, but I also know you never would have said those things if you hadn't just received devastating news."

"That's still no excuse for treating him so terribly. Especially when he had just risked his life to save mine."

"Maybe the next time you call, he'll answer and you'll be able to clear the air."

I looked at my brother like he had just grown a second head. "Hell no, I'm not calling him again. He made his feelings towards me all too clear last night and it made me realize that it was way past time to put this whole thing behind me. I've already moved on, plenty of other fish in the sea and all that shit." I folded my arms over my chest to show him I was serious.

Caleb held his hand out in front of me, palm up. "If you've already moved on, then you won't mind showing me your wallet so I can check to see if you threw away the card he gave you, with his number on it, right?"

"Shut up," I grumbled as Caleb smirked at me knowingly. Brothers sucked sometimes.

Isaac hung up the phone and came around his desk to see us.

He seemed even more nervous than usual as he stood in front of us, wringing his hands.

"What's going on, Isaac, and how can we help?" I felt bad for him as his eyes filled with tears.

"I've messed everything up and Matt is going to be so disappointed in me."

I exchanged a look with Caleb. Matt was the person who had started Agape House. He was a quiet and kind man, who fiercely advocated for the teens in his care. I couldn't picture him ever getting upset with someone who was as gentle and sweet as Isaac was. "Why don't you tell us what the problem is and maybe we can figure out how to fix it."

Isaac took a deep breath, calming himself before he spoke. "Matt had a great idea for a fundraiser for the center because, as you know, there's never enough money to keep this place running; no matter how hard Matt works." We nodded our heads, we knew how tight the funding was for a place like Agape House. Government leaders didn't want anything to do with helping LGBTQ teens who were too young to vote for them in the next election and most of society made the bulk of their charitable contributions around Christmas, when they happened to think of the less fortunate. That left the rest of the year for Matt to scramble, as he tried to find creative ways to raise the necessary funding to keep the center running.

I shook my head at my thoughts and then realized Isaac was still talking. "So anyway, I have all of the guys waiting and I forgot to schedule a photographer. Now there's no way we'll get it done and Matt won't have the funding he needs to keep the center going."

Caleb put his arm around Isaac, who was now sobbing. "It'll be okay, Isaac, I promise," he said soothingly.

"How?" Isaac wailed into his hands.

Caleb was quiet for a minute as he tried to think of a solution. Suddenly, a wide smile split his face and I squirmed in my seat, wondering why he was looking at me like that. "Carter!" he exclaimed.

"What?" Isaac and I said at the same time as we looked at Caleb in confusion.

"Carter has worked as a photographer before. He can go there and take the pictures and Matt will never know there was a problem."

My eyes widened in shock. I was in no way a professional. Photography had always been more of a hobby for me, except for the year I was hired to take children's school pictures, which had ended in tears and no, it wasn't the children's tears. Thanks to my rambling thoughts, I wasn't even sure what I was being asked to take pictures of.

"Oh, Carter, thank you so much. You have no idea how you've saved the day." I looked from Isaac's relieved face to my brother who was wearing a devious grin.

"Sure, no problem." I murmured to Isaac, narrowing my eyes at Caleb suspiciously.

"I'll call and let them know you're on your way over. They'll be waiting for you," Isaac said excitedly.

"Wait, what? I'm going *now*?" I turned to Isaac, who was already running down the hall and calling over his shoulder that he'd be right back with a camera. I turned to glare at Caleb, who still looked at me like he was in on a great joke. "What the hell did you just volunteer me for?"

He shook his head at me. "I knew you weren't listening. I told Isaac that you'd help with the fundraiser, by taking pictures for the calendar."

I sighed. "Oh, okay. So what do I need to take pictures of? Nature? Kittens?"

Caleb started to laugh harder as he backed away from me. "It's not that kind of calendar, Carter. It's a sexy calendar…of local firemen."

My eyes felt like they were going to fall out of my head, they were opened so wide. "You've got to be kidding me. I can't do this," I hissed at him. "Seriously, Caleb, what if Ryan's there? You have to go for me. It's not hard, just aim and shoot."

Caleb walked back towards me when he felt my panic. He wrapped his arms around me and rubbed soothing circles on my back. "It will be fine, Carter, I promise." He stepped back to look me directly in the eyes. "I hope Ryan is there, because I think you need this, if for nothing else than to get some closure. You need to tell him you're sorry for what you said and you still need to thank him for saving you. Now you can do both and he can't walk away from you because he has to sit still for the picture." He smiled at me triumphantly as I shook my head at him, still unsure.

I opened my mouth to give him another excuse when Isaac came bounding into the room, all smiles as he handed me a black, professional looking camera bag. "Thank you so much, Carter, you're a real life-saver."

"Um, Isaac, the thing is…" I started to say, but he interrupted me as he grabbed my arm and dragged me towards the door.

"Okay, they're waiting for you so you need to hurry. Just go to the station right down the street from here. Thanks again, Carter." Isaac gave me a kiss on my cheek and shoved me out the door. I looked back through the window, not quite sure how I had just ended up in that mess. I saw Caleb waving to me with a toothy smile on his face, I would have to remember to kick his ass later.

My heart was racing and my palms were slick with sweat as I walked up to the firehouse. How had I had the guts to perform in front of thousands of strangers over the past few years, but the thought of coming face-to-face with one particular man scared the shit out of me?

If it was for anything other than to raise money for Agape House, I would have told Isaac to forget it, but there was no way I could refuse when the money raised would help keep the center's doors open. There were too many kids out there that needed a place like Agape House, so I would push down the dread that threatened to choke me and do it for them. *Get your shit together, Carter. You can do this. Besides, this may not even be Ryan's firehouse.*

The giant garage doors were open, revealing three sparkling clean fire trucks. I felt very small and more than a little intimidated as I looked up at the massive machines. I couldn't imagine the amount of work it would take to keep the trucks looking so pristine. It showed a great amount of dedication and pride on the firemen's end.

I made my way up and down the trucks, looking for someone that could tell me where I needed to go.

"Can I help you?" I jumped in surprise at the sound of a voice and spun around, trying to find who had spoken. "Up here."

I looked up at the top of the truck that I was currently standing by and saw a man looking over the edge at me, wearing a broad grin as he chuckled at my confusion. "Uh, hi. I'm here to take some pictures for a fundraiser calendar."

"Oh yeah, the stud of the month calendar," the man snickered as he climbed down the side of the truck and landed next to me. He wore a friendly smile as he stuck his hand out for me to shake. "Follow me, the guys are in the rec room." I followed him through a door and down a narrow hallway. He spoke over his shoulder as we made our way. "My name is Joe by the way."

"Carter," I said back.

I almost slammed into the back of him when he suddenly stopped walking and spun around to face me. He tilted his head at me and I wondered if I had said something wrong. "What's your last name, Carter?"

"Greene." My voice shook. I was already nervous about coming here and the guy was not helping to put me at ease as he continued to stare at me through narrowed eyes.

"This is going to be awesome." He chuckled to himself before turning and walking away again. I shook my head at his odd behavior, but followed him until we reached a door at the end of the hallway.

He opened the door, revealing a spacious room with several couches and chairs. A large flat screen TV hung on the wall and a small kitchen area took up the space to my right. Several men were lounging around on the couches watching a football game, and a couple of guys were in the kitchen having a snack.

I took a deep breath and willed my racing heart to slow its pace. I kept my eyes down as I fought the temptation to search their faces for Ryan.

"Hey, guys, turn the TV off, it's time to get your pictures taken. Make sure you all look sexy, although that will be harder for some of you than others," Joe teased. Someone shut off the television and everyone turned to look at me. "This is the photographer, Carter Greene." One of the men in the kitchen began coughing as if he were choking, but I refused to look because I would have bet money it was Ryan. Joe turned to me with an amused gleam in his eyes. "Where do you want us?"

Luckily, Isaac had thought to put the written plans for the calendar in the camera bag or I would have had no clue where to start. There was a long, brick wall to the left of the room that had nothing hanging on it. I decided it would work well as a backdrop so I prepared the camera lens for a wide-angled group shot of the firemen.

I focused all of my attention on the camera in my hands so I wouldn't have to make eye contact with anyone. At that point, I was just hoping to take the pictures as quickly as possible and get out of there, but then Caleb's words filled my mind. As much as I hated to admit it, he was right, it may have been my last chance to finally say what I'd been wanting to say to Ryan. Maybe then I could finally get the man out of my head.

I took a deep breath as I stood to face the group of men who waited patiently for my instruction. "Let's line up along the brick wall and then I'll see where I need to move everyone." I raised my eyes long enough to scan over the men and when my gaze landed on Ryan it felt like all of the air had left the room. I couldn't look away as our eyes locked together. I gave him a small, nervous smile, but he frowned at me and looked away. I felt my heart sink at his reaction, but I took a cleansing breath. He wasn't going to make this easy at all, but I was determined to talk to him.

I walked around the group of men, arranging them by height so everyone would be seen in the photo. Isaac's written instructions said that they wanted this to be a tasteful, but sexy calendar. I was to take one group shot and then individual poses that would be used for the remaining months.

After the group shot was done, we moved around to various locations, both indoor and out of the station, to take their individual pictures. I took several of each man so that Isaac and Matt would have plenty to choose from.

The firemen seemed to get a kick out of their assignment and joked with each other about who was the sexiest and which month would be most popular. As it usually happens when a group of guys get together, the talk turned pretty crude. I found myself becoming more relaxed as I laughed at their antics. I noticed that they seemed like a very tight knit group, which wasn't surprising, considering their line of work. I imagined you would get pretty close to the people who you counted on to have your back in life or death situations.

I was laughing as one of the firemen, I think he said his name was Paul, began doing a sexy dance around the fireman's pole. The other men were all whistling and making cat calls when Joe shouted out between fits of laughter, "Man, I feel sorry for your wife, if that's all the hip action you've got."

"Your wife sure didn't give me any complaints last night, Joe," Paul shot back. Everyone laughed, including Joe, and I turned to find Ryan leaning against a wall, his eyes following my movements. He looked away quickly when he caught me staring and took a long drink from his water bottle; his Adam's apple sliding up and down his throat as he swallowed. *He's so fucking hot!* I felt my dick stir in my jeans.

I bent down to switch camera lenses, trying to hide my growing problem before anyone noticed. I was there to take pictures as a fundraiser for a youth center, it wouldn't look very good if I was walking around sporting an erection inside my pants.

"How much more do we need to do? I'm starving and I want to eat before we get called out on a run." I glanced up at the group of men who were looking at me questioningly.

I flipped through my saved pictures, quickly counting in my head then I stood so that I could shake their hands. "It looks like I only have two more firemen to photograph. The rest of you are all done. Thank you very much for doing this for the center, we appreciate it a lot."

One of the men clapped his hands. "Okay, assholes, whoever hasn't gotten their pretty picture taken needs to stay here and finish up. The rest of you, let's eat and rest. It's been too quiet around here today so we're bound to get a call soon." They all grumbled their agreement and made their way out of the room.

It was suddenly very quiet now that the large group was gone and I turned to see who was left. I felt my nerves kick in again when I saw that I had been left alone with Joe and Ryan, but then I realized that this would be the best opportunity to talk to Ryan without a large group of people around. I cleared my throat. "So, who wants to go first?"

"I will, I need to get something to eat." Joe wore a wide, toothy smile, but was looking at Ryan as he spoke and I was glad I wasn't on the receiving end of Ryan's glare.

"Okay then. I don't have any pictures with the fire trucks. Would it be alright with you guys if we took your pictures out there?"

"Sure," Joe said agreeably. I looked at Ryan who simply nodded and followed Joe out the door. I quickly grabbed my equipment and followed Ryan back down the narrow hallway I had come in through.

I couldn't help but take advantage of the fact that I was walking behind a very fine male specimen. My mouth watered as I ogled Ryan's perfectly rounded ass and I longed to grab it with both of my hands to see if it was as firm as it looked. What I wouldn't give to strip him out of those jeans, spread him wide with my hands, and bury my tongue in the crease of that ass.

A groan escaped my lips and I blushed as Ryan looked at me over his shoulder, catching my eyes on his posterior. A knowing smirk appeared on his lush lips and when he winked at me I nearly dropped the camera I was carrying. *Sexy bastard!*

CHAPTER
Four

Ryan

I WAS STILL REELING FROM THE FACT THAT CARTER WAS EVEN there at the firehouse. When Joe finished with his photos he walked out of the truck bay with a chuckle, leaving me alone with the incredibly attractive man. I was going to have to kick Joe's ass later for the pleasure he'd gotten out at my shock of seeing Carter again.

Carter was shorter than me, which was a huge turn on. I would guess he stood around 5'7", while I was a much taller 6'2". His lean, firm body made it clear that he took care of himself and when he focused his bright emerald green eyes on me, I felt my heart trip. He had light brown hair that was longer on top and flopped into his eyes in a sexy way. I fisted my hands at my sides as I resisted the urge to smooth it back.

He seemed very nervous and almost unsure of himself, a complete contradiction to the outgoing man I had seen performing on stage and I wondered if I had anything to do with his nervousness. I figured I was reading him wrong, so I shook off the ridiculous thought. I doubted this man was ever unsure of himself.

Carter knelt on the concrete floor, fiddling with the lens of his camera. I leaned against the fire truck and crossed my arms, hoping I looked as if his presence had no effect on me. "So, you're kind of a jack of all trades, aren't you?"

He peered up through his long lashes and I felt my cock stir at the sight of him kneeling in front of me. "What do you mean?"

"Well, I know you worked at Romero's, you obviously play in a band, and now I find out you're a photographer."

He gave me a shy smile as he stood. "Yeah, I guess I am, but only one of those is what I really want to be doing. The rest are just a way to make money; except today, this is all volunteer."

"The band." Carter tilted his head curiously at my statement. "Being in the band is the one you really want to be doing."

"How did you know?"

"Because you were born to be on a stage. You're very talented and you had the entire crowd eating out of your hand last night. It's obvious that music is your passion."

His face lit up as he smiled wide and I felt an unexpected fluttering in my stomach when I caught a glimpse of dimples at the corners of his mouth. "Thank you," he said sincerely, "but I don't think I had *everyone* eating out of my hand. Some people left the show early."

I smiled at his teasing. "It wasn't a reflection of your talent."

"Ryan." His face turned serious as he stepped closer to me and my heart began to beat faster at the sound of my name on his lips. "I want to apologize for the way I spoke to you at the hospital. That's not who I am and I felt horrible as soon as I said it, especially when I realized who I had said it to."

From my position as I leaned against the truck, I was able to look him directly in his eyes. I studied his face and saw nothing but sincerity and honest regret. "It's okay."

"No, it's not," he said firmly. "There's no excuse for what I said to you. All I can tell you is that I had just received very difficult news from my doctor and my head was killing me from the concussion. I was at my worst when you walked in and, unfortunately, I took it out on you."

"Are you alright? Are you sick?" I didn't know why the thought of him in pain or being ill caused my chest to hurt, but I found myself reaching for him, wanting to offer comfort.

He looked down at where my hand touched his arm and I wondered if he felt the same jolt of electricity flowing through us that I did. His eyes found mine again and he nodded his head at me. "I'm fine, now. The beam that had trapped me in the fire caused some nerve damage to my arm. The doctor did surgery to try to fix the damage, but he said that he didn't know if I would ever gain the full use of my hand. Playing music has always been all I wanted to do with my life and when you came to see me that day, I had just been told that I may never be able to play anymore."

It all made sense, if I had just been told that all of my dreams may have been destroyed, I would probably lash out at the closest person too. I looked down at his hands. "You're all better now though, right? I mean, I thought you were pretty incredible last night."

He gave me a gentle smile. "Yeah, after months of physical therapy and a lot of hard work, I'm able to play like before."

"That's good. I'm happy for you, Carter, and I understand why you were so angry that day. It was just shitty timing on my part I guess."

"No, it was really nice of you to come to the hospital to check on me and I shouldn't have taken my anger out on you," he insisted so I nodded my head once at him in acceptance and he breathed out in relief. "Good. I also wanted to thank you for saving my life."

I felt myself blush, I had always found it difficult to accept praise from people that I had rescued. As far as I was concerned, it was all part of being a fireman. "I was just doing my job."

"It was more than that. My brother Caleb told me how he begged all of the firemen to go look for me based on his twintuition." He made quotations with his fingers on the catch phrase. "He told me that you were the only one willing to listen, the only one willing to take the risk of going back into the building to search for me. I had been trapped down there for a long time. I was in pain and quickly losing consciousness from lack of oxygen. I knew I didn't have much longer and I was just hoping to go as quickly as possible. Then I heard your voice."

He shook his head solemnly. "For you it may have just been another day on the job, but for me…I would have died down there if you hadn't come to save me and I will forever be grateful to you. Thank you, Ryan."

I stared at his beautiful face for a long moment, my stomach twisting painfully at the thought of how close he had come to dying. He was such a vibrant man, so full of light, that it was difficult to think of the possibility of a fire snuffing the life out of him. "You are very welcome."

The noisy city just outside the doors, the people walking by the firehouse, cars driving by, nothing else existed as we stared at each other. Carter cleared his throat, breaking our trance. "So anyway, that's why I called you. I had finally worked up the nerve to apologize and to thank you."

"So that *was* you." I smirked at him.

He looked at me sheepishly. "Yeah, sorry about that. I hope I didn't cause any problems between you and your boyfriend by calling you at home."

My smile grew at how adorable he looked when he was embarrassed. "It's no problem and that wasn't my boyfriend; there is no boyfriend. The man that answered was Joe, who you've already met." I pointed over my shoulder with my thumb. "He's my best friend and he's also very straight, married, and not my type at all."

"Oh, good." His shoulders visibly relaxed as he smiled at me, and then seemed to realize what he had said. His eyes grew to the size of saucers. "I mean, it's good that you have a best friend…and that he's married…to a woman." He hung his head and I laughed. He took a deep breath and looked at me, holding his hand out to shake. "Can we start all over again please? My name is Carter Greene and it's nice to meet you."

I slipped my hand around his, enjoying the delicious chemistry between us. "It's nice to meet you, Carter. My name is Ryan Marshall."

He barked out a laugh. "Marshall? You're a *fire Marshall*?"

I rolled my eyes at his joke. "Like I haven't heard that a million times already. And for your information, I'm a lieutenant."

Carter chuckled as he held the camera up. "I should finish taking pictures before you get called out on an emergency." He told me where he wanted me and began snapping pictures. I stood near the fire truck with my arms crossed and then he had me sit casually on the back bumper of the truck. He finished with a few provocative poses where I gripped a long length of fire hose in my hands. I felt ridiculous, but he insisted they were sexy and if the look in his eyes was any indication, he was right.

My cock stirred in my pants as I watched his bright green eyes turn a darker shade when they traveled the length of my body. It was a heady feeling to know I was having that kind of an effect on such a sexy man. I looked longingly at his perfect features. I wanted to taste his plump lips and feel their fullness sliding against my own.

His voice sounded strained as he startled me from my thoughts. "You mentioned that Joe isn't your type. I'm curious, what exactly is your type?"

He stepped closer to me and my senses were assaulted by the delicious scent of him. He smelled clean and woodsy, like he'd been walking through a forest. I breathed his scent in and felt my head swirl as I tried to recall his question. "My type," I said, clearing my throat. "Hmm, let's see. My type is shorter than me, trim and toned." I let my eyes slide over his sculpted chest and the cut of his biceps which I could just make out beneath the tight shirt he wore. "With hair that flops down over his sparkling green eyes and dimples next to the most kissable pair of lips I've ever seen."

Carter gasped at my words and without another thought, I slid my hand around the back of his neck, pulling him towards me. I slanted my mouth over his and trembled when he opened up to me, allowing my tongue to taste the deep recesses of his mouth. He groaned into my mouth and I felt his hands slide around me, reaching down to cup my ass. "You are so damn sexy. I want to fuck you," he whispered huskily.

I pulled back and rested my forehead against his as I tried to catch my breath. I was shocked that I had allowed myself to lose control like that. It was dangerous that he had made me forget where I was.

I was glad that we had been able to clear the air between us and was pleased to find that he was really a nice guy after all, but I was afraid we were looking for two totally different things. I wasn't interested in just a quick fuck. At that point in my life I wanted something more substantial, I wanted a relationship.

I gave him one more soft kiss on his lips and then pulled away from him reluctantly, with a small smile. "I saw all of those men and women at the bar who would do anything to get in your pants. I'm not going to be just another notch in your belt, Carter. I'm looking for more than that, I want to get to know you. You have my number if you decide that's what you want too."

His mouth was hanging open when I walked away from him. As the door shut behind me, I said a little prayer that that wouldn't be the last time I would see Carter Greene. Because after just one taste of his mouth, I was hooked.

I walked into the kitchen area of the firehouse as the other guys were finishing up lunch, hoping that my face didn't give away the fact that I had just been making out with the sexiest man I'd ever met. We had all learned early on to eat as quickly as possible because if a call came through, we had to be ready to go, whether we were done or not. I had spent one too many nights with my stomach growling in hunger because the alarm dropped just as I was getting ready to eat.

I made my way through the group of men and put together a quick sandwich from the lunch meat laid out on the counter. I spread mustard on my ham and cheese then leaned against the counter to eat as I listened to the conversations around me.

I loved the constant flow of activity around the firehouse. There was always someone to talk to or watch a movie or play video games with. After working together for six years, most of those guys had become like brothers to me. We counted on each other to keep everyone safe and I trusted them completely. We often got together outside of work, meeting up for drinks after a long day or having cookouts at one of their houses.

Much like any other siblings, we often teased each other relentlessly and pulled pranks as often as possible. It helped to pass the long, often monotonous hours between emergency runs and made it easier to get through some of the more stressful days at work.

As close as I was with the guys from my station, I had never told any of them that I was gay, except for Joe. Despite his supportive reaction, I had decided early on that I would keep my sexuality to myself at work. I was proud of who I was and if anyone figured it out I wouldn't deny it, but in a testosterone fueled career such as mine - where you had to depend on others to have your back and keep you safe - you couldn't be too careful. I had never felt the need to create an imaginary girlfriend as some men had been forced to do, I just let the guys draw their own conclusions as to why I never brought a date to any of our gatherings.

It had become increasingly difficult over the years as we

celebrated several of the guys getting married or having children. I longed for a day when I could openly share my life with my friends, but I had heard about some terrible things that had happened to members of the LGBTQ community who came out at work, particularly within the police and fire departments. Besides, I figured it was a moot point until I actually found someone worth introducing them to.

I had been telling Carter the truth, I wasn't interested in casual hookups any more. There was a time in my life, mostly during college when one night stands had been fine. Now that I was older, I wanted someone to come home to; someone who I could tell about my day and enjoy the long dark nights with. I was lonely and I wanted someone to share my life with. Could that someone be Carter? I had to admit that there was definitely a strong chemistry between us, but chemistry would fizzle out if there was no deeper connection made. I had made it clear to Carter what I was looking for. So it was up to him, I guessed I would just have to wait and see what he decided.

I was pulled from my thoughts as I heard the obnoxious sound of Dan's voice. Dan Turner was a forty-six-year-old fireman with a shaved head and inky black eyes that reminded me of a shark. Of course that may have had more to do with his views on homosexuals, or women, or basically anyone who wasn't an American, Caucasian male for that matter. He was never shy about sharing his opinion with anyone in the room, whether you wanted to hear it or not, and was too self-involved to notice that most of us rolled our eyes and tuned him out when he started yet another tirade. He was famous for strutting around the firehouse calling himself "Dan the Man." Although I seriously doubted he attracted as many women as he claimed. If he did, I would have to worry about the mental health of those women.

I usually chose to walk away when he got started on one of his tirades because I didn't need his verbal poison in my life. I drank my water quickly and turned to the sink to wash my dishes, planning my escape in my head, when I heard him start talking about Carter.

"I don't know about you assholes, but I didn't appreciate the way that little fairy was eyeing me while he took my pictures. He looked like the type that would drop to his knees for any man that walked in. It's fucking disgusting, he's probably jerking off to my picture right now."

I felt my blood beginning to boil and gripped the glass in my hand so hard I was surprised it didn't shatter. I was just about to say something when I heard Rodrigues speak up. "I don't know, I didn't think he looked desperate enough to go for you, Dan. And he definitely seemed too smart for you."

Everyone started laughing as Dan's face turned beet red. He glared at Rodrigues who crossed his arms and smiled innocently at Dan like he hadn't just insulted him. After glancing around the room and seeing that no one was going to agree with his little rant, Dan finally stormed out of the room, grumbling about "fucking faggots."

"That man is a waste of perfectly good oxygen," Rodrigues said with a shake of his head. The others grumbled their agreement and then began filing out of the room when someone suggested a game of basketball.

Joe sidled up to me and threw his arm around my shoulders. He spoke quietly to me. "Come on man, you know he's an idiot. The guy has no clue what he's talking about and he's not worth your time." I nodded my head, feeling my anger beginning to fade. "Let's get out there before the teams are already formed. I don't want to get stuck guarding Teddy again, the man is a beast on the court." I laughed and thought, once again, how lucky I was to have a friend like Joe.

CHAPTER
Five

Carter

"SO, HOW DID THE PHOTOSHOOT GO? DID YOU SEE RYAN?"

I quit shoveling pasta primavera in my mouth long enough to glare up at my brother. "Of course I saw him. Isn't that why you set the whole thing up?"

Caleb smiled at me unapologetically as he wiped down the counters in his state of the art kitchen. My brother was a chef who could honestly work anywhere in the world with his talent. Luckily for me, he found and married the love of his life who happened to live in Chicago. I got to keep my twin close by and he fed me delicious food each time I visited him. "If you will remember correctly, I didn't set anything up. Isaac was in crisis mode and needed help fixing his mistake; I was simply trying to help out a friend. If I happened to push you into doing something you should have done a long time

50

ago, like finally facing the man who saved your life, then more power to me, right?" He gave me a pointed look as he tossed the dish cloth into the sink.

"Yeah, I guess so," I admitted with a smirk. "It could have gone very badly though and then I would be here kicking your ass."

Caleb laughed. "Well, since you're not making a feeble and somewhat useless attempt to kick my very fine ass, can I assume that it went well?" I shrugged my shoulders and returned my focus on the food in front of me. As usual, I would tell Caleb everything, but after the way he manipulated the situation with the photoshoot, I figured he deserved to wait for the information. He waited for me to take exactly three bites before grabbing the plate out from under me. He arched a brow at my protests as he held the plate behind him. "No more food unless you start talking. Now spill it!"

I chuckled. "Damn, you found my weakness, you know I'll do anything for your cooking. Now give it back." Caleb laid the plate back down and leaned his elbows on the counter, looking at me like a child waiting to hear a bedtime story. I rolled my eyes at the eager look on his face. "I was so nervous when I walked up to that firehouse, I wanted to turn back around and almost did a couple of times, but I couldn't do that to Isaac or the kids. I'm sure Ryan was shocked to see me there, but he didn't let it show. In fact, when I first got there, he wouldn't even look at me and during the group photos he acted like he didn't even know me. That finally changed when I got him alone though."

I paused to take a couple of bites, cleaning my plate of food. I started to take it to the sink, but Caleb waved me off. "I'll get that, you finish your story. What did you say to him? What did he say to you? Was he still really angry about what happened at the hospital? Does he have a boyfriend?"

I laughed at Caleb's excitement. "I apologized for the way I had spoken to him and explained that I had just found out about the damage to my hand and what that could have done to my career.

He seemed genuinely relieved to find out that the physical therapy worked and I was back to playing like before. He's a really nice guy." My words trailed off and I felt a fluttering in my stomach as I pictured Ryan's smile and his smoky, blue-gray eyes.

"Earth to Carter, come in Carter," Caleb said, mimicking a character from an old sitcom. "You can't leave me hanging, what else happened?"

"He accepted my apology and then I finally got the opportunity to thank him for saving my life. He was very humble about the whole thing. Then I took some more pictures of him for the calendar and I left."

"Wait, wait, wait. Back it up right there. I know there's more you're not telling me. Does he have a boyfriend?"

I rolled my eyes. Caleb was acting like this was a soap opera. "No, he doesn't have a boyfriend. The man that answered his phone was his best friend, Joe, who is also a fireman and very straight, thank God." I mumbled that last part under my breath, but Caleb smiled at me knowingly.

"What else?"

"We might have kissed…and I might have told him I wanted to fuck him."

Caleb's wide-eyed expression was almost comical. "Damn, boy, you don't mess around, do you?"

I shrugged my shoulders. "I've always been very honest about what I want, and I wanted *him*. God, Caleb, the man is sexy as fuck and he really knows how to kiss." I felt my cock lengthening at the memory of Ryan's mouth on mine.

"What did he say? Did you two…"

I cleared my throat. "No, we didn't. He said he saw how all of my fans acted around me at the bar and he doesn't want to be like that. He said he wants to get to know me." I could hear the wonderment in my voice as I spoke. I had never met anyone who wanted to know me for more than one night. Even in high school, I usually ended up messing around with guys who were hiding the fact that they were gay from their girlfriends or just beginning to explore their sexuality. I'd never had a boyfriend.

After high school, music took up all of my time which left none for a relationship, and I was fine with that. At least that's what I had told myself as I flitted from one random guy to another. That's not to say I didn't have a great time with my explorations. I had always had a very healthy sexual appetite and I loved trying new things with my partners. New positions, new toys, new locations. There really wasn't a whole lot I wouldn't do or at least try, sexually, other than golden showers and anything involving feces. The thought of a man urinating or defecating on me did nothing for me, but to each his own.

However, I had found myself becoming increasingly disappointed in my sexual encounters. I still got off and made sure the guy I was with did too, but it just seemed like something was missing. I hadn't even had the desire to be with anyone since the fire. I tried telling myself it was because I was focusing on getting better, but the photoshoot proved that it had more to do with a certain sexy fireman.

The sound of Caleb's voice brought me back to the present. "Of course he wants to get to know you, who wouldn't? You're an amazing guy, Carter."

I smiled at him. "Thanks, Caleb." I could always count on him to have my back.

"What are you going to do?"

I took a deep breath and released it slowly. "I'm going to ask him out on a date and maybe we'll have a great time or maybe we'll find we have nothing in common, but, either way, I want to try. I want to see what can happen with this guy."

An exuberant smile spread across his face and he clapped his hands together in excitement. "Yay! I'm so happy for you! There is absolutely nothing that compares to being with someone you care about. And on a side note, I have to applaud your choice in men. Ryan seems like a really sweet guy, and *HOT!*" Caleb fanned his face as his husband, Giovanni, stepped into the kitchen. *My brother had chosen an extremely handsome man himself,* I thought with a smile.

"Who's hot?" Giovanni said with a sexy growl as he slid his arms around Caleb and began placing kisses along his neck.

"You are. I missed you while you were at work." Caleb turned in Giovanni's arms and I watched as they devoured each other's mouths, obviously forgetting they had company. I loved seeing my brother happy, but it was a strange sensation to experience his excitement towards his husband through our "twin telepathy" or whatever you wanted to call it. Being able to feel each other's emotions was useful when I was trapped in a burning building, but not so much when he was getting hot and heavy with his husband.

"I'm just gonna go…" My voice trailed off as Giovanni lifted Caleb into his arms and Caleb's legs wrapped around his waist. I hurriedly let myself out the door before the clothes started flying and sighed with relief when I stepped onto the elevator. As I rode down the building, I chuckled to myself as I wondered if those two would ever get out of the honeymoon phase of their relationship. I seriously doubted it.

As I drove home, I plotted in my head what I would say to Ryan. I had never asked a man out on a date before. Most of the men I met only required a simple nod of the head or a wink to get things going. Of course, I had never asked those men to share a meal with me before. I pulled into the driveway and turned off my car. My heart began to race and I was surprised to find my hands were visibly shaking as I searched for Ryan in my contacts and hit the call button.

The phone rang twice before his smooth, sexy voice came over the line. It was the strangest thing, but the minute I heard his voice, my nerves calmed and I was able to breathe normally again. "Hello?"

I cleared my throat. "Hey, it's Carter. How are you?"

Ryan sounded surprised but pleased as he answered. "I'm good, how about you?"

"I'm great. Are you working right now, I don't want to interrupt anything."

"You're not interrupting anything. I actually just got home from work and was putting away some groceries."

"Ryan, I was wondering if you would like to go out with me tonight? Maybe we could go to dinner and a movie or whatever you'd like to do." I crossed my fingers that he couldn't hear how nervous I was. I didn't want to come across as pathetic, but damn it, I really was hopeful. I liked how I felt when I was near him and I wanted to spend more time with the man that was making me feel all those new and exciting things.

"I'd love to go on a date with you, Carter." He sounded happy and I could picture him smiling, his perfect teeth showing past his perfect lips, his perfect eyes shining...*okay, I just totally turned into a teenage girl there.* I rolled my eyes at my infatuation, glad that no one else could hear my thoughts. "But my shift was really long and I'd kind of like to just take it easy." I felt my heart plummet with disappointment. "Would you mind coming over here and we could just order in some food and watch a movie?"

I sighed in relief and my heart rate picked up at the thought of being alone with Ryan in his home. "That sounds great, thank you."

"It's my pleasure, I would love to feed you." My dick stood up and took notice of the double meaning behind his words and I let out a low groan before I could stop myself. I heard him chuckle and the sound made my pants fit that much tighter. He obviously knew what he was doing to me. *Time to flip the tables on him.*

"Well, I'm ready to swallow down whatever you want to put in my mouth." I smiled, proud of myself as I heard him hiss through the phone. "Just text me your address and I'll see you around seven."

"I'm looking forward to it."

I hung up and climbed out of my car, still smiling as I let myself inside my apartment. I went to my room and began digging through my closet to find something to wear. Was I supposed to dress up? Since we were staying at his place, I figured I should probably dress more casually than if we were going to a fancy restaurant, so I could forego a tie. On the other hand, this was our first date and hopefully not our last, so it deserved more than the t-shirt and sweatpants I would wear if I were going to hang out at Caleb or Landon's house.

I had finally settled on a new pair of jeans that I thought hugged my ass pretty well and a long sleeved, gray Henley that reminded me of Ryan's eyes. I threw the clothes on my bed along with a clean pair of boxer briefs and socks.

I had just started towards the bathroom to take a shower when my phone chirped with a text. I ran to get it and quickly swiped across the screen. It was strange, but thrilling, how excited I got just by seeing his name light up on my phone.

Ryan had texted me his address and I smiled as I read the message he sent. *Forgot to ask, do you like Chinese food?*

It's one of my favorites, thanks.

I'm really glad you called, Carter.

So am I. My cheeks hurt from smiling as I set my phone aside and headed to the shower. I would be seeing Ryan Marshall in one hour and I needed to get ready, I wanted to look my best for him.

I pulled up outside of what appeared to be an old warehouse of sorts and glanced around at my surroundings. The building was located in a remote section on the outskirts of Chicago and there wasn't anyone else around as far as I could see, but I saw a light glowing from one of the windows so I pulled my phone out of my pocket to check the address one more time. Yep, this was the address Ryan had given me.

For a split second I wondered if Ryan could be a serial killer, luring me into his web so that he could murder me, but then I laughed the ludicrous thought off. He had saved my life once already, so that kind of cancelled out the idea that he wanted me dead. *Unless he had saved me from the fire so my skin wouldn't burn because he wanted to be able to wear it as a coat.* I rolled my eyes at the direction my thoughts had taken. I loved horror movies, but maybe watching "Silence of the Lambs" right before bed was a bad idea.

Shaking my head at my own ridiculousness, I decided to call Ryan. "Hey, I just pulled up at the address you gave me and I wanted to make sure I was at the right place."

Ryan chuckled, obviously picking up on the trepidation I was trying to hide. "You're at the right place. As a matter of fact, I see you." I looked up through my windshield and saw him standing in front of the lit window, waving to me, and my heart began to beat faster for an entirely different reason. "Hang on, I'm coming down to get you."

I hung up and quickly checked my reflection in the rearview mirror then climbed from the car, locking it behind me. I walked towards the building and a door opened off to the side. Ryan stood in the doorway, looking ethereal with the light shining behind him.

He wore a pair of jeans that fit him perfectly and a tight, dark blue Chicago Fire Department t-shirt that showcased his broad shoulders and sculpted biceps. My mouth watered as my gaze trailed lower to see a noticeable bulge in his pants and my eyes shot to his. He was busy slowly running his eyes down my body and I was suddenly thankful for every second I had ever spent in the gym. I would gladly spend hours working out each day, if it made Ryan keep looking at me the way he was.

"Come on in," he said in a husky voice. I followed him inside and quirked my brow at him when he locked the door behind us. He smiled sheepishly as he answered my unspoken question. "It can get a little creepy around here at night sometimes."

I breathed out a sigh of relief. "Oh, thank God, it's not just me. I was freaking myself out a little when I saw the place." Ryan laughed and I was mesmerized by the sound.

I turned to follow him and let out a low whistle. "Dayum, this has to be the ultimate man cave. I apologize in advance for the drool, but my mouth is literally watering right now." Ryan chuckled as I wandered around the large open space that housed an impressive home gym, a game room that included a pool table, as well as air hockey, foosball, and ping-pong, and what appeared to be a fully stocked bar. "I bet you entertain a lot, don't you?"

"Not really." I looked at him as he shrugged his shoulders. "I'll have a few of the guys from the station over once in a while for a poker night and Joe and his wife stop by all the time, but other than that, it's usually just me here. I'm a pretty private person." I stared at him for a long moment, surprised that he didn't allow people over to his house often and touched that I had been included in the select few.

I sensed that there was more to the story, but I didn't want to pry, so I kept quiet. If the night went well, then hopefully I would be learning a lot more about him soon enough. Normally, I didn't care about getting to know the men I spent time with, only focusing on getting each other off and then parting ways without so much as an exchange of phone numbers. With Ryan, it was just different; I wanted to know everything about him. I wanted to know if he had any childhood pets and if he was allergic to anything. I wanted to know his happiest memory and if he'd ever had his heart broken. I wanted to learn all about that incredible man and for the first time in my life, I wanted to share all of those things about myself with him.

"Well, I wouldn't mind spending some time in here. I haven't played pool in a long time. My parents have a game room at our family cabin in Tennessee, but it's not nearly as spectacular as this."

"Thanks, I always loved playing games as a kid, so this game room was the first project I started as soon as I moved in. Come on and I'll show you the rest of the house."

I followed him up the stairs, enjoying the way his jeans showcased his perfectly shaped ass. As we reached the second floor, he turned to say something and caught me ogling him. I winked at him, ready to defend myself for being a healthy, warm-blooded American man, when I became distracted by the room laid out in front of me. "Wow! Ryan, this place is amazing! Did you do all of this yourself?"

I looked around in awe of his home. The massive warehouse had been designed with an open floor plan, so I could easily see from one end to the other. The floors were genuine hardwood, the kitchen had more equipment than I would know what to do with, but I was sure it would be a dream to Caleb. The living room was furnished with a large, leather sectional couch and matching chairs. The entire area was filled with antiques and I wondered if they had been passed down throughout the generations of Ryan's family, or if he had purchased them himself.

I smirked as I eyed the large flat screen television, because what bachelor pad would be complete without one, right? The smile slid from my face a moment later when I moved my eyes to the other side of the room. There, along the back wall was an enormous California king bed, Ryan's bed, and just like that, all I could picture was him, lying naked between its sheets.

Luckily, Ryan seemed unaware of my wandering thoughts as he answered my question. "Yes, it's been a lot of work and there's still a long way to go, but I've enjoyed remodeling it over the years."

I forced myself to turn away from the bed and focused my attention back on him. "You've done an incredible job. I never would have guessed from the exterior that this place could be so warm and inviting inside." Ryan smiled at my praise and my heart tripped over itself. He was so gorgeous.

"Would you like to see my latest project?" I nodded my head and followed him up a small flight of stairs and through a door that opened up onto the roof of the building. "Keep in mind this is a work in progress."

I was surprised at the welcoming, yet sophisticated, outdoor living space he had created. He had obviously put a lot of thought into the design, as shown by the slate tiles that covered the floor, the comfortable outdoor furniture that sat in a cozy circle around a fire pit and a large hot tub nestled within a pergola. A string of lights gave the space a romantic feel and the view of the stars from up there was fantastic.

"What are you going to do with that?" I pointed to where a bunch of bricks were piled neatly in a corner.

Ryan became very animated as he described the outdoor kitchen he was building. It was clear that he was passionate about the home he had created and I enjoyed seeing his enthusiasm as he talked about the changes he still wanted to make.

"I am very impressed, Ryan. I always enjoyed working on things around our house as I was growing up, but I've never taken on a project of this magnitude. You are truly talented," I said sincerely.

Ryan looked at me with surprise and shook his head. "I've seen you playing guitar, you're the talented one."

I stepped closer to him, inspired by the romantic setting of his rooftop and hoping for a kiss, but Ryan's phone sounded an alarm, making us both jump.

"The delivery guy is here with our food, come on." Ryan held his hand out towards me and I took it, letting him lead me back down to his living area. "I'll be right back, make yourself at home, there's beer or water in the fridge. Help yourself to whatever you want."

He started to walk away, but I pulled him back as I pulled my wallet out of my back pocket and handed it to him. "I was the one that asked you out, so it's my treat." When he started to object, I cut him off. "I'll let you pay on our second date."

"I like that plan." He gave me a sexy smile and then ran down the steps to get our food.

I quickly used the bathroom and washed my hands, then went to the kitchen to get drinks for us. I heard Ryan as he walked up behind me and laid the food on the counter. "You want a beer?" I grabbed one out for myself and then looked over my shoulder when Ryan didn't answer.

He was looking at me with an odd expression on his face and he slid my wallet across the counter towards me. "Um, here you go."

"Is everything okay?" I couldn't imagine what might have happened in the few moments he was gone to make him act so strange.

"Yeah, it's just, I opened your wallet to pay and this fell out." My eyes widened as he held up the card that had been in the flower bouquet he brought to the hospital. "I figured it would have been thrown away at the hospital. I can't believe you kept it all this time."

I walked around the counter to stand in front of him, looking up into his expressive eyes. "I pulled it out, I don't know how many times, trying to gather enough courage to call you. I don't know why exactly, but I just couldn't throw it away. Even though I had fucked everything up when you brought it to me, I guess I wasn't ready to give up yet."

His mouth lifted in a beautiful smile as he placed his hands on my hips and pulled me towards him. "I'm glad you kept it and I'm glad you finally called me."

My heart beat wildly as he leaned down and slid his lips against mine. I opened for him and moaned when his tongue tangled with my own. He tasted like mint and my new favorite flavor, Ryan.

All too soon, he stepped back and I groaned in frustration. Ryan kissed the tip of my nose. "There will be time for that later, let's eat before the food gets cold."

"Fine, but I'm going to hold you to that."

"I'm a man of my word." Ryan held up his fingers in the Boy Scout sign of honor.

"Were you even a Boy Scout?"

Ryan grinned sheepishly. "Nah, but I always wanted to be, so I figured that should count for something."

I laughed. "Okay, you get points for effort."

I was amazed at how comfortable I felt around Ryan. Not that I had a lot of dating experience, or any at all for that matter, but I had expected there to be awkward moments where neither one of us knew what to say. That wasn't the case with Ryan, instead it was as if I had known him my entire life.

We bantered back and forth as we dished our food out onto plates and then settled onto the wide couch in the living room. We each took an end, leaning our backs against the arms of the couch so we could face each other as we ate. The food was delicious. Ryan had ordered a variety of dishes which we shared, sampling them all.

"So, tell me about your band." Ryan looked at me with genuine interest.

"Well, let's see." I finished taking a drink of my beer and set the bottle back down on the coffee table. "I started putting Carter's Creed together right out of high school. It took me a while to select all the members of the band. I was very particular about who I wanted in the group. It was more than just their musical talents, they had to get along with me and with each other. We needed to have mutual respect for one another and be willing to listen to each other's ideas."

"The five of you seemed to really mesh up on stage, so I'm assuming you found what you were looking for?"

"Yeah, I did. We're all really close and I couldn't imagine a better group of people to work with. We all have the same goals in mind for the band, which helps keep us moving in the right direction. Steve is pretty shy around most people, but once he considers you a friend, he opens up and shows his wicked sense of humor. Tyler and Kalia just recently started dating. We all knew they were crazy about each other, but I think they held back because they were afraid of messing with the dynamic of the band. After a while, I guess they just couldn't help themselves because they're together now and I've never seen either one of them look happier. Rocko, our drummer…what do I say about Rocko?"

Ryan looked at me cautiously. "Is there a history between you two?"

I was thankful I didn't have any food in my mouth or I would have spit it everywhere. "Oh, hell no!" I shuddered at the thought of me and Rocko as a couple. "There will never be anything except friendship between us, trust me. Don't get me wrong, he is one of my best friends and I know he'll always have my back, but the guy is crazy. He's always getting himself into these insane situations and we all end up having to bail him out. I have my own share of kinks, but nothing is off limits with that guy. He'll literally do anything, say anything, and fuck just about anything."

Ryan laughed at that description. "And you still picked him to be in the band?"

I shrugged my shoulders. "He's a hell of a drummer and loyal to a fault. The man would lay down his life for any one of us."

"They sound pretty awesome. Maybe I'll get to meet them someday."

I smiled at him. "I'd like that. So, that's everyone in the band, except my brother Landon, who is our manager. He's done a great job of setting us up with the right people so we can keep moving forward."

"Wow! That must be great to have someone you can trust as your manager. How many siblings do you have?"

"There are five of us all together. Michelle is the oldest, then Emma, Landon, and finally me and Caleb, the surprise babies of the family. My poor parents had their hands full with all of us."

Ryan looked at me, thoughtfully. "Do your bandmates and family know you're gay?"

I set my empty plate on the coffee table next to Ryan's and settled back into my seat. "I told the members of my band during their auditions. I wanted to be clear from the beginning and rule out anyone that might be a homophobic asshole. None of them had a problem with it at all, especially Rocko, who's bisexual."

"And your family?" Ryan took a sip of beer and for a moment I forgot what we were talking about as I watched, mesmerized as the tip of his tongue slipped out to capture a drop of moisture from his bottom lip. His plump lips lifted in a cocky grin and I realized he had caught me staring, yet again.

"Uh…yeah, my family knows too. Landon came out first and kind of paved the way for Caleb and me. Our parents were very supportive, they immediately joined PFLAG and learned everything they could about gay sex so they could have *the talk* with us. That was quite interesting, let me tell you," I said with an exaggerated shudder.

Ryan laughed and I smiled back, loving the sound. "I'm sure it was, but it sounds like you are very lucky to have so much support."

I nodded. "I know I am, believe me. There are a lot of kids who aren't as fortunate."

"That's true," he answered solemnly.

"What about you? Are you out to your friends and family?"

I watched him take a deep breath. "I'm not out at work."

My face must have registered my surprise. "But you kissed me at the firehouse."

"Yeah, that was a risky move, but I couldn't help myself." Ryan blushed and I wanted to climb onto his lap and kiss him until we were both gasping for air.

"I'm glad you took the risk." I smiled at him wolfishly and he rewarded me with a beautiful smile. "So, no one at work knows?"

"Joe knows. He's my best friend and it didn't feel right to keep such a big part of who I am from him. I'm sure some of the other guys have their suspicions, but I just let them think what they want. Unfortunately, in my line of work, people who are gay have to be very careful. When you become a firefighter you become part of a brotherhood, much like with the police and military. We've come a long way, but there are still a lot of old-school, good old boys in those organizations who frown on gays. That can make things pretty tricky when facing life or death situations alongside those same men. So, sometimes it's just smarter to keep quiet and blend in. If anyone ever asked me, I wouldn't deny it, but I don't go around announcing it. I'm not ashamed of being gay and I'm very comfortable in my own skin, I just have to play it smart."

I frowned, thinking about the dangerous consequences he could face if he came out. "I understand. It's important that you're safe." I scooted closer to him on the couch and reached for his hand, twining our fingers together. "What about your family? Do they support you?"

Ryan studied our clasped hands as he spoke quietly. "I don't have any family. Well, other than Joe and his family, they've kind of adopted me, but..." He looked up at me and I tried to school my features so he wouldn't see the sadness I felt at his words. I couldn't imagine not having my family. "My mom was sixteen when she got pregnant with me. When she told the twenty-year-old guy who got her pregnant, he took off. I don't even know his name. My mom was basically still a child herself and she wasn't prepared to be a mom, so as soon as she turned eighteen she took off and left me with my grandfather. We never heard from her again."

"I'm so sorry." I squeezed his fingers.

"Don't be," he said as he gave me a brilliant smile. "My grandfather doted on me, showering me with enough love to make up for both of my absent parents. I grew up feeling loved and secure, even if I was a bit lonely sometimes. I would have loved to have had a brother or sister to play with. My grandma had passed away years before I was born, so it was just my grandfather and me. He was retired and had lots of money, so we travelled and had many adventures together. He was the best father figure I could have asked for. He never even batted an eye when I told him I was gay, just reassured me that he would always love me."

"He sounds wonderful," I whispered, grateful for a man I didn't even know, for the love he had shown Ryan.

"He was. He died suddenly right before my high school graduation. He had a massive heart attack and never regained consciousness. He left everything he had to me, including this building."

"I'm sure wherever he is, he's very proud of the man you've

become and all of the things you've done to this place."

Ryan looked at me for a long moment before he leaned forward and pressed his lips to mine. Without breaking our kiss, he put a hand behind my head and eased me back until I was lying flat on the couch, his firm body hovering over mine. "There's something else I want to know," he said as he kissed his way down my neck.

I had never been kissed like that in my life and I was a little disappointed that he wanted to stop and continue our conversation. I was going to die of blue balls around the guy. "What?" I asked, my voice sounding thick with tension.

Ryan licked his way up my throat and then leaned up on his strong forearms so he could look into my eyes. "You mentioned earlier that you have your own kinks. I want to know what they are."

I arched a brow at him. "And why do you want to know what my kinks are?"

"So I can help fulfill them." His words, along with the husky sound of his voice, had my cock straining against my zipper and I moaned. He pressed his groin down against mine and that small bit of pressure had me nearly coming in my jeans. "Tell me," he commanded.

"There's not much I won't do. I like to try new positions, toys, and role-playing. I like watching and being watched." Ryan bucked his hips against me and my eyes rolled back into my head with pleasure.

"What else?" His voice sounded strained and I thrilled with the knowledge that he was as turned on as I was. I had always wondered if I would ever be able to find someone who was as sexually adventurous as me.

"I like bondage, being at the mercy of my partner or controlling the situation myself. I'm versatile so I like both fucking and being fucked, sometimes at the same time." Ryan furrowed his brow at me in question. "I've been known to enjoy a few threesomes in my day."

His eyes widened, but instead of looking shocked, he looked… intrigued and extremely turned on. "I've never had a threesome, but I've always wondered what that would be like," he whispered breathlessly.

I was relieved that I hadn't scared him away with my admissions and decided to push things just a little bit further. I captured his lips in a powerful kiss and reached around him to tease my finger under the elastic of his briefs. When he didn't object, I slid my hand inside his underwear and began kneading the taut globes of his ass. "There's nothing like the feeling of fucking into a man." I lifted my hips and pressed my aching erection against his. "While another man pounds into your ass at the same time."

Ryan shuddered in my arms and I slammed my eyes shut and gritted my teeth. *Why did I let things go so far?* With a willpower I didn't know I possessed, I pulled my hands out of his pants and placed them on his chest, pushing him back slightly. "Ryan, we have to stop."

"What's wrong?" He was panting as he looked down at me questioningly through hooded lids. His lips were plump and wet from our kisses and I wanted nothing more than to pull him back on top of me, but there was something more important I needed to do.

"Nothing's wrong. You're perfect, but we have to slow things down. I told you I wouldn't treat you like another notch on my belt and I meant it." A slow smile lit up his face making my brain scramble with its brilliance. "You're different from any man I've ever met. There's a connection I feel with you that I've never experienced before and I think we both deserve to see where this could go. For the first time in my life, I don't want to rush through this. I want to take my time and really get to know you."

Ryan searched my eyes and then leaned down to brush his lips against mine sweetly. "It's easy to get carried away when I'm with you. You make me forget where I am and what I'm doing, but I feel the connection too. I've felt it from the very first time I laid eyes on you. You're a very special man, Carter."

"I think you're pretty incredible too." I gave him a lingering kiss before pulling away with a reluctant sigh. "I better get going."

Ryan looked at me as if he were struggling with something. Finally, he climbed off the couch, held his hand out to me and pulled me to a standing position. We held hands as we made our way downstairs.

"Sorry we never got to watch the movie."

I shrugged my shoulders. "I had more fun talking to you anyway," I said honestly.

As we reached my car, Ryan leaned down and placed his forehead against mine. His eyes were serious as he looked at me. "I really like you, Carter. I hope you'll let me take you out again sometime."

I reached up and gently cradled his face between my hands. "I like you too. I would love to go out with you again."

He breathed out a sigh of relief and I felt his warm breath ghost across my face, right before his lips sealed over mine. I had no idea what would happen between Ryan and myself, but I was quickly becoming addicted to that man.

CHAPTER
Six

Ryan

I TURNED THE WATER OFF IN THE SHOWER AND REACHED PAST the curtain for the towel I had left on the rack. Drying myself off, I couldn't help but smile as the sounds of my friends floated through the air. Having lived all alone since my grandfather died, my home was often too quiet, so I found it comforting when I heard the laughter and noise that was present day and night in a busy firehouse.

I finished drying off and pulled on a pair of soft jeans. I grabbed my shirt and tugged it over my head, wincing as the muscles in my back protested the movements. When the alarm had sounded for an apartment fire, I hadn't expected to have to haul a fully-grown, three-hundred-pound man from his home. The room had been quickly filling with smoke, but the man refused to leave without his most prized possession, a collection of over two hundred Elvis figurines. Joe assured him he would do his best to save the King of Rock and Roll, but I still had to forcefully pull the man, as he shouted instructions the entire way on the proper handling of the ceramic figures.

I shook my head as I thought of what some people were willing to risk their lives for as I made my way past the living area, where a baseball game was blaring from the large screen television. Five of my friends were gathered in there, trash-talking each other and sharing inappropriate jokes. Most days at the firehouse were like being at a college frat house, all that was missing was the empty beer cans, since drinking on duty was prohibited.

I went to the kitchen and grabbed a bottle of water from the fridge. I had just twisted the cap off and lifted it to my lips when my phone alerted me to a text. My heart raced as I wondered if it could be from Carter.

We had gone out a few times since our first date and things had gone very well. He had shown me the studio where the band practiced and I had taken him to my favorite antique stores. I felt like we had gotten to know each other much better and had been surprised by how easily the conversations flowed. Carter was a very interesting man and I found that the more I learned about him, the more I wanted to know.

I had to admit, I was very intrigued when he told me about his kinks. My sexual experiences had been pretty limited to casual hookups, where we got each other off as quickly as possible. I had never found someone I trusted enough to explore my own sexual desires with. I really couldn't even say what my kinks were, but I had nearly swallowed my tongue when he mentioned a threesome, so I guess it would be safe to assume that was one of them.

I took a long drink of water and sat the bottle on the counter so I could pull my phone from my pocket. I smiled when I saw that the text had in fact been from Carter. I guessed that meant he was still thinking about me.

Hey, Lieutenant Marshall. How are you?

I chuckled at his teasing. *Hey, rock star. I'm good, how are you?*
Better now that I get to talk to you.

My pulse raced as I read his words and I decided to throw caution to the wind. *Me too. I haven't been able to stop thinking about our date the other night.* I held my breath as I waited for his response, hoping I hadn't scared him off with my honesty.

Same here, I want to see you again. I'm playing at the same bar tonight. Would you come and watch? Maybe we can spend some time together after my set.

I'd love to, thanks.

Great! Give your name to the bouncer when you get there. I'll have a table waiting for you.

You don't have to go to any trouble, I can just sit wherever.

Don't be silly. You're my date and I want to know where to look into the audience.

I smiled as I realized that Carter really was interested in me. *Okay, sounds good.*

I slid my phone back into my pocket as Joe walked into the room, his happy smile grew bigger when he saw me smiling. "Hey, man, I picked up an extra shift. You want to stay and watch the game with me until a call comes through or do you have a hot date with a sander?" he teased. Joe knew all too well that I spent most of my time off at home alone, working on whatever home improvement project I had going on at the time and he loved to give me a hard time about it.

"Actually, I do have a date, but it's not with a sander, smartass."

"Oh, is it the drill's turn?" he deadpanned.

"You're hysterical," I said, rolling my eyes.

Joe leaned closer so anyone walking in wouldn't hear what he was saying. "Are you going out with a certain musician again?" Joe had already pulled as much information from me about Carter as he could, claiming that he couldn't go home without some details or Suzy would make him sleep on the couch. Knowing Suzy as well as I did, I believed him, so I told him as much as I was willing to.

"As a matter of fact, yes. He just asked me to come to his show tonight." I glanced down at my watch. "I better get going if I want to go home and get changed. I'll see you later. Be safe tonight."

"Safety's my middle name," Joe quipped as he turned to rummage in the fridge for something to eat.

"I thought your middle name was Delbert." I laughed heartily as I dodged the water bottle Joe threw at me. He had always despised his middle name, claiming that his parents must have hated him as a baby to name him something so horrible. It was a closely guarded secret that Suzy had unknowingly let slip one night while I was at their house for dinner and one that I had threatened to reveal to the other guys at work, just to taunt him.

"The man thinks he's a comedian," I heard him grumble, which caused me to start another fit of laughter that continued as I made my way out of the firehouse.

I felt nervous excitement as I walked up to the front door of the bar. Once again the place was very crowded and I wondered if that had mostly to do with the talent performing that night. After hearing only a couple of Carter's Creed's songs, I could understand why they had developed such a large fan base already. There was no question that they would go extremely far, the question was when.

Carter had told me about the big-wig from Golden Entertainment Studios that his brother Landon had arranged to come listen to them. If he liked what he heard, it could really launch Carter's career. I knew that was what Carter had always dreamed of and why he had fought so hard to recover from his injuries brought on by the fire. I was happy for him, but at the same time I wondered what the changes in his near future would mean for us.

I was getting ahead of myself, we'd only had a few dates for crying out loud. Just because I was completely smitten with Carter didn't mean his head was in the same place. I needed to chill out so I didn't scare him off.

The bouncer working the door was a giant of a man, with arms that looked like they could easily lift a truck. I was comfortable enough in my manhood to admit that I was more than a little intimidated as he towered over me; arms crossed and a deep scowl marring his face.

"Um, I'm here to see Carter Greene. He told me to tell you." I wanted to slap myself for sounding like such a bumbling idiot.

"Yeah, you and everybody else." His expression never wavered as he continued to glare at me.

"He said he would have a table waiting for me." I wasn't sure what I was going to do if this guy didn't believe me. The band would be taking the stage soon, meaning it was too late to text Carter.

You could have knocked me over with a feather when the bouncer suddenly started laughing. "I'm sorry," he said between fits of laughter. "You should have seen your face. It was priceless."

"Excuse me?" I asked, bewildered.

When he had finally calmed down, he answered my question. "My name's Jacob. I'm an old friend of Carter's; went to school together. He asked me to watch for you and show you where to sit, I just decided to have a little fun first."

"Ryan," I said in answer. "How did you know who I was?"

"Carter told me you were tall, blond, and gorgeous; he wasn't lying. Plus, the fact that you knew he was holding a table for you, kind of gave it away." I blushed more from Carter's description of me than the compliment Jacob had just given.

He showed me to a table directly in front of the stage. I didn't miss the looks I got from the people at other tables as they probably wondered who I was to have garnered a reserved table up front.

Jacob clasped his beefy hand on my shoulder as I sat down. "Sorry about messing with you, no hard feelings?"

"Nah, it's no problem." I smiled at him when he looked like he needed assurance.

"Okay then, I'll have Carla bring you a beer. It was nice to meet you, Ryan. I'm sure we'll be seeing a lot more of you." He winked at me before walking away. *Strange guy. Nice, but strange.*

I looked at those who were seated near me, interested in what kind of people Carter's music attracted. They were a fairly mixed group of mostly twenty and thirty year olds, dressed in anything from ratty jeans to high end duds. Men and women talked excitedly around me, some with piercings and tattoos while others looked like they had just left an office job to come to the bar. I smiled as I realized that Carter had managed to draw a crowd that was as uniquely individual as he was.

I was pulled from my thoughts when a waitress, who I assumed was Carla, laid a beer down on the table in front of me. "Thank you," I said as I smiled at the vivacious redhead. She wore tight black shorts and a blue tank top with the bar's logo on the front that rode up on her waist, revealing a belly button ring.

"You're welcome. Holler if you need anything else. Carter said to put anything you want on his tab, so just let me know." She gave me a friendly smile before walking off.

I looked down at the beer in my hand with a sappy grin. Carter had gone out of his way to make me feel special. I loved the fact that he hadn't been afraid to tell the people who worked there that I was someone important to him.

The lights went down, just as they had the first time I saw him perform and I felt my heart race with the anticipation of seeing him again. Even though we had seen each other several times throughout the week, it still seemed like forever since I'd looked at his beautiful face. I tried to convince my heart to move slowly, but I couldn't help how quickly I was becoming attached to him.

The music started before I could see him, but the hairs that had begun to stand up on the nape of my neck told me that he was close.

It surprised me, how in tune my body had become to his, in such a short amount of time. I heard his voice and, just like the first time I heard him sing, my cock started to swell. That time, however, was accompanied with memories of how he felt in my arms.

The lights came up and suddenly there he was. He wore low slung jeans that showcased his trim waist and a simple white t-shirt that hinted at the perfection that lay beneath. On each wrist was a leather cuff, which I found unbelievably hot. *I guess I have a leather kink.* I had a feeling I would discover many new kinks in the time spent with Carter. He had a way of making me forget my previous inhibitions and look forward to exploring new things.

Around me, men and women pushed their way closer to the stage, reaching their hands out to try to touch him as he neared the edge. I shocked myself with the level of possessiveness I felt surging through my body. I wanted to shove them out of the way and scream at them all that he was *Mine!* but I hadn't earned that privilege yet and so I took a deep breath to calm myself.

I looked up into his eyes and my breath caught at the pure joy I saw on his face as he looked down at me. *Could he have missed me as much as I had missed him?* Suddenly, no one else in the room mattered, in fact they ceased to exist as he held me in his gaze. It was as if he were singing only to me.

Finally, he turned to show some attention to his audience, but continued to glance at me every so often throughout the next few songs. I watched as he worked the crowd, singing directly to some and reaching down to touch the hands of others. He had an amazing stage presence. He made each person feel as if they were the most important person in the room and I saw many of his fans singing along, obviously familiar with his music.

When their set ended, the band exited the stage and I hurried to the bathroom to relieve my bladder. I returned to my seat in time to hear a conversation between two men at the table next to mine.

"I'm telling you, I'm gonna tap Carter's ass before he makes it too big. This is the perfect time to cash in on something like this. If I wait until they get a contract, I'll have no shot. Everybody knows famous people only trust the people they knew before they became rich." I turned to see a large guy with a buzzed haircut. He wore a football jersey, probably from his glory days in high school, and my stomach roiled at his words.

"You're not even gay, dude."

"It can't be any different than fucking a woman's ass. I'll consider it gay for pay." The guys laughed loudly and my vision turned red. Carter was an amazing man and he didn't deserve to be treated so badly.

I was out of my chair before I knew what I was doing and had grabbed the loud-mouthed, crew-cut asshole by the collar of his shirt. I leaned over him, my face inches from his. "Look, you little pencil dick. Carter Greene is one of the finest men I know and he deserves better than the way you've been talking about him. You're nothing but a leech, trying to ride on other people's coattails, instead of acting like a man and making something of yourself. You could only dream of being lucky enough to be with someone like Carter, but it doesn't matter anyway because he's way too smart to spend any time with an asshat like you."

The man's eyes opened wide in shock as I heard a voice behind me. "Ryan?" I swiveled around and my shoulders slumped when I found Carter looking at me, an expression of disbelief on his face. I would need to apologize to him for losing my cool on one of his fans, but I refused to do it in front of the money-hungry douchebag. I had to get Carter alone so I could explain.

"Carter," I started, but my anger fled as he leaned up, reached his hand behind my neck and pulled me down into a blistering kiss. My head swam from the sensations firing through my body and I felt my cock lengthen within the confines of my jeans.

My hands found their way to his waist and I pulled him up against me. We broke the kiss to suck in a much needed breath and it was only then that I noticed everyone else around us. The crowd looked a bit shocked, and for some, a bit disappointed to see the lead singer of the band obviously claimed for the evening. If I had any say in the matter, Carter would be claimed by me for much more than just one night. Someone started clapping and before we knew it, more had joined in and several people were letting out loud whistles and cat calls.

I was relieved that Carter wasn't pissed at me for my behavior. He smiled up at me and took my hand as he began leading me behind the stage. When we got to a dark hallway, he pulled me towards him and circled his arms around my waist. "I'm sorry I lost my cool back there," I said.

"Don't be, I heard some of what that guy said. I've met a lot of assholes who are just trying to get a piece of us on our way to the top. You're the first person who's ever stood up for me that way against one of them. Thank you for that." His face showed his sincerity and I leaned forward to slide my lips over his. I pulled back when I heard him chuckle and looked at him questioningly. "It seems like you're always saving me in one way or another, aren't you?"

I was embarrassed by his assessment so I pulled him closer and swept my tongue over his lips until he granted me entry. He tasted sweet and I sucked on his tongue, drinking in the flavor of him.

He growled low in his throat and pulled back with a tender smile on his face. "Come on, I want you to meet my friends."

We went into a room that wasn't much bigger than a storage room and may have been at some point. The members of the band were sprawled out on the loveseat and various chairs that were available. They looked tired but happy after the show they had put on.

"Hey, guys, I want you to meet Ryan." All eyes turned to us and I waved my hand in greeting.

"It's nice to meet all of you, I've heard a lot about you."

"Don't believe everything you hear. I'm sure we're much nicer than Carter made us sound. I'm Steve." The man I recognized as the bass guitarist stood from his chair to shake my hand. He had a friendly smile and the way his curly brown hair kept flipping into his eyes made him appear much younger than he really was.

"It was all good," I assured him with a smile.

The couple who had been snuggling on the loveseat came over next. "I'm Tyler." The man stretched his hand out to shake mine, but before we could, the tiny woman pushed past him and threw her arms around my waist.

"Thank you so much for saving Carter. You don't know how much he means to all of us. I don't know what we would have done if we'd lost him in that fire. You're a real hero."

Tyler laughed and pulled her back to his side. "Okay, Kalia, I think you've embarrassed the man enough for one day," he said as he noticed the deep blush that had spread over my face.

"I'm sorry, but it's true," Kalia continued. "You're like a real live Superman."

"I was just doing what I've been trained to do, but thanks." I could still feel the heat on my face as I glanced over at Carter who wore a proud grin. I would never get used to people calling me a hero. To me, I had only done what anyone else should do in that situation: help in any way you can.

"Well, you're a hero to me," she said with a smile as she curled up next to her boyfriend once again.

"I don't know about being a hero, but I do have to thank you for inspiring our boy here." I looked over at the large tatted drummer who was sitting with two very well endowed girls on his lap. They had been making out with him, but when he turned his attention to me, they began to kiss each other. It was a bit odd, trying to talk to him while two people were playing tonsil hockey on his lap, but from everything Carter had told me, this was very normal for Rocko.

I looked at Carter questioningly, but he was too busy glaring at his friend. "Rocko," he growled warningly.

Rocko didn't seem scared in the least as a wolfish smile spread across his face. "What, you haven't told him about all of the songs you've been working on?" He turned to look at me then. "Seems like quite a coincidence that Carter here has been cranking out one new hit after another ever since he met a certain fireman, don't you think?"

Everybody laughed at Rocko's obviously friendly teasing. I looked at Carter who stared down at the floor in embarrassment. I reached over and squeezed his hand. I was touched that I had in any way influenced the creative genius beside me to write new songs.

"Okay, that's enough of an introduction. We need to get going. See you guys tomorrow." We said goodbye quickly and walked back out into the dark hallway. "Sorry about those idiots," he mumbled as he turned to walk away.

I pulled him back and circled my arms around him. "I liked your friends. It's obvious they care a lot about you. Besides, I think it's incredibly sexy that I could inspire someone as amazing and gifted as you." I kissed him deeply, our tongues mating with each other as I cradled his head in my hands.

"Well, you are pretty inspiring, Superman." I growled at the new nickname which made him laugh. His hand reached down to clasp the quickly growing bulge in my pants and I drew a quick breath in through my teeth. "Why don't we go back to your place and you can show me why they call Superman, The Man of Steel."

I couldn't get him back to my place quickly enough. He laughed loudly as I dragged him down the hallway and out the front door of the bar. As we neared my truck I turned to him. "Did you drive yourself here?"

Carter smiled at me sheepishly. "I took a cab here. I was kind of hoping I wouldn't be going home alone tonight."

I tried to hide how his words affected me. Logically, I knew that he had meant that he wanted to go home with me, but I still felt a little anxious when I thought about the numerous people who vied for his attention each and every night.

I must not have hidden my reaction well enough because his expression became very serious. "What did I say wrong?"

"Nothing," I assured him. "You didn't say anything wrong, I'm just being stupid. Let's go." I held the door of my black Ford 350 open while Carter climbed in.

As I got behind the wheel, he turned to me and placed his hand on my thigh. "I want to be very clear. I want to go home with you and *only you*. I heard what you said about wanting more than a one-night stand. I can't make any promises right now other than to tell you that I can't stop thinking about you and I want to keep seeing you and getting to know you better."

My heart swelled with his words and I leaned over to place my lips against his. The kiss was sweet, a promise of much more to come. "Will you come home with me?"

"I'd love to," he said, flashing his dimples at me.

We held hands on the way to my place, where I leapt from the truck to open his door for him. I locked the door behind us and led Carter upstairs. "Would you like a drink?"

"Just water please, I'm always thirsty after I perform."

I handed him a bottle of water then leaned against the counter with my own. "I enjoyed the show. You guys were really incredible up there. Do you write all of the songs or do you collaborate?"

"Thanks, I'm glad you liked it. So far I've written all of our songs, but occasionally the others will help me compose the music to go with the lyrics."

"It must be so rewarding to create something new like that. I'm not creative at all."

"Are you kidding me? When I look around this room, I can see all of the things you've created. You've got very talented hands." He smirked at me sexily.

I arched my brow at the double meaning in his words. "You think so?"

"I would imagine, but maybe we should test it out just to be sure."

I walked over to where he stood and placed my arms on either side of his body, trapping him against the counter. "I want to hear more about your kinks," I whispered in his ear.

"No way, I told you mine already. I want to hear *yours* now."

I looked into his eyes that had turned a darker shade of green as we spoke. "Well let's see, after tonight, I think I have a leather kink." He arched his brow at me questioningly. I slid my hands down his arms until I reached the leather cuffs on his wrists. I circled the bands with my fingers and then closed them around his wrists, holding him secure. "I'm not sure if it was the leather itself or what they represented; the thought of you being bound by your wrists, completely at my mercy. Whatever it was, it turned me the fuck on."

"Fuuuccckkk!" he moaned. The lust in his eyes was obvious.

I licked a long line up the side of his neck and he arched his head to the side, giving me better access. I bit down gently on the lobe of his ear and felt his body shiver against mine. "So, Carter, what do you want tonight?"

He captured my bottom lip between his teeth and bit down, sending a jolt of pleasure through my cock, which began leaking in my underwear. "Tonight, I want you to tie me up and fuck me. Show me what it's like to be at your mercy, Ryan."

I captured his mouth in a heated kiss, sweeping my tongue in to explore the texture of his tongue on my own. When we broke apart, each of us gasping for air, I pulled him out of the kitchen and stood him next to one of the large wooden posts in the middle of the room. "Don't move one inch." The command in my voice surprised me. I had never played any games with any of my past lovers, but with Carter, I felt safe enough to explore new sexual avenues. That included my newly discovered domination kink. I didn't want to ever hurt him in any way, but the thought of him giving himself to me completely, unable to move and completely trusting of me, had my cock harder than it had ever been in my life.

I hurried to the table next to my bed and quickly dug in the drawer, giving a victorious fist pump in my mind when I found what I was looking for. I turned and my breath caught at the sight of Carter, standing exactly where I had left him. He had followed my command and waited patiently for me.

I didn't waste any time getting back to his side and chuckled at the look of surprise when he noticed the handcuffs in my hand, as well as lube and condoms. "The cuffs were a gag gift from Joe on my last birthday. I never thought I would have a reason to use them, but I'm really glad I didn't throw them out."

"Me too," he said with a wicked smile. "Where do you want me?"

"I want you to stay right where you are," I told him firmly. "I want to see what you have hidden under these clothes."

I let the palm of my hand glide down his firm chest, feeling each ripple of muscle that lay beneath the thin fabric of his shirt. When I reached the bottom of his shirt, I grabbed it with both hands and slid it slowly up the length of his torso. The backs of my fingers brushed against his smooth skin as the material drew away from his body and I watched in fascination as goose bumps prickled along his flesh with my touch. I pulled the shirt over his head and tossed it to the side, then stepped back so I could take in the perfection of him. Carter Greene was even more beautiful than my limited imagination had been able to envision.

He watched me through hooded eyes, waiting for either my approval or denial, as if the latter were even possible. I couldn't deny this man any more than I could deny my need for air. "You're perfect, Carter." I reached for him, needing to feel his bare flesh. I traced my hands over his smooth chest and circled his nipples which pebbled under my ministrations. He looked up at me with fire in his eyes and I sealed my lips over his. The passion between us ignited and my need for him reached a fever pitch. His hands slid around to cup my ass, but I backed away. "Huh uh, I'm in charge tonight." I smirked at the whimper that escaped his throat, but then he folded his hands behind his back in an act of submission and I struggled not to bend him over and bury myself in him right that second.

I let my eyes glide all over him as I tried to decide where to start. I wanted to taste him everywhere. I pressed a gentle kiss to his lips and then let my tongue trail down his silky throat, enjoying the delicious salty taste of his skin. I nibbled along the tender area where his neck met his shoulder and breathed in his intoxicating scent then moved lower until my mouth hovered over his pert nipple.

"Please," he begged. His voice sounded strained.

"Don't worry, I'll take care of you." I pulled his erect nipple between my lips and sucked hard. His back arched away from the post as he cried out. I swirled my tongue around his nipple before moving over to show the other one the same attention.

I lowered myself to my knees as I kissed my way down his rippled abs and over the smooth plane of his stomach. He trembled when I reached for the button of his jeans and I looked up at him. He watched me intently through hooded eyes clouded with passion. I opened the button of his jeans and slowly slid his zipper down. I pulled his pants down and threw them out of the way. My mouth watered at the sight of the impressive erection that strained behind the material of his bright blue Andrew Christian underwear. I nuzzled my nose against him, breathing in the scent of him along the apex of his thighs.

I paused when I noticed the tattoo on his left hip. It was a heart with 2:34 a.m. written in the middle of it. "What's this?"

"Caleb and I have matching tattoos with the time we were born." I smiled up at him, loving that he was so close with his twin. After all, it was that closeness that had led to me finding him that night. I pushed away thoughts of the fire and concentrated on giving him pleasure.

"You are so sexy," I whispered as I removed his underwear.

His cock was thick, long, and glistened with pre-cum. I leaned forward and blew warm air on the tip of his shaft and it jerked in response. Carter growled at my teasing and I watched as his hands fisted at his sides.

"You've shown a lot of restraint," I praised him.

"It's not easy," he said through clenched teeth.

"You deserve a reward." Before he could say anything else I swallowed his cock down to the root, his trimmed pubic hair tickling my nose. He screamed my name and bucked against me, causing the large mushroomed head of his cock to hit the back of my throat. I swallowed around him and he let out a strangled cry.

I bobbed up and down the length of him for several minutes, hollowing my cheeks to bring him the ultimate pleasure. I reached up, cupped his balls in my hand, and tugged on them gently; just enough to ward off his impending climax.

He panted as I stuck a finger into my mouth, wetting it thoroughly, then reached behind him to circle it around his puckered hole. He flexed his hips, letting me know that he needed more. I was all too happy to oblige him and let my finger gently breech him. I groaned as I felt how tight he was and I couldn't wait to feel him wrapped around my aching shaft.

I wet another finger and slid it inside of him as my tongue teased the sensitive bundle of nerves under the head of his dick. I lapped at the trail of juices that ran down the side of his cock and then kissed the tip before swallowing him once again. "You taste so good, baby."

I fingered his crinkled hole, stretching him, and I rubbed relentlessly against his prostate until he had trouble standing. I removed my fingers slowly and licked his pre-cum one more time before standing and sliding my tongue into his eager mouth. He moaned and sucked on my tongue greedily, obviously enjoying the taste of himself.

"Please, Ryan."

"What do you need?" His pupils were dilated, only a tiny ring of green still showing.

"I need you to fuck me, Ryan. Right here. I want you to cuff me to this pole and use me for your pleasure."

I had to fight off the orgasm that threatened to wash over me with his erotic words. "I promise, we will both experience pleasure tonight."

I felt his eyes roving over me as I quickly removed my clothes. When I was finished, I looked at him. The heat in his gaze threatened to scorch me. I had never felt so desired in my life, nor had I ever wanted someone with the intensity with which I wanted Carter.

"Before I cuff you, I want you to get me ready." I was surprised by the controlled sound of my voice, because the rest of me felt like it was about to break apart. I needed to be inside him, to become one with that incredible man.

He stepped forward, looking relieved. "Thank you, I needed to touch you."

I pointed to the condom and lube I had placed on the floor, but he walked over to his pants instead and fished out a foil wrapped package. He smirked at my questioning look. "I have a thing for specialty condoms. There's no reason safety can't be fun, right?"

He tore the wrapper open with his teeth and my head fell back as his warm hand curled around my cock. "Fuck," I hissed through clenched teeth when I felt the callouses on his fingers from playing the guitar. The roughness sent shock waves of pleasure throughout my body.

I gazed down at him as he slicked my cock with lubricant. I was about to stop him, afraid I would embarrass myself if he continued to touch me, but it was then that I noticed the condom he had enveloped me in. I laughed as I saw it had red flames down the sides and the words "It's getting hot in here."

"That's awesome!" I said between fits of laughter.

"That's what I thought!" Carter exclaimed happily. "The flames are perfect for you. I'm just glad I got the extra-large." He winked at me saucily before he turned and placed his hands around the pole, pushing his ass back. "Is this what you had in mind?" He smirked over his shoulder as he wiggled his ass at me tantalizingly.

"Apparently I'm not the only one who likes to tease," I grumbled. Carter laughed which earned him a swat to his right ass cheek. He gasped at the sensation and I discovered another new thing about myself. I *really* liked the pink imprint of my hand on his smooth skin. I leaned down and placed a gentle kiss against the mark.

As much work as it had been, I was very grateful for the countless hours I had spent sanding down the large wooden beam until it was completely free of splinters and smooth to the touch. I pulled his wrists towards me and quickly removed the leather straps before replacing them with the handcuffs. I felt his breath quicken as the metal clicked into place and I marveled at his trust in me. "Are they too tight? I don't ever want to hurt you."

There was a tender look to his eyes as he answered, "You won't. They're fine."

I moved behind him and we both gasped as our naked bodies slid against each other for the first time. "You feel so good," I whispered into his ear. I rubbed my hands over his broad shoulders and let them glide along his arms until they reached his bound wrists. I pulled gently, testing the security of the cuffs. "You're not going anywhere now, baby."

"Nowhere else I want to be."

I slicked my fingers with lube and traced them down his crease. His breathing hitched as I pushed in just the tip of one. He pushed back against me until my finger had disappeared completely inside his warm hole.

I added a second and then a third finger until he was grinding against me, riding my fingers wantonly. I pulled them out and he whimpered in frustration. "Are you ready for my cock?"

"Yes," he yelled. "Now, Ryan. I need you now!"

I didn't waste any more time before lining my cock up with his delicate entrance and sliding into him. The sensation of being inside the man was overwhelming. His channel gripped me in its tight hold and the heat from his body threatened to blister me, but it was so much more than a physical reaction. Inside Carter, holding him so closely to my body, sharing this moment; I finally felt like I wasn't alone anymore. I felt like I had finally found the one place in the world where I was meant to be. I had never experienced such a deep connection to anyone else before and I was stunned by the sudden surge of emotions that threatened to erupt.

As if sensing my inner turmoil, Carter turned his head and offered his mouth up to me. I drank from his lips and feasted on him as I drove into him with long, sure strokes. I tilted my hips so that I could peg his prostate and was rewarded when he cried out into my mouth. "That's it, baby, let me hear you. Don't hold anything back."

He bent in half with his arms still cuffed around the pole and pushed his ass towards me. I grasped his hips with my hands and began to thrust into him, his screams of pleasure urging me on. Sweat ran down the side of my face as I fought for control, but I wanted him to find his pleasure first.

I could tell he was close so I reached around him and circled my hand around his dripping cock. Pre-cum ran down my fingers and I couldn't wait to taste him again.

He thrust into my hand several times. "I need to come, Ryan."

"Do it, Carter. I want you to shoot all over that pole."

I thrust only a few more times before he screamed and I felt his hole spasm around me. His body jerked in my arms from his powerful orgasm and it was enough to send me over the edge. I shook against his sweat slicked back as wave after wave of ecstasy washed over me and I filled the condom. I was lightheaded by the time it ended. I had never come so hard in my life.

We stood there for a few minutes, each of us trying to catch our breath as the room spun around me. I felt his laughter against my chest. "Oh my God. That was amazing! I think I finally figured out why they tell you on those commercials to check with your doctor to be sure you're healthy enough for sex. I'm pretty sure my heart stopped. I guess it's a good thing you know CPR."

I laughed as I carefully pulled out of him. "I know what you mean, but I'm not sure how much help I'd be since I was about to pass out myself. I'm still a little dizzy."

I walked around the pole, smiling at his cum sliding down the sides of it and opened up the cuffs. I gasped when I saw the angry, red marks left behind on his wrists. My eyes flew to his. "Carter, I'm so sorry."

He quickly pressed his lips to mine, silencing my words. "Don't you dare apologize. I loved every single second of what we did. I'm glad I'll have the marks to look at when we're apart." Seeing my doubt, he added, "If it makes you feel better, I'll keep my leather cuffs on when I'm around other people."

"It's not that I'm worried about other people seeing, well, except for your family. I'm upset because I don't ever want to cause you pain." The thought of hurting him in any way made my heart squeeze painfully in my chest.

Carter placed his hands on either side of my face, forcing me to look at him. "Ryan, listen to me. It doesn't hurt. It's just a little bit tender, like my ass." He smirked up at me, his eyes dancing in amusement.

I chuckled, finally able to see the humor in the situation. "Your ass hurts, huh?"

"Well, you *are* a big boy..."

I hugged him to me. "We need to get cleaned up. Will you stay the night?"

"I've never done that before, but yeah. I'd love to stay."

After sharing a long hot shower where we spent more time exploring each other's bodies, we climbed into bed, exhausted. Carter reached for me in the dark and scooted closer. I gladly wrapped my arms around him and he lay his head against my chest. I had begun to think he was asleep when he spoke.

"Thank you for tonight, Superman."

I snorted. "Don't you start that hero crap too."

He yawned loudly. "But you are a hero. *My hero.*"

I could tell he had drifted off to sleep by his even breathing. *I don't know about being a hero, but I'd love to be **your** anything.* I closed my eyes and enjoyed the best night of sleep I'd had in years.

CHAPTER
Seven

Ryan

I T HAD BEEN A WEEK SINCE I HAD SEEN CARTER AND THE NEED to be near him was like an itch I couldn't scratch; consuming my thoughts and leaving me irritable. We texted each other as much as possible, sending funny anecdotes from our day or random thoughts that popped into our heads. I felt warm all over each time I saw a new text from him, knowing that he was thinking of me as much as I was him. It was surprising how quickly he had become such an important fixture in my life.

It had been a particularly busy week at the station, with several of the guys out sick and a surprising increase in the number of emergency calls coming through. The calls ranged everywhere from house fires and car accidents, to a drunk man threatening to end his life as he stood on the ledge of his apartment building.

I had ended up crashing exhaustedly into one of the bunks provided to us at the firehouse. It was easier than dragging myself home when I couldn't keep my eyes open long enough to drive. Through it all, my thoughts constantly drifted back to Carter.

He had been busy too, practicing well into the night with the band to make sure everything was perfect for when the CEO of Golden Entertainment Studios came to hear them. The past three days he had been travelling, playing several nights in a row at a casino in Indiana. According to his text, which came through while I was battling a fire, he had arrived back home around two in the morning and was going straight to bed. I didn't know his plans for the evening, but I was off for the next two days and I was hoping to spend as much time as possible with him.

I had just finished carrying the last of the groceries up to my kitchen when my phone signaled that I had a text. My heart raced and I hurriedly laid the bags of food down on the counter so I could get my phone out of my pocket. A smile spread across my face as I saw Carter's name on the screen and I chuckled when I saw his words.

What are you wearing?

Well, I just walked in my door so jeans and a t-shirt. What are you wearing?

I just woke up, so nothing but a sheet and a smile. I groaned loudly as I saw his reply. My cock was instantly hard and I had to reach down and adjust my zipper, which was threatening to cut off circulation.

I was trying to figure out how to respond when another text came through, that time a picture. Carter was lying in his bed, one arm bent behind his head and a sexy smirk on his face. He had a shadow of scruff that he hadn't yet shaved and his green eyes shone bright with mischief. My eyes roamed over the smooth expanse of his flawless skin until they reached the white sheet that covered his perfect cock. The barest hint of his happy trail peeked out from the top of the sheet, taunting me. All of my blood rushed to my cock at the sight of him and I would have given up everything I owned if I could have been in that bed with him.

Are you still there? His text ripped me from the daze I had fallen into.

I'm here, but I'd rather be there. It was several long moments before he responded and I hoped he was as turned on as I was.

And what would you do if you were here? I smiled at his playfulness and quickly sent back my reply.

I'd spend some time discovering what other kinks I have, besides bondage obviously.

The bondage was very, very hot. I'm happy to assist you in your other discoveries. Where should we start? I felt heat wash over my body as I remembered some of his own kinks he had named off. Many of them had sounded hot, but I wasn't really sure what I would like until I tried it. I clearly hadn't been as adventurous as Carter, but with him, I wanted to try everything.

Voyeurism? I held my breath as I waited to see what he would say. I didn't have to wait long.

Nice choice. Do you want to watch or be watched, Ryan?

I don't know. I've never done either. Maybe both?

Are you interested in a threesome? I stopped to consider his question. Carter had admitted to having enjoyed threesomes in the past and if I was being completely honest, the thought made me feel hot all over. My pulse raced as I pictured Carter, kneeling before me, sucking my cock as another man teased my nipples.

I'd be willing to give it a try if you are.

I think I just swallowed my tongue. I'll pick you up at 8:00. I'm taking you dancing.

I can't wait. I wanted to laugh as I hit send. I had never tried anything so provocative in my life. The thought of two mouths on me at the same time had me nearly coming in my pants. I reached down to press the heel of my hand against my aching dick and gasped at the pleasure it brought me. I was teetering right on the edge of release.

I quickly strode to my bathroom, tossing my clothes to the floor as I went. I turned the water of my shower to all cold and climbed in, sucking in a harsh breath as the icy blast hit my body. It helped to calm my raging passion and I got out and dried off. If I was going to experience my first threesome, I didn't want to waste time with an orgasm brought on by my own hand.

Carter picked me up promptly at 8:00 and I rushed out and climbed in his car. It had felt like years since I had felt his skin beneath my fingers or breathed in his intoxicating scent. He seemed just as anxious to see me as he leaned over the console and thread his fingers through the hair at the nape of my neck and pulled me in for a passionate kiss. Our teeth clashed and our tongues danced around each other as we tried to make up for the time we had been apart.

When we finally pulled back, each of us gasping for air, he laughed. "God, I've missed you. A week was way too long to be away from you."

"Longest week of my life," I agreed. I licked my tongue across his bottom lip and drank in his happy sigh before leaning back in my seat and buckling up. "So, where are we off to tonight?"

He waggled his brows at me as he turned the key to start the engine. "We're going to one of my favorite clubs. Drinks, pulsating music that will let me grind my body up against yours. Sound alright to you?"

"Hell yeah!" He laughed at my enthusiasm.

We drove through the city streets holding hands. Carter told me all about the positive response the band had received from the fans at their shows and a funny story about a woman that asked him to autograph her newborn baby. She hadn't liked it when Carter refused to mark the infant with a permanent marker and security had ended up being called. I told him about the couple who were so caught up in the throes of passion that they hadn't realized their condo was on fire.

"I can understand that," Carter said with a glance in my direction.

"You can?"

"Yeah. I'm pretty sure the world could have ended while you were fucking me against that wooden beam and I wouldn't have cared. All I was focused on was the feel of your long, thick cock sliding into my ass."

I moaned and had to force myself to relax the tight grip I had on his hand. "If you keep talking like that, we won't be leaving this car at all. I'll just have my way with you in here instead."

"As much fun as that sounds, I have other plans for you tonight." I swallowed thickly at the wicked smile that spread across his face.

We pulled into the parking lot of the club and Carter turned the car off. Before I could open the door, he lay his hand on my arm, stopping me. I turned to him and was surprised to see he looked nervous.

"I think we should set some ground rules for tonight. It's always better if everyone's on the same page so there's no miscommunications."

I nodded my head in agreement. "Well, you're the expert in all things kinky. What kind of ground rules do you suggest?" I teased.

Carter rolled his eyes at me. "Nothing too detailed. I was just thinking that we should both agree on the guy; we each need to feel comfortable with who we leave with."

"That makes sense. What else?"

"We need to decide where we're going to go with him."

"Not my place," I nearly shouted, causing Carter to jump. "I'm sorry, it's just that I'm a private person. I've never taken a man back to my place before." A dazzling smile spread across Carter's face and I was unable to breathe as I got a glimpse of the dimples at the corners of his luscious mouth. "What are you smiling at?"

He leaned over and kissed me sweetly. "*I've* been to your place."

I still didn't understand what had him smiling so much, until I replayed my words in my head. I cradled his face in my hands. "*You* belong there." I pecked at his lips a few more times before backing up. "So, a hotel room then?"

"Or his place if he offers," Carter suggested.

"Anything else? Do we need a secret word or code to communicate with each other?" I joked.

Carter leaned forward once again to whisper in my ear as he made little circles along my thigh with his fingers. "Yes, in fact there is. If there's anything you don't like or you want to stop for any reason, all you have to do is say…Superman." He winked at me before throwing his door open and climbing out.

I finished drinking my beer and set the bottle down on the bar beside me. I sat on a stool while Carter stood between my legs, playing with the collar of my shirt as he laughed at my story. "I've seriously got to meet Suzy. She sounds like she really keeps Joe on his toes."

"Yeah, she's the best and she's dying to meet you too. Joe said she hasn't been able to talk about anything else since she found out we were dating." I licked a lingering drop of beer off his bottom lip and heard him sigh contentedly. Carter leaned forward, pressing his warm lips to mine.

"We better get out on the dance floor if we're going to find a third," he suggested. He watched me closely as he waited for my response and I caught a glimpse of something in his eyes that I might have categorized as anxiousness or doubt, but I couldn't be sure because it was gone as quickly as it had appeared.

We had been at the club for over an hour and I had to admit that

I was perfectly happy spending time alone with him. My excitement over trying something new had waned in comparison to getting to know Carter better. I had promised him I was going to try a threesome though so I nodded my head, took his hand, and led him to the crowded dance floor.

We made our way through the press of bodies that were grinding on each other as if there were no one else in the room. The alluring mixture of sweat and sex clung heavy in the air, making my pulse beat wildly in my chest with anticipation.

When we reached the middle of the floor, I turned Carter to face me. As musically gifted as he was, I shouldn't have been surprised by how well he could dance. However, I hadn't expected him to be pure fluid sex in my arms. My brain went fuzzy as he rubbed his body seductively against mine to the pulsating beat and I gripped his hips tightly in my hands.

I was lost in the smell of his skin, the heat of his body writhing against my own and the feel of his hands as they glided over the muscles of my back before landing on my ass and squeezing. I moaned as I felt his hard cock rub back and forth over mine.

I turned him in my arms so his back rested against my chest and I wondered if he could feel my heart as it beat wildly against him. I licked a trail of sweat that ran down the side of his neck, the salty flavor of him bursting on my tongue, then I closed my eyes and let the music and his seductive movements carry me away.

A few moments later, I felt Carter stiffen in my arms and opened my eyes to see a man standing in front of him with his head cocked to the side, as if waiting for an answer to some unspoken question. Carter looked over his shoulder at me, his brow arched in question. Nerves plagued me, but I took a deep breath and looked the man over carefully. He was average height with strawberry blond hair and bright blue eyes. A smattering of freckles graced his nose and cheeks, giving him a boyish appearance. He was dressed in a green and white checkered shirt and tight blue jeans, complete with cowboy boots. I wondered idly if he really was a cowboy or if he just liked the look. Either way he was adorable and appeared safe enough. I nodded my head slowly at Carter, who turned and nodded to the man. He gave us a sexy smile that lit up his entire face and I felt my cock give a twitch in my pants. *I can totally do this.*

I watched as the stranger slid his hands along Carter's chest appreciatively and began moving his body against Carter's in a seductive dance. I felt the rumble of Carter's moans as the man pushed his hips up into Carter's groin and a fiery heat race through me.

I glided my fingers down Carter's arms and pulled his hands up until they lay clasped behind my neck. This caused him to arch his body further into the other man, whose pupils were almost completely dilated. I reached around Carter's body and pinched his erect nipples between my fingers, making his hips rock wildly as he gasped in pleasure.

The man reached his hand up around my neck and pulled me towards him. His lips were firm and insistent as his tongue plunged into my mouth. The taste of him was foreign and my body immediately stiffened at the intrusion. I pulled away and saw the man cupping Carter's cock through his jeans.

Suddenly, I felt cold all over. I loved watching Carter find pleasure, I just wanted it to be *me* giving it to him. My heart twisted painfully in my chest. My eyes flew up to Carter's face and I was surprised to find him staring at me over his shoulder. He wore an odd expression, but I couldn't decipher what he was thinking behind those brilliant green eyes. I didn't want to let him down, but I just couldn't do this anymore, it felt all wrong.

Without breaking our gaze, I spoke up. "Superman." Our eyes widened in surprise as the same word came out of Carter's mouth at the exact same time.

Carter turned and whispered something to the man who gave him a curt nod and disappeared back into the crowd. Carter turned to me with a mixture of guilt and confusion on his face. I took his hand and led him outside because I needed to know what had happened and it was impossible to hear over the music without screaming at each other. We walked around the side of the club and I leaned against the brick wall, enjoying the refreshingly cool air on my overheated skin.

"What happened? Are you okay?" My eyes wandered over his body as I searched for a clue. I knew why *I* had used our code word, but I needed to know why Carter had. It had seemed like he was enjoying himself, but if that guy had done something to upset Carter, I would kick his ass.

"I'm sorry, Ryan. It's just…" Carter stared at the ground until I took his face in my hands, forcing him to look in my eyes.

"What?"

"I couldn't do it," he huffed out, then moved away from me and began pacing back and forth, running his hands through his hair in agitation. "I tried, I really did. I've always enjoyed threesomes before and I know you really wanted to try something new. I'm so sorry if I disappointed you, but I just can't. I told myself all day that this would be okay, that I'd be able to share you. I wasn't even able to get that far though. As soon as his lips touched yours, I knew I couldn't do it and I just had to stop it. If I had to watch him put his hands on you, I would have lost my mind." He stopped pacing and faced me, his eyes begging me to understand.

A smile had already begun to spread across my face as he spoke and warmth filled my chest. I was relieved that he didn't want to share what we had with anyone else. It proved to me that we were on the same page.

I backed him up against the wall and placed my forearms on either side of his head, caging him in. "I'm not sorry at all. When he kissed me it felt all wrong because they weren't your lips and yours are the only ones I want to feel. That's why I said the code word too."

Carter searched my face. "But you wanted to try a threesome. I'm sorry if I ruined that for you."

"I'll admit, talking about threesomes turned me on, but just in the abstract. When I had to watch that guy pawing all over you and touching what doesn't belong to him, it made me sick. I didn't know whether to punch the guy or throw up."

Carter threw his head back as he laughed then wrapped his arms around my neck, letting his forehead rest on mine. I slid my arms around his waist and breathed him in, feeling peaceful for the first time that night. We stood that way for several minutes before he broke the silence. "Ryan, I don't want to scare you off or anything, but I just have to put this out there. I don't want anyone other than you." He chewed his bottom lip nervously and I reached up to pull it free with my thumb, then kissed his lips gently, soothing them.

"Why would that scare me? I don't want anyone else either." I gave him another warm, slow kiss.

"Well, it scares the fuck out of me because I've never done this before. I have no clue how to be in a relationship, but I want us to be together. I want us to be exclusive."

I smiled, my heart felt like it would burst. "That's what I've wanted all along, baby. This is new for me too, but I want to see what can happen between us. Will you come home with me? I need some time alone with you."

He looked up at me, his eyes shining. "That sounds perfect."

I kept my eyes closed, still caught in that hazy period between sleep and wakefulness and let my mind sift through the events of the previous night. From the tantalizing way Carter's body had swayed against mine as we danced to the tender way he looked at me as we made love last night. I smiled as I finally opened my eyes and saw him lying next to me, still sound asleep.

I propped my head in my hand as I looked over his flawless body. His brown hair was messy from me running my fingers through it as he slid into me the night before. His long eyelashes swept along his cheeks and he held his plump lips in a slight pout while he slept. I wanted to run my hands all over his smooth skin and memorize every curve and edge to him, but I forced myself to climb quietly from the bed, leaving him to rest peacefully.

After rummaging through the contents of my cabinets, I discovered I had no coffee. I quickly brushed my teeth, threw on some clothes, and scribbled out a quick note to Carter that I was running out to get breakfast for us and would be back soon.

I scooped up my wallet and keys from the counter and headed for the door, smiling when I saw Carter's guitar leaning against the wall. He had insisted on bringing it in from his car last night, claiming that it was a part of him and therefore should never be left out in the cold like a piece of garbage. I had teased him about it, but really, I loved seeing his stuff mixed in with mine; it felt right.

I hurried to my favorite bakery, not wanting to be away from him any more than I could help. It was rare for us to have an entire day where neither of us had work or prior commitments and I intended to make the most of every single second. I wasn't sure what he liked so I chose several pastries and two cups of coffee before I drove back home.

I heard the strumming of a guitar as I reached the top of the stairs and my pulse sped up in anticipation of seeing him. I found him in nothing but a pair of red briefs, stretched out on my bed with his guitar across his chest and a pair of headphones in his ears. His eyes were closed, obviously unaware that I had returned. I had to cover a laugh as he belted out a lively rendition of "The Lazy Song" by Bruno Mars. He was a mixture of adorable and sexy, all wrapped up in one perfect package and I realized in that moment how hard I was falling for the man.

I quietly moved to the kitchen and laid our breakfast on the counter before making my way over to him. When I reached his side, I carefully lifted my leg over his body and eased myself down until I straddled his waist. He jumped with a start and his eyes flew open as he let out a blood curdling scream. He whipped the headphones from his ears and glared at me when he saw me holding my sides, laughing hysterically.

"You asshole," he said, shoving me off of him. I fell to the floor, still laughing so hard there were tears running down my cheeks. He peered over the side of the bed wearing a scowl on his face, that was completely ruined by the grin that tugged at the corners of his mouth.

"I'm sorry, baby. I couldn't help it," I said as my laughter died down. I crawled back onto the bed and pulled him down to lie next to me. "You were so fucking adorable singing that song that I just needed to be close to you, but then you screamed like someone was chasing you with a chainsaw and it was just so damn funny."

"I didn't think it was funny at all." He narrowed his eyes at me, his shoulders pulled back and his nose turned up in a haughty manner. This of course started another round of laughter from me. "Are you done yet?" He tilted his head, looking at me like a parent trying to be patient with an unruly child.

"I think so, but I'll let you know for sure in a few minutes." He playfully punched me in the arm and I wrapped them around him, pulling him until he straddled my waist. "I am actually really sorry I scared you," I told him sincerely. "I loved seeing a side of you that your fans don't get to see though. They only see the sexy performer, I get to see all of your sides: the sexy, goofy, sweet, and even the scared little girl side of you." He swatted at my chest at the last part, but then leaned down and placed his lips on mine.

"What about my hungry side?"

"I wasn't sure what you liked so I got several things to choose from."

"I wasn't talking about breakfast." He waggled his brows at me playfully.

"I like how you think." He squealed in surprise as I quickly rolled both of us until he was lying under me. I knew exactly how I wanted to spend the rest of the day.

CHAPTER
Eight

Carter

I PULLED MY SHIRT ON AND CHECKED MY REFLECTION IN THE full length mirror that hung on the back of the door in the tiny dressing room. I slipped my favorite beanie from the back pocket of my jeans and tugged it down over my head. I pursed my lips and let out a long breath, trying to slow my heart that was about to beat out of my chest.

I couldn't remember the last time I had felt so nervous about performing. Most nights I felt a rush of adrenaline as I got ready to go on stage, but that was no ordinary night. Everything needed to go perfectly because Mr. Edwards would be in the audience and if he liked what he saw, the sky would be the limit on what could happen with our careers. After all of the hard work we had put in, the years of practicing and refining our craft, it all came down to one night and one man. It was one of those do or die, once in a lifetime moments; hence the swarm of butterflies that had taken up residence in my stomach.

A knock at the door pulled me from my thoughts. "Carter? You decent?" Hearing my older brother's voice relaxed me and I smiled as I swung the door open.

"Hey, Landon!" He pulled me in for a hug and kissed the top of my head.

"You doing okay, kiddo?"

"Yeah, just trying not to throw up." Landon chuckled, but then his face morphed into what I referred to as his "manager face." Sometimes it was as if he were two totally different people. On one hand, he was my big brother who picked on me mercilessly and still laughed about the time he switched my toothpaste with diaper cream. On the other hand, he was a shrewd businessman who knew his way in and out of the music industry and was able to negotiate deals for his clients better than any shark on television. I was so grateful that I had both sides of him in my corner. I knew the agent in him would always fight tooth and nail to help me achieve success, all while watching over me with the protectiveness of an older brother.

"Take a deep breath and relax. You guys know what you're doing, better than any other band I've worked with. You've practiced until your fingers have bled. Carter's Creed is ready for this. Besides, this is more of a formality. Mr. Edwards is an extremely busy man; he wouldn't waste his time coming to hear a band he wasn't already pretty sure about. Just treat this like any other night and go out there and play up to the crowd. Pick out some hot guy in the audience and sing just to him."

"I've already got that covered."

"Really?" Landon arched his brow at me. "When did you have time to scope out the crowd already?"

I started to answer him, but was interrupted by the door opening. Caleb walked in, holding hands with Giovanni and I peered around their shoulders. "Don't worry, I'm sure he'll be here soon." Caleb gave me a knowing smile.

I hugged him and then turned to his husband. "Do I get sugar too?" Giovanni waggled his brows at me.

"Always. I'm just waiting for you to realize you picked the wrong twin and come crawling back to me." I wrapped my arms around him and squeezed his ass playfully. Giovanni was a great guy and we had become very close. I liked to tease him about how gorgeous I thought he was, but everyone knew he had become another brother to me.

"Hands off the merchandise." I laughed as Caleb pretended to push me away from his man.

"Merchandise?" Giovanni sputtered.

"Don't even act like I don't own you," Caleb said in his best diva impersonation. Complete with a finger snap and weaving of his head back and forth.

"God, that was hot," Giovanni said, wrapping his arms around his husband and kissing his neck. I laughed at their antics.

"Wait a minute. Who were you waiting for, Carter?" Landon asked in confusion.

Another knock came at the door and I opened it to find Ryan. He was dressed in tight black jeans and a blue button down shirt with the sleeves rolled up, revealing strong forearms that were covered in the same golden hair that graced his head. He gave me an almost shy grin when he saw me checking him out. "Hey, sorry I'm late."

I pulled him towards me and leaned up to kiss him. He moved us further into the room, his lips never leaving mine and kicked the door shut behind him. He licked at the seam of my lips and I opened up to him, welcoming the flavor of him on my tongue.

The sound of laughter behind me had us pulling away from each other in surprise. *How did I forget my brothers were there?* I looked up at Ryan who was blushing furiously as he finally noticed the three other men in the room.

"Well, I felt *that*," Caleb said a bit breathlessly.

"Serves you right after I have to be around the two of you always going at it like bunnies," I said with a smirk. "Ryan, you remember my brother Caleb and his husband, Giovanni, don't you?"

"Hey! It's good to see you again."

"I'm glad you could make it. I know Carter really wanted you here." They all shook hands and then I heard Landon clearing his throat.

"Am I invisible? Because I've had dreams like that before, but never thought it would really happen." We all laughed at Landon's sarcasm.

"As much as we all wish that were true, no, we can see you just fine," I quipped. "Ryan, this is my brother Landon. Landon, this is Ryan Marshall."

Landon reached his hand out to shake Ryan's hand. "Ryan Marshall, are you..."

"He's the fireman that saved Carter," Caleb jumped in.

Landon's eyes grew soft and I heard Ryan let out a surprised gasp as Landon pulled him in for a hug. Landon whispered something in his ear and then let him go. "I hate to take off, but I need to make sure everything's set for tonight. It was really nice to meet you, Ryan. I hope we see you around some more."

The door shut quietly behind Landon and I turned to Ryan who looked flustered. "What did he say to you?" I knew how overly protective Landon could get when it came to someone in his family and the look on Ryan's face had me worried that Landon may have crossed a line.

"Don't worry, it was nothing bad. He just thanked me for saving you and said that he would always be in my debt." Color flooded his cheeks and I wrapped my arms around his waist.

"You're going to have to get used to praise if you're gonna keep saving lives, Superman." I teased as he swatted my ass.

There was a loud noise as the door banged opened and the rest of the band poured into the room. It was chaotic as everyone greeted each other, but soon conversation turned to the evening ahead. We all shared the same nervous excitement, almost like a graduation of sorts where everything you'd ever worked for was about to come to fruition.

"We better head out and let you guys finish getting ready," Caleb said. They gave me one last round of hugs before he and Giovanni walked out, promising they would save a seat for Ryan.

I pulled Ryan over to a corner of the room so we could have a bit of privacy. I needed just a moment of quiet with him. I had never had anyone that made me feel so centered and at peace like Ryan did. As if sensing what I needed, he leaned down and rested his forehead to mine. We held each other close, our eyes closed as our breath mingled and we shut out everyone else in the room. For just a few moments, nothing existed outside of our little bubble. It was exactly what I needed; *he* was exactly what I needed.

His lips pressed against mine in a sweet kiss. "You're going to be great out there, I promise. If you get nervous, just look at me. I'll be watching you and picturing you spread out, naked in my bed. Exactly like you will be later tonight." His words made me groan. He backed away with lust clouding his blue-gray eyes and it was in that moment that I knew, Ryan Marshall had ruined me for anyone else.

I stepped into the tiny shower stall that was available for the bar's employees and entertainment and let the cool water wash away the sweat that had soaked my body as I had worked my ass off. I smiled proudly, knowing that no matter what happened with Mr. Edwards, we had *owned* that stage.

It was one of those magical nights for a musician where everything seemed to just come together perfectly. We had played our hearts out, blending so perfectly we sounded as if we were all parts of just one instrument. The crowd had picked up on the excitement in the room and responded by singing along and shouting out their encouragement. I had never been more grateful for our fans.

When I had first stepped on stage and stood behind the mic, I made the mistake of glancing around the room. Landon had warned me which table Mr. Edwards would be at so I could avoid looking at him, but my eyes landed on him before I could stop myself. His eyes were narrowed as he studied each of us shrewdly and suddenly my mouth was dry and my mind went completely blank. I couldn't remember a single word to any of our songs.

As panic threatened to take over, I moved my eyes over to where I knew my brothers and Ryan would be sitting. It was only when my eyes locked with Ryan's that I felt like I could breathe again. He gave me a single nod of encouragement and everything came back to me. The rest of the show flew by in a blur.

I turned off the water and quickly dried myself and got dressed. Landon had given us fifteen minutes to get cleaned up and then he wanted to introduce us to Mr. Edwards. David, the bar owner, had graciously offered us the use of his office for our meeting so we would have some privacy.

I hurried out of the bathroom and made my way through the crowd who showered me with congratulations. We had played the same bar for several years and had developed a rather large following of dedicated fans. I hoped I never got to a point where I would forget that they were the reason we got to do what we loved most in the world.

I took the time to sign a few autographs and then swallowed hard as I looked up into the steady gaze of Mr. Edwards as he stood in the doorway of David's office. He was a strikingly handsome man with dark brown hair and eyes the color of warm honey. I offered him my hand to shake. "Hello, I'm Carter Greene. Thank you so much for taking the time to come out here, Mr. Edwards."

"'Please call me Lachlan. It's a pleasure to meet you," he said as he shook my hand. I was surprised to hear a strong British accent when he spoke. The rest of the band joined us and introduced themselves as a waitress came in and took our drink orders. We settled around the office and made small talk until she returned with our drinks. When she had shut the door behind her Lachlan cleared his throat. Even with the noise of the crowd just on the other side of the door, it was quiet in the room as we all seemed to hold our breath, waiting to hear what he had thought of our performance.

"I've been in this business a long time. I pride myself on being able to listen to a band and know exactly how far they will go in our industry. I look for musicians that not only have talent but the whole package. They have to be able to engage the crowd, to have a stage presence, if you will. They have to understand that it's just as important to interact with their fans as it is to produce quality music. With what I've seen tonight, I can tell that if you are willing to put in the hard work that comes with this job, there's no limit to how far you can go. I'm very impressed with not only the level of talent you each possess, but also the relationship you have obviously developed with your fans."

I looked across the table and caught Landon's eye. His face gave nothing away, but I could see the excitement in his eyes. He winked at me discreetly before we turned our attention back to Lachlan.

"You should all be very proud of a job well done. It would be my pleasure to work with you. Now, I suggest you all get out of here and go celebrate because tomorrow you will be offered a temporary contract with Golden Entertainment Studios."

It was quiet for a moment as we looked around at one another in shock. Then Rocko let out a loud whoop and we all started yelling and hugging one another.

I stood and shook Lachlan's hand. "Thank you so much for this opportunity." My face hurt from the giant grin that refused to leave my face.

Lachlan returned my handshake with a broad smile. "You're

welcome. I expect great things from you all."

"We won't let you down, sir," Kalia said through her tears. Tyler threw his arm around her neck and kissed the side of her head.

As my friends followed Lachlan out of the office, I felt a pair of strong arms wrap around my waist and lift me off the ground, spinning me around in the air. I laughed hysterically as Landon let out a loud shout before setting me back down on my feet. I spun around to look at him as I struggled to breathe again.

"I am so fucking proud of you, Carter." Even at twenty-three years old, I still beamed under the praise of my older brother.

"Thanks, Landon. Thank you for setting all of this up and for always watching my back."

"I always will, man, don't you ever doubt that." I hugged him and he patted my back gently. We turned when we heard a knock at the door and saw Caleb peeking his head in.

"Is it safe to come in? We saw everyone else coming out."

"Hell yeah, get in here," Landon answered.

Caleb walked in, followed by Giovanni and Ryan. Each wore matching anxious expressions on their faces. "Well?" Caleb prodded.

"We just got ourselves a temporary recording contract." It still didn't feel quite real even as the words left my mouth.

"Oh my God! Seriously?" Caleb squealed as he rushed forward and threw his arms around my neck. I laughed as he jumped up and down, making me jump with him. "I knew this day would come and I'm so happy for you! I love you!"

"Thanks. I love you too."

I was still smiling as Giovanni grabbed me up in his strong embrace. I hugged him back, but looked over his shoulder, searching out Ryan. I found him standing back a bit, his hands shoved into his pockets and a small smile playing on his lips. I suddenly really needed to feel those full lips on mine and I saw his eyes fill with heat as he caught me staring at his mouth.

I forced my attention back on Giovanni when he spoke. "This

calls for a celebration. Why don't we head over to Romero's; my treat, of course."

"Thanks, G. Ryan and I will meet you guys there." I got one more hug from Caleb before they left and chuckled as he whispered into my ear. "He's so yummy. For the first time in our lives, I *want* details." He winked and then closed the door behind him. Oddly enough, for the first time I had someone so special that I wanted to keep things about us private, even from my twin. That realization was enough to have my head swimming. I was really falling hard for the man.

"Why are your hands in your pockets instead of on me?" I gave Ryan my most naughty grin and was rewarded with a low growl.

"I didn't want to interrupt anything. You needed to have that moment with your family."

I stalked towards him slowly. "What I *need* is to feel you wrapped around me, your lips on mine, and your cock in my ass."

"Holy fuck!" he breathed out as he lowered his head and swept his tongue into my mouth. My hands moved over his strong arms and I clung to him as I felt my legs tremble and threaten to give out. Ryan swirled his tongue over my teeth and the roof of my mouth, leaving no crevice unexplored. He kissed me so thoroughly, I was almost positive I could have come from just that, but he pulled away before I could test that theory. I made a mental note to try it sometime.

He was panting as he leaned his forehead against mine and I was happy to see that I hadn't been the only one affected by our kiss. "As much as I would love to bend you over that desk and bury myself in your tight heat, we need to go. Your brothers are waiting for us at the restaurant."

I stuck my bottom lip out in a pout. "I love them, but I'd really prefer a more private celebration, if you know what I mean."

"I'll make you a deal. We'll have a nice dinner with your brothers so I can get to know them better and when we're done, we'll go back to my place and take turns fucking until neither of us can walk tomorrow. Sound good?" He brushed his lips against mine and my eyes rolled back into my head as he cupped my straining erection through my pants.

"Deal. Just eat fast," I agreed quickly.

"Wow! This place definitely looks a lot better than the last time I was in here," Ryan said as we walked into Romero's. I took a look around, appreciating the changes and updates Giovanni and Caleb had made to the place, but I couldn't help the cold chill that swept through me as I spotted the door that led down to the wine cellar. My nightmares had almost completely stopped since I started seeing Ryan, but I hadn't been back in the restaurant since the night of the fire and my stomach churned as I remembered the pain and the terror I had felt that night.

"Are you okay?" Ryan asked, saving me from the horrific memories. He put his arm around my waist and pulled me closer to him.

I looked up into his concerned eyes and suddenly I felt calm and safe again. I had discovered that Ryan seemed to always have that effect on me. I liked teasing him about it, but he really was like my very own personal Superman. When he was near, it was as if I had a shield of protection around me, like nothing and no one could hurt me.

"Yeah, I'm great." I sighed happily as I leaned forward and kissed his chest.

"Hey, Carter! It's great to see you again." Lauren, Giovanni's assistant manager, walked up at that time with a big smile on her beautiful face.

Lauren was an incredible woman with a great sense of humor and we had quickly become friends in the short time I had worked at the restaurant before the fire. I reached for her and gave her a kiss on the cheek. "You too. I've missed you."

She gave Ryan a curious glance. "Ryan, this is a friend of mine,

Lauren. Lauren, this is my boyfriend, Ryan. He's the fireman that got me out of here."

Lauren's eyes grew wide. "Oh, it's so nice to meet you. Thank you for taking care of Carter. We're all pretty fond of him around here, he's part of our restaurant family." Ryan looked shocked as she pulled him in for a hug and I chuckled at the blush that colored his face. He was so damn modest.

"Um…you're welcome. It's nice to meet you too." He patted her on the back awkwardly until she finally released him.

"Follow me, guys, G has a table in the back for your group. I hear congratulations are in order, huh?" She looked at me excitedly.

"Yeah, I guess so," I answered. "It still doesn't feel real yet."

"Well, I've heard you play so I know that you deserve it. I'm so happy for you."

Lauren led us through the expansive dining area to the back of the room and I saw Landon, Giovanni, and Caleb already enjoying a beer. "Thanks," I said before she left us to go attend to the other guests.

"I see you got started without us," I motioned to their beers as we sat down.

"This is already our second round. We weren't sure if you'd actually make it here or if you'd go off to celebrate on your own," Landon teased.

"If it had been up to me, we would have chosen option B," I quipped back and everyone laughed.

"I couldn't give up an opportunity to meet the people who can tell me embarrassing stories about your childhood, now could I?" Ryan gave me a mischievous grin.

"Oh, we can definitely do that," Landon answered.

"We've got some really good ones." I narrowed my eyes at Caleb as he jumped in.

"I warned you about paybacks," Giovanni said with a devious smile.

I groaned in defeat. "Just take it easy, I'm pretty crazy about this guy. I don't want you scaring him off." I heard Landon gasp at my words and I realized what I had just said out loud. I had never liked a man enough to introduce him to my family, much less announcing to them how much I liked the guy.

I bit my bottom lip as I stole a peek at Ryan out of the corner of my eye to see his reaction. I was relieved to see him smiling warmly at me. He leaned forward and placed a gentle kiss on the corner of my mouth. "I'm crazy about you too." My dick instantly hardened in my jeans as his breath ghosted across my lips. I swallowed hard and tried to adjust myself discreetly, but nothing got past my brothers who snickered at my obvious reaction.

"Shut up, assholes." I couldn't wipe the smile off my face though. I looked around the table and realized that I had never been happier in my life. My musical dreams were coming true, I was with my family, and I had a man next to me that meant more to me than any other man ever had. I never wanted the night to end.

We stayed way past when the restaurant had closed. The food was delicious and I enjoyed watching Ryan become more and more relaxed with my brothers as we shared endless stories. I told about the time I had first met Giovanni. He hadn't known that Caleb had an identical twin and when he saw me dancing with a guy at a club, he mistook me for Caleb. Giovanni had gone all caveman and ripped me away from the guy, only to be shocked when Caleb walked up behind him and he realized what had happened.

I laughed as Giovanni hung his head in embarrassment, but Caleb lifted his husband's arm, wrapped it around his shoulders, and kissed him gently on his jaw. "I loved it," he said happily. "That was the first time you showed me that I meant something to you." They gave each other a tender look and Giovanni kissed my brother gently. I glanced over at Ryan and was surprised to see him watching me. I felt his hand reach for mine under the table and I quickly linked my fingers with his.

We talked for several more minutes before I excused myself to go to the bathroom. When I returned, I heard everyone laughing and I smiled to myself. My family was extremely important to me and I had always hoped that whoever I brought into my life would fit in easily with them. Apparently, Ryan did.

They quieted as I neared the table and I eyed my brothers suspiciously. "What did you do?"

They glanced at each other innocently. "I don't know what you mean," Caleb said.

"*We* didn't do anything," Giovanni said with a chuckle.

I turned my glare on Landon who simply smiled at me. "As your manager, I need to remind you that with this contract, will come a lot of hard work."

"I realize that." I squinted at him as I wondered why he had thrown out that random comment. I noticed everyone else at the table trying to hold back their laughter and my suspicion grew.

Landon continued. "What I'm trying to say is, you're going to be incredibly busy from now on. There won't be time for anymore lounging around in your Snuggie."

"Or clicking to MTV so they can teach you how to Dougie," Giovanni chimed in.

I swung my head to Ryan, my eyes widening in shock and I pointed my finger at him accusingly. "You didn't," I gasped.

He grinned at me apologetically. "I'm sorry, it just kind of slipped out. We were talking about your performance and I mentioned that it was nowhere near as good as the private show I walked in on at my place."

I dropped my chin to my chest with a groan as my brothers laughed hysterically around me. I would never hear the end of this now, I thought as Landon and Caleb broke out in a very off-key rendition of "The Lazy Song."

"You're all a bunch of assholes." This started another round of laughter. There was no heat in my words and my brothers knew I could take a joke. I stood from my chair and held my hand out for Ryan. "I think we better go before any more damage is done." I hugged each of my brothers and Ryan shook their hands before we left.

I climbed into Ryan's truck and buckled my seatbelt then turned to look at him when I realized he hadn't started the engine yet.

He was biting his lip as he studied me apprehensively. "What's wrong?" I asked.

"I'm really sorry if I crossed a line in there. Are you mad at me for telling that story?"

Normally, I would have teased him and tried to make him feel bad, but I could tell he was afraid he had really upset me. I leaned over the console and held his face in my hands. "You will find out that I can both give and take a joke, Ryan. I grew up with four siblings who love to tease and torment each other. This is not the first or the last time they'll have something to use against me. I'm not mad in the least. In fact, I was really happy to see you hitting it off with them so quickly."

Ryan leaned his forehead against mine and his shoulders relaxed as he breathed out a sigh of relief. "Thank God. I don't have much experience with how siblings interact and I was so afraid I had upset you."

"Not at all." I kissed him deeply and ran my fingers through his hair. "But you could still make it up to me if you want to." He laughed as I waggled my eyebrows at him suggestively.

"I think that can be arranged." He leaned in for another deep kiss before starting the engine. I twined my fingers with his as he drove us to his place and wondered just how much better our night was about to get.

Ryan held my hand as we made our way through the darkened lower level of his home. He led me over to the spiral staircase, but before he could start climbing the steps, I pulled him back to me.

I ran the palms of my hands over his broad chest, feeling my way over each muscle until I clasped my hands behind his neck. "Thank you for coming to support me tonight. It meant everything for me to be able to see you in the audience." I pulled him towards me and gave him a lingering kiss which soon became heated as we thrust our hips together, seeking friction against our growing erections.

Ryan broke our kiss and when he spoke his voice was deep and gravely from his arousal. The sound of it had my cock fighting to get out of my suddenly very tight pants. "Unless you want me to take you right here on these steps, we need to get upstairs. Now!"

"These steps don't have enough room for everything I want to do to you tonight so lead the way." As I followed behind him I enjoyed the way his black jeans hugged his delectable ass. I couldn't resist reaching out with both hands to cup his taut globes, squeezing them. He looked over his shoulder at me. "You're lucky I didn't bite them. *Yet.*" I gave him a playful wink and a low growl rumbled from his chest. I loved it when he did that.

When we reached the top of the stairs Ryan pulled his shoes and socks off and set them neatly near the stairs. He walked around, turning on some softly lit lamps. It gave the open space a warm, seductive, and very private feel. I watched him as he made his way around the space and I wondered how I had gotten so lucky to be with such an amazing and stunning man. *Whatever it is, I hope it never ends.*

"I'm going to get a glass of water. Would you like anything?"

"No thanks, I'm fine." He got a glass out of the cabinet then reached into the fridge for the pitcher of cold water while I made my way over to his massive bed. I kicked off my socks and shoes, and sat down on the foot of the bed.

Ryan shut the fridge door and turned to find me. Even across the room I could feel the heat in his gaze as he studied me. "I like seeing you in my bed."

"It would be much better if you were over here with me." I licked my lips slowly and patted the mattress beside me.

He took a long drink of water, his eyes never leaving mine. His Adam's apple bobbed as he swallowed and I felt my briefs grow wet from my weeping cock. He set the glass down on the counter and gave me a knowing smirk.

"I agree, but first I need to make it up to you for telling that story to your brothers."

"That's exactly why you should hurry up and join me in this gigantic bed," I quipped.

He gave a low chuckle and I felt it from the base to the tip of my aching shaft. I reached down and popped the button of my jeans and lowered my zipper just a fraction. I looked up through my lashes and found Ryan watching my hands intently.

He wet his lips with his tongue as he saw the tip of my cock peek out from the waistband of my red boxer briefs. I reached down and swiped my finger over the tip, drawing it through the moisture. I lifted my finger, letting him get a good look at the string of pre-cum that formed between my cock and it, then slowly raised my finger and swiped my tongue over it. I moaned as I tasted myself.

"You don't play fair," Ryan ground out. I smiled to myself at the effect I was having on him, but was surprised when instead of joining me on the bed he turned his back to me and walked over to his entertainment system. *What the hell was he doing?*

I didn't have to wait long to find out because he turned to me with a shy, boyish smile and I felt my heart skip a beat as I saw yet another side to Ryan Marshall. I watched him, wondering what was about to happen as he took a deep breath. "Even though I found it both adorable and incredibly sweet to walk in and hear you singing that song, I owe you for telling an embarrassing story about you and giving your brothers more ammunition to use against you. Soooo… here goes nothing." He released a nervous breath through pursed lips and then hit a button on the remote he held in his hand before tossing it to the side.

Through the various speakers that were strategically placed around his open living space I heard the clear voice of Charlie Puth as he started singing "Marvin Gaye." My eyes grew wide and a huge smile spread across my face. I loved that song and had always thought it was incredibly sexy. Ryan started unbuttoning his shirt in a strip tease and I leaned back on my elbows so I could enjoy the show.

I laughed as he pulled his shirt down his arm and spun it around his wrist a few times before letting it drop to the floor with a flourish. He bit his bottom lip, watching me through hooded eyes as he unbuckled his belt and pulled it free of his pants then whipped it against the bed. The snapping sound it made sent a jolt of lust through my body like an electric shock. I pulled my shirt over my head and threw it to the side of the bed. If Ryan was going to get naked, I wanted to match him step for step.

He turned away from me and my eyes travelled over the planes of his back. I saw the tight muscles rippling beneath the surface of his skin and my fingers itched to touch him. I quickly slid out of the rest of my clothes and moved up the bed until my back rested against the headboard.

With his back still to me, he rotated his hips several times and then slowly lowered his pants before kicking them away from him. Standing in nothing but a pair of black boxer briefs he glanced over his shoulder at me and blessed me with a seductive wink.

I was mesmerized at the sight of his fingers as they teased the waistband of his briefs down until they laid nestled just below his pert ass. My head dropped back against the headboard with a thud as I zeroed my sights in on his crack. I wanted to pull him towards me and bury my tongue in his seam until he begged for my cock to take him, but I restrained myself; barely.

I wrapped my hand around my cock, using the moisture that dripped from the tip like a leaking faucet to make the glide easier as

I began jerking up and down, my hips thrusting upwards in search of friction. I needed to touch him, to feel his strong body covering my own. As if he heard my thoughts, Ryan turned around and his eyes shuttered as he saw me fucking my own fist.

He dropped his briefs then before I knew what was happening, he grabbed me by my ankles and pulled me towards him until I lay flat on my back. He climbed on the bed and began crawling his way up my body like a predatory animal until we were at eye level with each other. He knocked my hand out of the way. "This is all mine and I didn't say you could play with it." He grabbed my cock in his large fist and held it, but didn't move. I wanted to yell at him to please just make me come, but I saw the challenge he held in his eyes. I gave him a single nod of concession and his lips spread into the most glorious smile.

"Thank you," he said before he lowered his body onto mine. He sealed his lips over mine in a possessive kiss, swallowing my gasp as our cocks aligned and rubbed against each other. I wrapped my arms around his neck and locked my legs around his waist. If I had my way, I would never let him go.

We devoured each other's mouths, consuming each other as the music continued to play. I closed my eyes as he began making his way down my body, scraping his teeth along my jaw and showering my neck with tender kisses. My body jerked under his as he landed on my nipple and teased the tight nub between his teeth before flicking it with his tongue. I placed my hand behind his head and held him to me, not wanting him to stop the sensual assault that was scrambling my brain.

He looked up at me with a smile. "I love how responsive you are." His tongue left a wet trail behind as he made his way across my chest and to my arm.

He paused, suddenly very serious as he peered down at the small scars that lined the inside of my bicep from the surgery I had after the fire. A lump formed in my throat as he leaned his forehead against the scars and squeezed his eyes shut tightly. I could see his lips moving as if he were saying a prayer and my eyes burned as he laid the gentlest of kisses along each jagged line. It was at that moment that I knew without a doubt that I belonged to Ryan Marshall; heart, body, and soul.

I cupped the back of his neck and pulled him to me. I was so overcome with emotion that words failed me, instead I poured everything I was feeling into a kiss. "I need you, Ryan," I whispered as I drew in a ragged breath.

"I'm right here, baby. Let me make you feel good." I held onto his shoulders as he lowered himself until I could feel his warm breath against my cock, causing it to twitch in response. He grasped my dick in his strong hand and I braced myself for the feel of his hot, wet mouth. Instead, he leaned down further and nuzzled his face into my groin.

My back arched up off the bed as he sucked the sensitive skin at the juncture of my thigh. I knew he was marking me and I felt it everywhere throughout my body. *I was his.* I wasn't brave enough to voice my feelings yet, but I already knew I would never want another man the way I wanted Ryan. He had quickly become the most important person in the world to me.

I groaned as he lapped at my balls, drawing them into his mouth one at a time. His hands pressed against the backs of my legs, bending me in half and lifting my ass off the bed.

I scrambled to find something to hold on to as he spread my cheeks and with a flattened tongue, licked a line up the seam of my ass. "Fuck, Ryan!" I yelled. I heard him chuckle as he buried his face and began eating my ass like it was his last meal. His wet tongue swirled over my hole several times and then snaked its way inside of me. I had never been rimmed with so much intensity before and I was soon delirious with need. "Please!" I whimpered.

It was a gloriously frustrating feeling because I never wanted him to stop, but I was also desperate for something more. As usual,

Ryan knew just what I needed and he didn't disappoint as he worked one finger inside me while he licked around my rim. He continued holding me up in the air and the feeling of being completely at his mercy brought a whole other level of sensuality to what he was doing to my body. I gripped the blanket in my fists as I let him take control and do whatever he wanted to me.

My eyes rolled in the back of my head as he added another finger and held me open so he could spear me with his tongue. "You taste so fucking good," he rasped as he lowered me back down to the bed. Before I could respond he sucked my cock down his throat and curled his fingers inside me until they swept over my prostate, making me scream. Stars burst behind my eyelids and sweat dripped from my brow as I struggled not to come.

"Pl..please, Ryan," I stuttered. "So close." I nearly wept at the emptiness I felt when he removed his fingers. He hovered over me as he reached into his side table for the necessary supplies. I leaned my head up and captured his nipple between my lips, sucking on him.

When he found what he needed he returned his lips to mine. We kept our eyes open, trained on each other as we kissed and I could see the hunger in his gaze. He pulled away long enough to rip the condom wrapper open with his teeth. I expected him to slide it down his own leaking shaft and so I gasped in surprise when he rolled it down mine.

"I want to feel you filling me up." I couldn't do anything but nod my head. No one had ever turned me completely inside out the way Ryan did.

I ran my hands over his sweat slicked chest, rolling his nipples between my fingers as he poured lube over his fingers and reached around to begin opening himself up. "That is so fucking hot!" I drawled. His eyes held mine as he raised himself over me, lining my cock up with his tight hole.

Ryan lowered himself slowly, allowing his body to adjust to my size. His heat seared me through the thin latex and I fought to be patient. Everything in me wanted to grab him by the hips and slam my cock into him, but I could never hurt him, so I ground my teeth and panted as I let him set the pace.

When he was fully seated on me he opened his eyes and my breath caught at the emotions I saw there. *Could he possibly be feeling all the things for me that I felt for him?* He nodded as if he had heard my thoughts and then he began rocking his hips and my ability to think disappeared.

I wrapped my hands around his waist, digging my thumbs into the V cut of his abdominals as he began riding my cock. I pressed my heels into the mattress and lifted my hips, meeting his downward movements with an upward thrust that pegged his prostate. He threw his head back as he got lost in the sensations.

Watching his complete abandon brought my orgasm much closer than I had expected and I grabbed his cock in my fist and began working it, hoping to bring him to the edge with me. After a few more thrusts he screamed my name and showered my chest with his hot seed. His tight hole gripped my cock like a vice and every muscle in my body tensed as my orgasm took over.

He collapsed onto me and I curled my arms around him as we lay there shuddering. I buried my face in his neck and breathed in the heady scent of cum, sweat, and Ryan. I decided that from that moment on, whenever life got rough, his body covering mine and my arms wrapped around him, would be my happy place that I would escape to.

CHAPTER
Nine

Ryan

I PULLED INTO THE STATION LOT AND PARKED MY TRUCK IN AN open space. A song played on the radio that reminded me of Carter. The singer was talking about being gone on the road for too long and how he couldn't wait to get back home to the person he loved. As happy as I was for Carter that his career seemed to be moving forward, I couldn't help being nervous about what the changes he was facing would mean for us.

I had no doubt in my mind that we were good for each other and I believed that he cared about me. I could already tell, through his actions and the way he looked at me sometimes, that he was feeling the same thing I was. I didn't know if he was falling as hard and as fast as I was, but I could feel him moving in that direction.

I had a lot to worry about, even though I was trying not to let it show. There was a good chance that Carter's band would have to relocate. Golden Entertainment Studios was located in Los Angeles and they could very well expect them to move there. Statistically speaking, most relationships didn't last once they became long distance. Considering the fact that we were a brand new couple, made the chances even slimmer.

Then there was the consideration that at some point they may be sent out on tour. Carter already had men and women throwing themselves at him and even though he didn't strike me as the cheating type, he could decide it was easier to break things off with me and enjoy the life of a rock star instead of holding on to someone he might not see for months at a time.

The whole thing was terribly depressing. It had already gotten to the point where I couldn't picture my life without him and even the thought of him walking away from me made my chest hurt. He was such an amazing man and exactly who I had been looking for. It would kill me if he decided to walk away.

I took a deep breath as I turned off the engine. Like my grandpa always told me, "There's no point in borrowing trouble, son." I definitely didn't want Carter to think I was clingy. I needed to trust him to make the best decisions for his future and I would pray that I would get to continue to be a part of it.

With a new resolve, I locked my door and headed into the firehouse. I heard laughter as I walked down the hallway toward the rec room and smiled to myself as I recognized the sound of Joe's teasing voice.

Joe and I had the same sense of humor, so working together always made our shift pass by much faster. Besides that, there was no one in the department I trusted more to have my back when we went into a fire. We had trained together and worked beside one another for so long that we could almost read each other's minds and followed the other's cues without ever having to speak a word. We automatically knew what role each of us would take in different situations and what we needed to do to help the other person. We were a great team.

His smile grew as I walked in the door and he stood, grabbing me in a manly hug and slapping me on the back. "There you are! I was just explaining to the guys here that it doesn't matter what challenge they throw our way; no one can beat us. We're the Dynamic Duo." I smiled back at his heavy New York accent. He'd lived in Chicago for several years, but would probably never lose that part of his hometown roots.

"Dynamic duo, my ass!" We looked over to see Billy, one of our friends who wore a smirk on his face. "You guys wish you were half the team that Jeff and I are." Everyone laughed at that. We were usually paired up into teams when we entered a fire, which then caused a friendly competitiveness between all of us over which team performed the best. We were always trying to outdo each other in all areas, whether it be a game of darts, basketball, or training courses. It kept everyone on their toes and helped pass the time during long, boring shifts when the alarm never sounded.

The laughter died out as Dan shoved his way through until he stood in front of me. He looked around the room as if he were making sure he had everyone's attention before turning back to me with a sadistic smile on his face. *What the hell was this guy's problem?* He cocked his head as he sneered at me. "Haven't you all heard? Ryan here has already partnered up with someone else. Although this person is much more than a workplace friend. From what I hear they're pretty close. Tell everyone, Ryan, how is your little fuck partner, Carter Greene? Kevin saw you two holding hands as you left a restaurant last night. Exactly which one of you filthy faggots takes it up the ass?"

I lunged for him, my arm cocked and my fist ready, but Joe grabbed me from behind before I could deliver the blow. "Calm down, Ryan. He's a piece of shit and he's not worth getting into trouble over," Joe said quietly, trying to soothe me.

I took a deep breath and straightened, knowing Joe was right. As much as I wanted to pummel the guy until he was unconscious, I would probably end up on paid leave and be required to go through anger management while he would walk away with a warning about using politically correct words. I needed to be smart about how I handled the situation, but that didn't mean I would back down.

"I think I can speak for everyone in here when I say that I don't *ever* want to know about your sex life, so why do you care about mine?" My eyes got very wide and I made an "O" with my mouth like I had just figured something out. I leaned towards him like I was going to tell him a secret, but spoke loud enough for everyone to hear. "Unless you want to know because you're *sexually curious*. Is that what this is about?"

Everyone started laughing and I watched as Dan's face turned a deep shade of purple. His whole body vibrated with rage and when he spoke, spit flew from his mouth. "You better watch your back, Marshall." He stormed out of the room letting the door slam behind him. Even though I had stood up to him that time, I wasn't foolish enough to think that he was going to let it go.

I turned to the other guys in the room. "Yes, I'm gay. If anyone else has a problem with that, speak up now." I crossed my arms as my eyes swept the room. I noticed Kevin standing off to the side, his gaze locked on the floor.

"No problem here."

"Doesn't matter to me." The guys all took turns answering and I was relieved that no one else seemed to have an issue with me having a boyfriend.

"Now maybe my girlfriend will quit talking about how sexy you are," Rodrigues joked.

"Are you kidding? Women find two guys making out totally hot! Now you have to worry about your girlfriend even more than before," Joe quipped.

Everyone cracked up at the look of horror on Rodrigues's face.

Now that the tension had been broken everyone began filing out of the room, eager to get something to eat before we were called out on a run. Joe squeezed my shoulder as he moved past me and I gave him an appreciative nod.

I waited until most of the guys had left before approaching Kevin who looked like he was going to be sick. He hadn't been with our department very long, having just graduated from the academy, and I knew he looked up to all of us as his mentors. "You okay, man?"

His head snapped up at my words and I was surprised to see tears in his eyes. I waited for the door to close behind the last guy before speaking again. "Do you want to talk about it, Kevin?"

He let out a warbled breath and then spoke quickly. "I'm so sorry, Ryan. I had no idea that he heard me talking or that no one else knew that you were gay. I just figured that you were kind of private about your personal life, which still gives me no excuse to have talked about you. It's just that I was so happy when I saw you holding hands with Carter. It made me feel like I wasn't the only one. So I mentioned to one of the other guys that I had seen the two of you leaving Romero's. I told him how great I thought it was. I had no clue that Dan was around to hear what I said. I'm so sorry, I never meant to cause you any problems."

I smiled at him gently, sensing how distressed he was and wanting to reassure him. "It's okay, Kevin. I'm pretty sure most of the guys had already figured it out. There's only so many times you can make excuses about why you don't have a girlfriend, especially with as many years as most of us have worked together. I just hadn't made any announcements because there's still a lot of narrow minded people in our line of work, like Dan, who could make things pretty rough when we're supposed to be protecting each other."

"Oh God, I hadn't considered that." Kevin's eyes grew wide in alarm. I lay my hand on his arm to calm him.

"It'll be alright. I just have to keep a close eye on Dan, but we work with a great group of guys and knowing what just happened here, I have a feeling they'll all be watching my back a little more closely too. Now, can I ask you something?"

"Sure, anything." He let out a long breath, relieved that I wasn't angry with him. I remembered what it was like to be a rookie and wanting to fit in with all of the more seasoned firefighters.

"You said seeing me and Carter together made you feel like you weren't the only one. What did you mean by that? Are you…?"

"Gay," he answered with a nod. "I was actually out with my boyfriend when we saw you. Toby didn't want me to tell any of you guys I was gay because he was afraid someone would hurt me. He's very protective." Kevin blushed and I thought it was sweet. He had always seemed a bit naïve to me and I was glad he had someone watching out for him. "Then when I saw you holding hands with Carter, I thought 'hey, that's a guy that's been here for a long time and everyone likes and respects him so they must be okay with it.' I'm really sorry."

"Hey, quit apologizing. It's not your fault that Dan's a dickhead. Just promise me you'll be careful around him, okay? I've been around longer than you and I'm better prepared to defend myself against his bullying. I don't want him to make you his next target, understood?"

"Yes sir!" He nodded his head so fast I was afraid he was going to hurt his neck.

I chuckled. "Let's get something to eat, kid."

I shrugged off the jacket of my fire suit and hung it on the hook. I was exhausted and everything hurt. I was sweaty and covered in ashes and needed to take a shower before going home, but as I neared the bathroom I saw Dan heading that way. Normally I wouldn't give him a second thought, but after the shift I'd had, I just didn't have it in me to deal with anything else. I felt completely drained.

Turning around, I pulled my keys out of my pocket and headed outside. I knew my truck was going to smell like smoke for a long time, but I didn't care. My only thought was to get away.

Some of the guys were going to the bar around the corner for drinks, but I wasn't in the mood to be around a crowd. It had been one of the worst shifts I had ever experienced on the job and I needed some time to process everything.

I drove down the darkened streets lost in my own thoughts, not really caring where I ended up. After a while, I stopped at a red light and wiped the tears from my eyes. As I waited for the light to change, I finally took notice of my surroundings and was surprised to see that I was almost to Carter's apartment building. I guess when my head became too full with the terrible images from earlier, my heart took over, knowing exactly what I needed.

I pulled up in front of his building and climbed out, praying that he was home. I made my way to his door and knocked. He swung the door open and his happy look of surprise soon turned into worry as he took in my condition. "Ryan, what's wrong, baby?"

He reached for me and then I was in his arms and I was sobbing into his shoulder. I don't remember him getting me inside or shutting the door. All I could concentrate on was the feel of his warm arms wrapped around me and his hands rubbing soothing circles across my back. I don't know how long we stood there, but he held me until I was cried out and all that remained was my gentle hiccups as I calmed back down. Carter was exactly what I had needed. He was my comfort.

I took a deep breath and wiped my eyes with trembling hands. "Thank you. I'm sorry about that, but thank you."

His eyes were filled with worry, but he gave me a beautiful smile that made my heart melt. "Don't ever apologize for coming to me if you need something. I want to be that person for you."

"You are," I answered quietly as he smoothed his hand over my cheek. I nuzzled into his warm palm. "Would it be alright if I took a shower here?"

"Of course. Do you mind if I join you? I want to hold you some more."

"That sounds perfect," I said with a little smile. I appreciated that he hadn't demanded answers from me right away. Instead he seemed happy to stay close to me, willing to listen whenever I decided I was ready to talk.

He took my hand and led me to a small bathroom. We somehow had always ended up at my place and so this was the first time I had been inside his apartment and I was surprised with just how at home I felt. Although I was beginning to suspect that had more to do with the man undressing in front of me than whatever place we happened to be in. Once he was completely naked, he started the shower before he turned and began undressing me.

I still felt a bit numb so I simply watched his hands moving lovingly over me as he removed each article of clothing. Neither one of us spoke and the silence, along with his nurturing touch, made the moment that much more intimate.

As the last of my clothes dropped to the floor, Carter took my hand and pulled me under the spray of water. He grabbed the shampoo and poured some into his hand before lathering my hair. I closed my eyes and felt my tense muscles begin to relax as he used his fingers to scratch gently at my scalp.

After rinsing my hair, he lathered my body with soap, paying loving attention to each part of me. There was nothing sexual in his actions. The moment was simply about him bringing me the comfort I needed and yet it was in that moment that I realized, no matter what the future held for us, I would never love another man the way I loved Carter Greene.

He turned off the water and reached for the towel hanging on the wall. I bent down so he could reach to towel dry my hair and I wrapped my arms around his waist, laying little kisses along his chest. "Thank you."

"You're welcome," he said simply. He kissed my lips before taking me to his room where he rummaged through his closet for a few minutes before presenting me with a long pair of sweats and a large t-shirt. I looked at him skeptically, knowing the clothes were much too big to be his. I appreciated his help, but I'd rather walk around naked than wear clothes left over from an old hookup of his.

Carter noticed my hesitation and rolled his eyes at me. "They're Giovanni's. This place used to belong to Caleb and he left some stuff behind when they got married." I shrugged apologetically and pulled the clothes on. "You're freaking adorable when you're jealous." He leaned up to kiss the tip of my nose then began getting dressed himself.

I followed him into a tiny kitchen where he handed me a beer from the fridge. I swallowed it down gratefully, not stopping until it was empty. He watched me, his expression full of concern and understanding. "You want another one?"

"Yeah, I think I need one more please." He handed me another and then he led me to the living room. Carter sat down, leaning his back against the arm of the couch, one leg up on the cushions and motioned for me to sit between his spread legs. I happily obliged and leaned my back against his chest. It amazed me that even with our height difference we seemed to fit together like two puzzle pieces.

He put his arms around me and nuzzled his cheek against mine. I reached for his hands that lay on my chest and threaded our fingers together. Carter waited patiently while I let out a long, slow breath and tried to figured out where to start.

I started by telling him about being outed at work. "Shit," he breathed out. "I'm sorry, I never thought about anyone from your work seeing us together. What did they say?"

"One guy there is a real douchebag, always runs his mouth about stuff. I think the only person that likes him is...*him*. I don't care what he thinks."

"What about the others?" I closed my eyes as he moved his hands and began massaging my shoulders, working his thumbs in deep to relieve the tension there. His hands were extremely strong, probably from all of the hours spent playing his guitar and piano.

"They were great. I don't think any of them were really surprised. And I found out that another guy there is gay also. When he saw us together he was thrilled to find out he wasn't the only one."

"Well, I guess it turned out pretty good then. I'm so glad I didn't mess things up for you."

I turned my head so I could kiss his neck. "You make everything in my life better," I whispered as I rubbed my lips back and forth over the line of his jaw.

Carter angled his head to kiss my lips. "Sweet talker." After a few lingering kisses he went back to massaging my shoulders. "Will you tell me what had you so upset earlier?" he asked quietly. I knew if I said no, that he would respect that and we'd move on, but I found myself wanting to unburden my grief on him. At some point he had become my rock, the one person I could count on to be there through both the good and bad times.

"We got called out to a fire. It was a tiny, run-down house. A neighbor had seen flames shooting out of one of the windows and called it in." Carter wrapped his arms around me securely when he felt me shudder. "Joe and I were the first ones to head in and we had to bust the door down because it was locked. When we got inside we found four kids. The oldest was probably no more than six years old, although forensics will have to determine that to be sure." I heard Carter's sharp intake of breath, but I forced myself to keep going. "They were all together near the front door. I assumed they were try-ing to get out, but the door had been locked at the top of its frame and they couldn't reach it." I choked on a sob and Carter rocked me in his arms, letting me get it all out.

Tears streamed down my face as I continued. "There was noth-ing we could do for them, so we just put the fire out before it could spread to any of the nearby houses. When we were finishing up I heard screaming from the front yard. The mother had just gotten home from work. From what the police were able to gather, her husband had been physically abusive to her and the kids so she ran away from him. She moved them to the little house about three months ago. She was working two full-time jobs just to keep them all fed, but she couldn't afford childcare and she was afraid if she applied for assistance and was put in the system that her asshole husband would track them down, so she left food out for the kids, turned on the TV and locked up the house while she went to work. She thought she was keeping them safe, first from their abusive father and then from strangers, but ultimately she locked them *in* when they needed *out* the most. I'll never forget the sound of her screams when she realized she'd lost them all."

Carter never let go of me while I spoke and I could feel his tears dripping onto my shoulder as he cradled me in his safe embrace. When I was with Carter, nothing else could hurt me. He called me his hero, but he was a hero to me every bit as much as I was to him.

Before Carter came into my life, I had been lonely. Growing up, it had always been just my grandpa and me. Then when Grandpa died, I had no one I could count on until I met Joe. Still, even though Joe was like a brother to me, he had his own family to go home to at night. The nights had always been the hardest for me; a time when my mind raced and my worries came to the forefront. I used to dream of a day when I would have someone that I could come home to and share not only my worries with, but the good things too. Carter had become that someone for me. I just prayed he felt the same.

I turned in his arms to face him and brought my hand up to wipe the tears from his cheeks. "Thank you for listening, I'm sorry for dumping all of that on you. I hope I didn't ruin any plans you had tonight."

He looked at me seriously. "I am so honored that you came to me when you were upset. I always want to be the one you turn to. As for my plans tonight, I was going to call you and see if you wanted to come over and watch a movie, so you didn't ruin anything." I closed my eyes and breathed in deeply, letting his familiar scent soothe my frayed nerves. "What do you need, sweetheart?"

My eyes fluttered open to find him watching me intently and my voice sounded raspy from crying. "Help me forget."

Without a word, Carter stood from the couch and held his hand out for me to take. I slid my hand in his and he led me down the narrow hallway to his bedroom. I stared at the large bed which took up most of the space in the small room as Carter moved behind me, sliding his hands around my waist.

He placed a gentle kiss between my shoulder blades then slowly pulled my shirt up and over my head before tossing it to the side. I turned in his arms, cupping his face in my hands and pressed my lips to his. My tongue slid along the seam of his mouth, seeking entry. Carter opened for me and our tongues dueled with each other as we each fought to climb further into the other.

When we broke apart, I grabbed his shirt and pulled it off of his slender body. His hand snaked inside the waistband of my sweats and I moaned loudly as I felt his callused fingers wrap around my shaft. I held onto his shoulders as my legs threatened to give out from under me. Our teeth clashed as we devoured each other's mouths in a passionate kiss.

"I need you to fuck me, Carter, and don't hold anything back. I want to forget everything but the feel of your cock stretching my ass."

"Whatever you want, baby!" Carter promised.

We each slid our pants off and then I climbed on the bed, positioning myself on all fours. My head hung down between my shoulders as I offered myself completely to the only man I had ever loved. I heard him moving around, but couldn't see him. Not knowing when or where he would finally touch me heightened my arousal and my cock began dripping onto the bedspread beneath me. I felt the bed dip behind me and he grabbed my ankles, spreading my legs wide. My heart beat wildly in anticipation as I felt him moving closer.

"It would be such a shame to let this go to waste." I let out a guttural moan when I felt his mouth close over the head of my dick. I peered down between my legs and saw him lying on his back, his head directly under my groin, as he sucked my cock like a starving man. His lips stretched wide around the bulbous tip and I felt the familiar burning sensation at the base of my spine.

"Stop!" I gasped. "I'm already close and I really want to come with your cock buried inside me."

Carter chuckled wickedly as he slid out from under me and knelt behind me. "Fine, but later I need to drink you down. You taste divine."

"Ugh! You're killing me." I let my forehead drop to the mattress and stretched my arms towards the headboard, completely surrendering to him. He could do anything he wanted to my body and I would be perfectly happy with it.

"No, baby, I don't want to kill you. I want you to soar." I let out a very unmanly whimper as I felt his tongue swipe over my puckered hole. "Mmmm, you taste just as delicious here."

I was lost to the sensations he brought to my body as his tongue forced its way into my eager hole, swirling around and intimately kissing me where no one else had ever kissed me before. I loved rimming, but had never trusted someone enough to allow them to do it to me. I trusted Carter with my entire soul and I quickly learned that I was a huge fan of being rimmed. I protested when he rose up behind me, I didn't ever want him to stop.

His voice sounded husky. "I'm sorry, sweetheart, I was enjoying that a little too much. If I don't get inside you in the next few seconds, I'm afraid this will all be over."

"Yes, please." I reached for my cock and stroked it as I heard him ripping open the condom wrapper and then I heard the snick of the lube bottle being opened. Carter slicked himself quickly and then slathered my hole.

My heart hammered in my chest as he pressed against my tight ring with the head of his cock and began pushing in. When he met resistance, he leaned his body over mine and licked the shell of my ear. "Push against me, baby. Let me inside so I can feel your smooth walls."

His sexy words flipped a switch in me and he was soon able to slide in all the way. I panted through the pain and burning sensation as I stretched to accommodate his size. Carter held steady, waiting for my cue. After a few seconds, I nodded and he started rocking his hips into me slowly.

"Harder!" I commanded.

Carter obliged by gripping my hips in his strong hands and tunneling his way into me relentlessly. After several minutes, I took over and began backing up onto his cock. The only sounds in the room were of our sweaty skin slapping against each other and the bed rocking against the wall. He held still, letting me use his body to seek my own pleasure. "That's it, baby, use me. Take whatever you need."

The tone of his voice gave me no doubt that he was experiencing just as much pleasure as I was, but I still needed more. I had to be sure that he was feeling the same way I was and to do that I needed to be able to look into his eyes. After all, they were the windows to his soul.

I pulled off of him and flipped over onto my back. I wrapped my legs around his waist as he pushed into me and pressed the heels of my feet against his firm ass, silently urging him to pound me harder. I wanted to feel the effects of our lovemaking for days afterwards.

Carter leaned over me and grasped my hands in his, linking our fingers together. His eyes were hooded with lust, but clear in their honest emotion. He held my gaze as he continued to rock into me at a steady pace.

"I love you so much, Ryan." My heart soared at his declaration, but before I could respond, he took my mouth in a primal kiss and angled his hips so that he pegged my prostate with every thrust. Lights burst behind my eyelids as my orgasm rushed through me and cum shot out of my cock, soaking my chest and making it slick between our bodies.

Carter followed quickly behind. Watching him orgasm was the most beautiful sight I had ever seen. His head was thrown back and his body bowed sharply as he screamed my name. I vowed then that I would do whatever it took to make sure my name was the only one he ever screamed again.

He collapsed onto me and we held each other, both shaking as we struggled to catch our breath. When my heart rate had slowed, I kissed the top of his head and ran my fingers through his hair lazily.

"Did you mean it?" I whispered into his hair. I was nervous about his answer, but needed it all the same.

He shifted so that his chin rested on his hands which were folded across my chest. He looked at me unapologetically and with complete adoration. "Of course I meant it. I love you, Ryan. I've loved you for quite a while now and I know you may not..."

"I do," I interrupted. "I love you more than I ever thought was possible to love someone else. I love you so much it hurts." I grabbed him under his arms and pulled him up so that we were face to face. He showed me my favorite smile, the one that made his dimples appear at the corners of his mouth. I leaned forward to kiss each one before rolling us quickly until I had his body pinned under mine.

Carter laughed in surprise and his green eyes danced. "I am so happy right now," he said as he swiped his tongue over my chin.

I tilted my head as I studied him for a moment. I felt a smile spread across my face. "It's really surprising, considering how this day started, but so am I. You've made me happier than I've ever been." I pressed my lips to his and felt my cock stir, ready for round two.

CHAPTER
Ten

Carter

I PULLED INTO MY PARENTS' DRIVEWAY AND SMILED WHEN I SAW that both of my sisters' cars were there also. My siblings and I had enjoyed the usual teasing and picking on each other growing up- *and still do to this day, if I'm being honest-* but we had also been extremely close. Now that we were older and had careers and significant others in our lives, it made it harder to find time to get together. I was very fortunate that I still got to see my brothers as often as I did. Of course it helped that Landon and I worked together. Unfortunately, I didn't get to spend as much time with my sisters as I would have liked.

As I walked in the house and shut the door behind me, I heard laughter as my oldest sister, Michelle, finished telling the others about some crazy do-it-yourself disaster she and her husband, Jason, had gotten involved in.

Mom spotted me first and jumped up with a delighted smile and gave me a quick kiss on the cheek. "Hey, baby! This is a nice surprise!"

Dad came over next and threw his arm over my shoulder. "We haven't seen you very much lately. Have you been busy with the band?"

"We've been working our butts off as usual. Mostly just to keep us from going crazy until we hear what all Landon and Mr. Edwards worked out."

"Oh reeaally?" my sister Emma drawled out. She looked at Michelle and they both faced me with their arms crossed and their eyes narrowed. As a kid they could make me confess to any wrong doing with just a look. As a grown man, their scrutiny could still give me goose bumps, even if I had no clue what I had done wrong.

"So there's nothing else that might be taking up all of your time?" Michelle chimed in.

"Make that *no one* else?" Emma added. "Because from what I heard through the grapevine, there most definitely *is* someone who you've been spending a lot of time with lately."

Michelle jutted her bottom lip out in a dramatic pout which made me roll my eyes in amusement. "Of course we had to hear about it from someone other than our baby brother here. Someone who has actually gotten to meet this special guy while we, his loving sisters, haven't."

They clung to each other as they pretended to cry and I couldn't hold back my laughter any longer. "Okay, I give up. I'm sorry. I'm the most horrible excuse for a brother that there ever was." I got down on my knees and clasped my hands together in a plea as I peered up at them through my lashes. "Can you ever find it in your hearts to forgive me?" I begged as I worked the puppy eyes.

Emma pretended to sniffle. "I don't know. Are you going to dedicate your first album to us?"

"No."

"Tell People magazine that you have only us to thank for your talent and success?" Michelle asked.

"No." I stifled a laugh.

"Interrupt Taylor Swift's next acceptance speech by jumping on stage and declaring that your sisters are the only reason you get up in the morning?" Emma tried to look serious, but it was ruined by her twitching lips.

"Hell no!" I burst out laughing. I stood up and wrapped my arms around both of them. "How about I promise to let you meet him instead?"

"Deal!" they said in unison.

"Jeez, that's all you had to say, Carter." Michelle snickered.

"Musicians! Always have to be so over the top with everything," Emma agreed, shaking her head. They both giggled when I swatted their butts.

"Wait a minute, I'm confused." We turned to look at Dad. "Does Carter have a guy or not?" His bewildered expression had me and my sisters rolling with laughter once again. Mom stood at his side looking very hopeful.

"Yes, there's a guy and he's very special." I couldn't help the sappy grin that spread across my face whenever I thought about Ryan.

"What's his name? How did you meet him? Is it serious?" Mom fired off her questions like a drill sergeant.

We all sat at the table as Michelle poured everyone a glass of lemonade. "I actually stopped by today to tell you about him." When I saw Emma start to bristle, I covered her hand with my own and looked at her pointedly. "And I was going to call both of you next." Feeling mollified, she settled back down in her seat.

"His name is Ryan Marshall. We met because he was the fireman who pulled me out that night." Mom gasped and then covered her mouth with her hand as her eyes filled with tears. Dad put his arm around her and pulled her closer so he could kiss her temple. "And I really hope it's serious because I'm crazy in love with him." I rolled my eyes as my sisters "Awwwed" me.

"We have to meet him for sure now," Mom said, slapping the table. "I've always wanted to thank him for saving your life and I can't wait to meet the man who has finally stolen your heart."

"Mom, you act like I'm ancient. *Finally* stolen my heart? You make me sound like a spinster."

Mom crossed her arms with a huff. "Well, I'm still waiting for grandbabies and I'm not getting any younger here."

"In due time, my love. In due time." Dad patted her arm reassuringly.

"On that note, I'm going to get going." I chuckled as I stood and pushed my chair in. "Sorry to rush off, but I really have to get to the studio and work on some stuff."

I leaned down to kiss my mom's head. "No problem. Your sisters and I will get busy planning a family cookout so we can meet Ryan. I'll call you later to let you know when to show up."

I raised my brows as I looked at my dad. "Do I even have a say in this?"

He walked with me to the door, keeping his voice low so he couldn't be overheard. "I've learned over the years that it's best if I stay out of the way and let her do whatever she wants. When your mom's happy, I'm happy," he said with a shrug.

I never used to understand when people would say things like that, but I completely got it since meeting Ryan. There really wasn't anything I wouldn't do if it brought a smile to Ryan's face. I hugged my dad and then walked down the front porch steps, smiling as I sent Ryan a text informing him that he was going to have to meet the rest of my crazy family. I just hoped they didn't scare him off.

I sat on a stool, my body bent over my guitar as I strummed a few random chords. I was thankful to have the rehearsal studio to myself for a while. I needed some time to get lost in my own head.

Everything in my life was changing so fast. Granted, it was all good changes, such as getting signed on with Golden Entertainment Studios. Of course having Ryan come into my life topped the list of good things, but still, with all of the changes, I needed some time with my guitar to help center myself. Music had always had a way of helping bring me back into focus when life seemed to be swirling too fast around me.

I closed my eyes and let the melody that had been playing on a loop in my head all morning come to life through the movement of my fingers over the strings. It was a sensual, almost hypnotic, melody that conjured up images of making love to Ryan. The notes flowed from me as I remembered the taste of his skin and the strength in his arms as he held himself above me. The tempo increased as I pictured him thrusting into me, making every nerve in my body come to life and behind my closed lids I could see the intensity of his gaze right before he leaned down and claimed my mouth. As the song neared the end, the notes reached a new high, just as I had when I found my release. My fingers teased and held the final note, willing it to last as long as possible.

When the strings had quieted and the room was once again in total silence, I opened my eyes slowly. I smiled, feeling completely back in balance and thrilled with my new creation. I jumped from my stool and raced across the room to grab my composition book and a pencil. I wasn't sure if I would ever play the song for anyone else or if I could even come up with words perfect enough to match my memories, but I knew one thing for sure: I needed to get it all written down so I could revisit it over and over again.

I sat down and began putting my music to paper. Awhile later, I heard the door open and glanced at my watch. I wasn't all that surprised to see that several hours had passed since I had begun composing. It wasn't the first time that I had gotten so caught up in my work that I lost all track of time.

My body was stiff from sitting still so long. I put my arms over my head and leaned back, stretching the aching muscles in my back and I wondered idly if I could talk Ryan into giving me a massage later.

I smiled as Landon walked in the room. He looked all business in his sleek black suit and wing tipped shoes, carrying a briefcase.

"Where are the others?" He slid his sunglasses on top of his head, slipped his jacket off and sat down.

"They'll be here in a little bit. I came in early to work on some stuff while it was quiet."

"Sorry if I interrupted. You working on a new song?"

"Uh, yeah. I just finished," I said as I quickly gathered up the papers I had been working on and gently pulled the one Landon was looking at out of his hands. Even though no one else would know what had inspired the song, I wasn't ready to share something so personal yet. "What have you been up to, Mr. Fancypants?" I stood up and tucked my papers away in my guitar case for safe keeping, looking at him over my shoulder.

"You wish you looked this good." Landon smirked at me as he ran his hands down his chest and I pretended to gag. "And what I've been up to is having a meeting with a certain Lachlan Edwards about a certain band I represent. Not that you'd be interested in hearing about any of that, right?"

I swung back around, my eyes wide and ran back over to sit across from him. "Tell me everything and don't leave anything out."

Landon's eyes danced with amusement as he leaned back in his chair and linked his hands behind his head as if he didn't have a care in the world. "Well, let's see. First, I got off the plane in L.A., then I took a cab to Golden Entertainment Studios, then I got on an elevator there, then..."

I narrowed my eyes at him. "Don't make me hurt you, Landon." He laughed at the absurd threat. We both knew I wouldn't stand a chance against him in a physical battle, but over the years I had learned other ways to fight back. "Tell me now, or I'll tell Mom you were the one who broke her great-grandmother's china platter when you and Tommy McGregor were playing football in the house; even though she told you a hundred times not to." I folded my arms across my chest smugly.

Landon rolled his eyes. "*That's* what you're going to go with? Tattling to Mommy? I'm twenty-eight years old. I don't think Mom's going to get upset about something that happened fourteen years ago."

I picked up my phone. "Then you won't mind me calling her now, right?" I smiled innocently at him.

I could see the moment I had him and I knew I had won this round. "You're a child, you know that?" he scoffed.

"You started it." I pointed my finger at him.

"Did not," he said with a grin.

"Did too." I smiled back. "Okay, now tell me *almost* everything. Skip to the important stuff this time."

"Okay." Landon sat up in his seat with a chuckle and picked up his briefcase. He rummaged through it for several seconds before finally pulling out a manila folder which he laid on the table. He opened his mouth to say something, but before he got the chance I heard the door open and the sounds of my bandmates filled the air.

They piled into the room, smiling at Landon. Kalia gave me a quick hug. "What's going on, guys?"

"You're just in time. Landon was about to tell me what happened at his meeting with Lachlan," I explained. My friends eagerly sat down so they could hear what Landon had to say. "Where's Rocko?" I asked, noticing his absence.

Steve rolled his eyes in exasperation. "Fuck if we know. Been trying to get ahold of him all day. He's not answering any of our calls or texts."

"I hope he hasn't gotten into trouble again," Kalia said, gnawing her bottom lip worriedly.

"Getting into trouble is what Rocko does best," Tyler said, taking Kalia's hand on top of the table and squeezing it gently.

"If so, he better get his act together. I have some really big news to share with you guys and we don't need any trouble at this point." Our heads swiveled to Landon, remembering that he had been about to tell us something important. Seeing that he had our attention he opened the file in front of him. "As you guys know, Lachlan was very impressed with what he heard the other night and he told you he wanted to offer you a temporary contract with his label." We all nodded, smiling at each other as the rush of that night came back to us.

Landon continued. "Well, when I met with Lachlan today it was clear to me that there was a lot he *hadn't* said."

"What does that mean?" I asked with a nervous feeling in the pit of my stomach. I was well aware that until the contract was signed by all parties, the whole deal could easily fall apart. *Please don't let this fall apart.*

Landon smiled at all of us. "It means; he's extended an invitation for you guys to be part of a three-month tour opening for another band. If everything goes well, at the end of the three months, your temporary contract will become permanent."

My ears buzzed as I sat in my chair, stunned. I couldn't believe this was finally happening. I looked around at my friends who wore the same stunned expression that I was sure I sported. I wanted to ask more questions, but my brain wasn't connecting with my mouth.

Landon chuckled. "You each need to look over your contracts to see if there's any changes you'd like to make, but in my professional opinion, Lachlan has made you a very fair deal. Not to mention, proposing quite a generous starting salary." He passed us each a copy of the contract and I thumbed through it. My eyes bulged at the amount of money being offered.

"Damn, that's a lot of money," Steve said, breaking us all from our trance. We all started laughing. Tyler hugged Kalia and whispered something in her ear that made her blush.

Finally finding my voice I asked, "So, how does this all work and who will we be opening for?"

"And when do we leave?" Tyler asked.

"The tour starts in a few weeks, so you only have a little bit of time to get everything ready. You'll be given a tour bus to travel in so I hope you guys all get along because you're about to get a whole lot closer." Landon rubbed his hands together dramatically. "Now, for the best part. Carter's Creed will be opening for Maximum Mayhem."

"No fucking way!" Steve shouted and we all looked at each other excitedly. Maximum Mayhem had gotten their start on a singing competition reality show a few years before and after winning the competition, shot their way to the top of the rock and roll charts. They were performing to sold-out crowds every night. Opening for them was definitely going to get us noticed. No doubt about it, this tour could make or break us.

"Yes fucking way," Landon said, causing the others to look at him in shock. They always saw Landon when he was being the straight-laced business manager, they didn't know him the way I did. He winked at me. "Okay, I have to get back to the office. Look over the contracts and we'll meet again in a day or so to finalize everything. Congratulations, you guys really deserve this." We all stood and took turns shaking his hand and thanking him.

When Landon had left we all looked at each other, grinning like fools. "Looks like we have a lot to take care of," Tyler said.

"Somebody needs to track down Rocko and let him know what's going on," Kalia added.

"I'll do it, I know most of the shitholes where he hangs out," Steve offered.

"Okay, let's meet back up here tomorrow to talk about the contract and figure out what kind of song list we want to put together for our show," I suggested. Everyone nodded in agreement and then took off to take care of business.

The door closed behind them and I peered out the window to

make sure they were gone before I let out a loud war whoop and broke into a celebratory dance, twirling my head and shaking my ass to a song only I could hear. I couldn't believe all that was really happening. Everything I had dreamed of as a kid was coming true.

I pulled my phone out of my pocket. I couldn't wait to tell Ryan the good news. When I unlocked my phone, Ryan's picture appeared on the screen. I had kept one of the photos that I had taken of him that day at the firehouse and made it the wallpaper on my phone. In it he was leaning back against the fire truck, his biceps bulging where his arms were crossed. His slate colored eyes sparkled with mirth as he fought back a grin at something I had said.

My smile slid from my face as I looked at the picture and my heart squeezed tightly. I wondered what my leaving for three months would do to us. Our relationship was so new; was it fair of me to ask him to wait around for me to return, even if that's what I wanted to beg him to do? And Ryan was an extremely private person. If our band became well-known, how would he feel about being thrust into the public eye just because he was dating me?

I shook my head. There was no use getting worried about something I had no control over. I would just be happy about this opportunity and pray that Ryan would be willing to go along for the ride. It was too painful to think of the alternative.

I hit the button, held my phone to my ear and waited for him to answer. After a few seconds his voicemail picked up. I checked my watch, noting the time and realized he was still at work. "Hey, sexy! Give me a call whenever you get this message. I love you." I hung up, smiling once again.

My earlier excitement started building again and I suddenly wanted to share my good news with my best friend. I sifted through my contacts and hit the button. "Hey, you got time for some company?"

"If that company is you, always," Caleb answered cheerfully.

My smile grew as I turned out the lights and locked the door behind me. "Great. I'll be right over."

CHAPTER
Eleven

Ryan

I CLIMBED OUT OF THE FIRE TRUCK AND WENT TO THE ROW OF lockers against the wall to put my gear away. I pulled off the heavy fire proof jacket and hung it on the hook then slipped out of my boots and lined them up neatly at the bottom of the locker. I slipped my suspenders down off of my shoulders and stepped out of the thick pants, sighing in relief once I was free of the cumbersome uniform. Stripped down to my own sweat soaked clothes, I made my way to the showers and began washing away the grit, grime, and frustration of the day.

My jaw ached from clenching it so tightly and I had a pounding headache. It had been another crappy shift at work. The call we had just returned from was pretty routine: a small car accident where luckily no one was injured.

My frustration came from having to deal with the constant homophobic garbage that Dan insisted on spewing whenever he was in my presence. You would think that with all of our co-workers telling him to shut up that he would eventually let it drop, but the man was like a dog with a bone. For whatever reason, he seemed to have decided to make it his life's mission to attack my love life whenever the opportunity arose. I tried to ignore him as much as possible, not wanting him to know that he was getting a rise out of me, but I honestly wasn't sure how much more I could take of his bullshit before I would have to lay him out. I had tried to behave as professionally as possible, but I refused to be someone's punching bag and I most certainly wouldn't allow him to talk trash about Carter.

I stepped out of the shower and dried off quickly, wrapping the towel around my waist. I walked through the locker room, thankful to see just a few of my buddies. I pulled my phone out of my locker and smiled for the first time that day when I listened to Carter's voicemail. Even though we had already said the words to each other, my heart still tripped over itself at hearing Carter say he loved me. Suddenly, the nastiness of the day disappeared and nothing else mattered.

I started to return his call, but at that moment the door swung open and Captain Jones's gruff voice filled the room. "Is Marshall in here?" All heads turned to him and everyone automatically stood when he entered the room. Curtis Jones was ex-military and built like a brick shithouse. He expected only the best from his team and accepted no excuses for failure. While we all had a healthy fear of the man, we respected the hell out of him too.

"Here, sir." I stepped forward, painfully aware that I was still only dressed in a towel.

"Get dressed, I want to see you in my office in five."

His demeanor brooked no argument so I nodded quickly. "Yes, sir." His eyes darted around the room and then he gave me a single nod before turning on his heel and retreating from the room.

Joe hurried over to my side. "What was that about?" He knew as well as I did that it was rarely a good thing to be summoned to the captain's office, and even more cause for concern that he had come to search for me himself instead of sending his assistant.

"I have no idea, but I better hurry." I shrugged off Joe's worried look because it was doing nothing to help my own nerves and quickly pulled my clean clothes on. I didn't have time to call Carter so I sent out a quick text instead, asking him to meet me at my place at six o'clock for dinner. I shoved my phone in my pocket and rushed out the door. I did *not* want to keep the captain waiting.

My hand shook a bit as I knocked on the closed door. "Come in," the captain's deep voice called out. "Shut the door behind you," he said as I walked in.

I did as he asked and then sat down in one of the chairs across from where he sat at his desk. I forced myself not to squirm under his close scrutiny and cleared my throat. "You wanted to see me, sir?"

"Yes, I did. It has been brought to my attention that there may be an issue between another member of the team and yourself. Can you tell me anything about that?"

I clenched my jaw. As much as Dan had pissed me off, I wanted to try to handle things myself before going to our superior about it. "It was just a difference of opinion, but I'm handling it, sir."

I was surprised when the captain leaned forward with his hands clasped on the top of his desk and his face softened as he looked at me. "I have a younger brother who's gay." He studied my face for a reaction, but I was too shocked to say anything. Not because his brother was gay, but because in all the time I had worked there, the captain had never divulged anything about his personal life to the men who worked for him. He said he preferred to keep his home life separate. The only way I knew he was married was the ring on his left hand, but I had no clue if it was to a man or a woman or if he had any children or pets. So the fact that he had just told me he had a brother, had me sitting up straighter.

150

"When he was in junior high, a boy he went to school with started bullying Scotty because he was gay. This kid was a real punk; came from a whole family of narrow-minded assholes. Anyway, I got tired of seeing my brother come home upset. I offered to take care of the kid, but Scotty refused, saying he wanted to deal with it himself. I respected my brother so I let him handle it, but I also didn't trust the other kid not to hurt him, so I followed Scotty home from school one day. Sure enough, the kid cornered Scotty in an alley and started pushing him around."

The captain's face took on a look of pride as he remembered that day. "Scotty stood his ground. He never raised his hand to the kid, just stood there and told the kid in no uncertain terms that he was an ill-informed, uneducated, narrow-minded jerk who didn't know his ass from a hole in the ground. Then he began listing famous gay people throughout history and all the ways in which they contributed to society and told the kid that he should try to do better with his life too." He chuckled at the memory.

"What happened next?" I said with a smile.

The captain shook his head. "The jerk backed off after that. I'm not sure if any of the things Scotty said got through to him or if he was just too confused by the big words Scotty used to waste any more time on my brother, but he walked away and moved on to other things. He eventually got in enough trouble and was kicked out of school. He and his parents moved to Arkansas last I heard."

He grew serious again as he looked at me. "The reason I told you all of this is because I want you to know that I get it. I know the kind of shit you're dealing with and just like with my brother, it's my job to keep you safe. I've received written complaints from several of your coworkers and Dan will be placed under review for his actions. I'll be speaking to him about this, but I wanted to make you aware of the situation first. With any luck, this will straighten him up, but I'll be keeping a close eye on him in case things escalate any further."

I nodded my head, humbled by the compassion in his eyes.

"Thank you, sir. I really appreciate that."

He tapped his knuckles against the top of his desk. "Okay, well, unless there's anything else, you can head on home."

I stood from my chair and shook his hand "Thank you, sir. Have a good night."

I smiled as I left the captain's office. It felt good to know that I had friends at work that would stick up for me against Dan's homophobic slurs. I just hoped it would be enough to stop him.

As I climbed into my truck, I shot off a quick text to Joe to let him know everything was fine so he wouldn't worry all night and then I headed to the store to get the ingredients for dinner. After the crazy roller coaster of a day I'd had, I was ready for a nice romantic evening with the man I loved.

At a quarter till six, I checked the chicken to make sure it was done and then set it on top of the stove to cool. The little red potatoes were just turning a nice golden color so I left them in the oven to finish baking. The tantalizing smell of herbs and spices filled the kitchen as I shut the oven door. I stirred the citrus glaze that would coat the chicken once it was carved and opened the lid on the fresh green beans that were steaming in a pan. Dinner was a little fancier than what I normally cooked, but I wanted to make something special for Carter.

I glanced around the room, double checking that the table was all set and the candles were lit. I pulled my apron off over my head and smoothed down my button down shirt, making sure it was tucked into my dress slacks properly then I turned on some music. I smiled, everything was ready and all I needed was Carter.

As if my thoughts conjured him, I suddenly heard the deep pulsing bass of his car radio as he pulled up to the house. I raced down the stairs and pulled the door open before he could reach for it. Carter stood there smiling, looking sexier than a man should be allowed to look in a tight white t-shirt, jeans with strategically placed holes, and a pair of black work boots. His guitar case was slung over his back and his bangs flopped over one eye, making him appear younger than he was. *Damn, my man is fine.*

He whistled under his breath as his eyes travelled up and down my body and it sent a shiver down my spine as if he had actually caressed me. "Don't get me wrong because you look fantastic, but are we going somewhere? I feel really underdressed."

I smiled at him. "You're dressed perfectly. The only thing that would be better is if you weren't dressed at all."

He smiled widely, his dimples popping at the corners of his mouth. "That can be arranged, but only if you promise to get naked with me."

I stifled a groan. I wanted to take him right there in the doorway, but I had other plans that needed to happen first, I reminded myself. "I will definitely take you up on that, later." I chuckled as he pouted adorably and I couldn't resist leaning down to suck his bottom lip into my mouth. He pressed his body to mine and I could feel his arousal as he ground himself against me. The man was a master of seduction and I had to force myself to pull back. I adjusted my dick which was begging to get in on the action.

Carter looked up at me through hooded eyes, knowing exactly the effect he had on me. I grabbed his hand and pulled him towards the stairs. "Come on, you little minx, before you ruin my plans," I growled.

"You planned out our sex? Whew, kinky! Is there a script? Am I going to be the patient or the doctor tonight?"

I laughed at his enthusiasm. "Sorry to disappoint, but I didn't plan any role playing tonight. Just this." As we reached the top of the stairs, I gestured to the room with my hand.

Carter's expression was unreadable as his laughter died out and he looked around the room. "What is all this? It's not my birthday or anything."

I shrugged my shoulders. "I just wanted to have a quiet, romantic evening with my boyfriend. Is that alright?" I suddenly felt a little foolish. Maybe Carter wasn't the romantic type. Maybe he would rather go out somewhere.

Before I could get too worried, he turned to me with a shy smile. "I've never had anyone do anything like this for me before. This is perfect, Ryan. Thank you."

I let out a sigh of relief and led him over to the table where I pulled his chair out for him. My grandpa had always told me that it didn't matter if it was a man or a woman, if you loved someone you showed them respect at all times and that included holding doors and pulling chairs out for them. Carter blessed me with a brilliant smile that took my breath away and I sent up a silent thank you to Grandpa for the advice.

"It smells heavenly in here. What did you make?" Carter asked.

I opened the fridge and held out a beer to him which he took then I started carving the chicken while we talked. "I made citrus chicken, roasted herb potatoes, and green beans."

"That sounds amazing. I didn't know you were so talented in the kitchen. I mean, I can attest to your talents in other rooms…"

I shot him a warning glance over my shoulder. "Behave yourself or I'll clear off this table and eat *you* for dinner instead."

He arched his eyebrow at me. "Was that seriously supposed to be a threat? Because I have to say, it sounded more like you fulfilling my wishes."

I pointed my finger at him teasingly. "Look, little boy, if you're good and eat your dinner first, I promise you can have *dessert* afterwards."

Carter laughed at my stern expression. "Little boy? Do I need to remind you what a big boy I am?"

"I'm well aware," I said with a laugh. Carter's phone buzzed with an incoming text, interrupting our banter. He glanced at it quickly, rolling his eyes before looking up at me.

"Sorry, that was my mom. She was reminding me for the tenth time today to invite you over for a family cookout this weekend."

"You told your mom about me?" I asked casually as I pulled the potatoes out of the oven and began carefully transferring the food to the table.

"Yeah," Carter said with a snort as we dished food onto our plates. "I went over to tell my parents about you and my sisters were there. Apparently one of my brothers had told them that they had gotten to meet you already and they put me through a huge guilt trip about how I hadn't introduced you to them yet. The next thing I know, the three women were planning a big family get-together so they can all get to know you. Is that okay? My family can be a bit overwhelming sometimes."

I smiled at him reassuringly. "It's fine with me. I'm glad you want them to get to know me."

He looked up at me through his lashes. "Of course I want them to know you. You're going to be in my life for a long time, aren't you?"

"I'll be here as long as you want me," I replied carefully.

He nodded his head, seemingly satisfied. "Good. Although I should warn you, that may be a very, very long time."

I grinned at him. "I can handle that." If I was lucky, Carter would want me forever.

"This is delicious," Carter exclaimed as he tasted the chicken.

"Thank you, I'm glad you like it."

As we ate, we told each other about our day and I loved how domestic it felt. He was angry that Dan was still harassing me, but relieved that the captain had gotten involved and that he would be keeping a close eye on the situation.

"Landon came to see me today. He had a meeting with Lachlan Edwards to go over our temporary contract."

"How did it go? Is everything okay?" I looked up from my plate to see him chewing his lip.

"It went good. Great, actually."

"Then why do you look nervous?" I asked.

Carter sat his fork down and took a deep breath. "Okay, here's the thing. Lachlan has made arrangements for us to do a tour as the opening act for Maximum Mayhem. If we do well and the fans like us, we'll get a permanent contract with Golden Entertainment Studios."

"That's incredible! It's everything you've been working for. I'm so proud of you." He smiled at me, but it didn't reach his eyes. I cocked my head at him. "Why don't you look excited?"

"I am excited and you're right, this is the kind of opportunity I've always dreamed about. It's just…I'm leaving. I'll be gone for about three months."

"And you're worried about what will happen with us?" Carter nodded silently. "Listen, Carter, I have to be honest. When I heard you were getting a contract, I knew this would happen. Hell, the first time I saw you up on stage I knew you were headed for big things. I admit I have my own worries. You already have tons of fans vying for your attention and now that number is about to quadruple. You may get on tour and decide you want to be with someone else." I covered his mouth with my finger, cutting off his objection. "But I've decided that you're worth the risk. I love you more than I ever thought possible and while it would devastate me if you ended this relationship, I'd rather have you for any amount of time you're willing to give me than not at all. So you go do this tour and enjoy the hell out of it and I promise to support you every step of the way."

Carter had relaxed a bit with my words, but still looked apprehensive as he said, "There's no chance of me wanting to end things, Ryan. You're the best thing that's ever happened to me, including this contract. In fact, it's more likely for you to decide you're tired of waiting for me to come home."

I stood and tugged his hand until he also stood and followed me into the living area. I pulled him in close and we began swaying to the music that played softly from the speakers. I kissed him softly then rested my forehead against his. "It feels like I've waited for you my whole life. And I promise, when you come home after the three months is up, I'll still be here waiting for you."

For the first time since we started our conversation, Carter gave me a genuine smile. "I like the sound of coming home to you."

"Me too," I said as he lay his head against my chest with a contented sigh. We danced for several songs, simply enjoying the other's company and the feeling of being wrapped up in each other's arms.

"Are you ready for dessert now?" I asked.

"Yeah. I brought dessert actually."

I pulled back to look at him. "You did? What did you bring?"

Carter gave me a mischievous grin then leaned up to whisper in my ear. "I'm wearing edible underwear."

My eyes felt huge as I stared at him, trying to determine if he was telling the truth. "Are you serious?"

He popped the button of his jeans. "Guess you'll have to find out for yourself."

"My pleasure." I dropped to my knees in front of him and held his gaze as I slowly lowered his zipper. I tore my eyes away long enough to spread the fly of his jeans open and laughed when I discovered he was in fact wearing a pair of red edible underwear. Carter was always full of surprises. *I will never have a dull moment with my man.*

I slowly pulled his pants down to his knees and licked the candied briefs. "Mmmm, cherry flavored." I grinned up at him. "It tastes almost as sweet as you."

I carefully used my teeth to peel the underwear from his body and swallowed his cock until it hit the back of my throat. He shouted my name as he held onto my head for balance. I slid my arms around the back of his thighs and grabbed the firm globes of his ass in my hands, squeezing and kneading them as I hollowed my cheeks and sucked him in deep.

His fingers gripped my hair in an almost painful hold, and he began pumping in and out of me. I relaxed my throat and allowed him to fuck my mouth. I quickly unzipped my own pants and reached my hand into my briefs. I wanted to weep at the relief I felt as I squeezed my cock.

Holding the back of my head, Carter slid down my throat as far as he could and held still. I swallowed around him, my lips stretched wide around his cock. My eyes began to water and he relaxed his hold on me. Saliva dripped down my chin as I pulled off of him, gasping for air. He looked down at me questioningly and I smiled up at him, telling him wordlessly that I loved everything he was doing to me. He leaned down and swiped his tongue into my mouth.

"Lie down on the couch, baby. I want to suck you at the same time." I had to squeeze the base of my cock to keep myself from coming as I pictured what we would look like in a sixty-nine.

We hurried to remove the rest of our clothing then I stretched out on the couch and watched as Carter stalked towards me. He was a wet dream come to life and I still couldn't believe he was all mine. He waggled his brows at me as if he had read my thoughts.

"Are you ready?" I nodded and he bent down to kiss me long and hard. "Good, because the next time my mouth is on yours, I want to be sharing the flavor of each other." I gasped and he winked at me.

Without another word, he turned and straddled me backwards. I saw stars as my cock was enveloped in a brilliant wet heat and for a few seconds I was lost to the overwhelming pleasure his mouth was bringing to me. I almost forgot that I was supposed to be taking care of him too, until he wiggled his ass in my face as a reminder.

I licked at his dripping cock like it was an ice cream cone in danger of melting in the summer sun. The low rumble that emanated from him sent electricity up my spine and I began sucking him in earnest. I soon realized he was mimicking my every move and so I played out for him how I wanted him to bring me pleasure. The dual sensation of sucking his cock while his mouth worked my own had me nearing the end much quicker than I had expected.

Not wanting to come without him, I wet a finger and circled his hole as I continued worshiping him with my mouth. Carter rocked his hips backward, searching for more. I slipped my finger inside his tight entry and gave it a few twists until, with a muffled shout, he came down my throat. Tasting his essence on my tongue had me finding my own release and I shot strand after milky strand of cum into his thirsty mouth.

I lay on the couch, boneless and shaking. Carter stumbled to his feet and twisted around until he lay on top of me, face to face. "Damn, that was good," he mumbled into the crook of my neck.

"Weren't you saying something about exchanging flavors with each other?" I reminded him.

"Ahh, yes I was." He tilted his head up and our mouths met in a languid kiss, happily tasting the bitter saltiness of each other. After several minutes he rested his head on my chest. "I think this is what I'll miss the most," he whispered.

"What? Mutual blow jobs?" I teased.

"Nah, this right here. Being safe in your arms and hearing your heart beat against my ear."

I sifted my fingers through his hair and pulled him tighter against me with my other arm. My throat felt tight as I answered him. "Me too, baby. Me too."

CHAPTER
Twelve

Carter

I looked at Ryan out of the corner of my eye and noted the white knuckles as he gripped the steering wheel and the firm set of his jaw as he clenched his teeth. He hadn't said one word since we got in the truck and only responded to my attempts at conversation with the occasional grunt of acknowledgement.

I reached over and placed my hand on his leg, letting my thumb trace soothing circles over his thick muscles. "Are you okay? If you don't feel like doing this, we don't have to."

Ryan looked over at me quickly, almost as if he was surprised to see me sitting there. He exhaled slowly and I watched his shoulders relax. He placed his hand over mine and I turned my palm up so that I could thread my fingers with his.

"I'm sorry, honey. I'm just a little nervous about meeting the rest of your family."

"Just a *little* nervous?" I teased lightly. "I wasn't sure if you were using the steering wheel to drive or if you were trying to rip it out of the dashboard." Ryan chuckled and I was happy to see my words had the desired effect of removing the last of his tension.

"Okay, I'm a *lot* nervous, but this is a really big deal. I mean, what if they don't like me?" My heart melted at the vulnerable look on his face and I wanted to erase the worried look in his eyes.

"Baby, there's no way in the world they won't like you. You're an incredible man with a good heart and they know you make me happier than I've ever been. Trust me, they're going to love you almost as much as I do."

Ryan gave me the first genuine smile since he had picked me up at my apartment. "Do I really make you happy?"

"God yes!" My voice took on a seductive edge. "Especially when you're taking me from behind and…"

"Oh my God, enough!" he said with a groan. "You can't say things like that right now. We're almost there and I refuse to meet your parents with a raging hard-on." He carefully removed my hand which had begun creeping further and further up his leg until my pinky finger was grazing the impressive bulge in his pants.

I held my hands up in surrender. "Okay, I'll be good." Ryan arched his brow at me disbelievingly so I amended my statement. "I'll be good for *now*. Later, when we're alone, I make no promises."

His lips turned up in a seductive grin and I wanted him to stop the truck so I could lick him all over. "Later, you can be as bad as you want to be."

With a chuckle, I leaned over the console to kiss him on his cheek then directed him down the small street that my parents lived on. "That's it," I said, pointing to the large two-story, brick home I had grown up in. It appeared as if we were the last to arrive, if the number of cars lining the driveway were any indication.

"Here goes nothing," I heard Ryan mumble under his breath as he climbed out of the truck.

I walked around the front of the truck and took his hand, giving it a gentle squeeze. When I opened the front door I heard the boisterous sounds of my family floating from somewhere further inside. I smiled at Ryan and led him towards the large kitchen that was the usual gathering place when we all got together. Every head turned and all conversation stopped when we walked into the room and I felt Ryan stiffen next to me.

"Way to make things awkward guys," I said, looking around at each of them.

"Don't make any sudden movements or you might scare him off," Emma's husband, Mark, whispered out of the side of his mouth.

"I've never actually seen one in person. I mean, I've heard tales about their existence, but an actual sighting is very rare indeed," Michelle chimed in.

"What are you idiots talking about?" I asked, rolling my eyes at them.

"I think they're referring to finally seeing someone who will put up with you," Caleb explained.

"Ha! Ha! Ha!" I said as everyone cracked up around me. "I'm glad you guys think you're funny because no one else does." I looked at Ryan and was relieved to find him laughing along with everyone else.

"I'm sorry about my children's behavior. I swear I raised them better," Mom said as she stepped around Caleb to stand in front of Ryan. She smiled up at him and I saw tears brimming in her eyes. "You must be Ryan. We have an awful lot to thank you for. Without you I wouldn't have my baby anymore." Ryan looked around in surprise when my mom threw her arms around him in a fierce hug.

"It's better if you just go with it. There's less chance of getting hurt then," Giovanni advised him. He knew all too well what my mom could be like when she was feeling affectionate.

"Oh, you brat," Mom said with a laugh. She brushed the tears from her eyes before swatting Giovanni playfully with the dishtowel she held in her hand.

Dad stepped forward and put his arm around her waist. He reached his other hand forward to shake Ryan's. "All kidding aside, thank you for what you did for our boy. Because of you, we still have our son." He glanced over at me and my chest felt tight at the love I saw in my father's eyes. "As much as we love to tease each other, our family just wouldn't be the same if things had ended differently that day."

Ryan smiled at them shyly. "You're welcome, sir."

"Please, call me Rick."

"You can call me Kathy…or Mom," my mother said with a grin.

I worried that this all might be a little too much for Ryan after his earlier bout of nerves, so I was relieved when he smiled warmly at my parents.

"Thank you. It's nice to meet you. And it was my pleasure to help that night. I can't imagine not having Carter in my life either." He held my gaze and we shared a private look that spoke volumes about our feelings for each other.

"Aww!" I heard my sisters say in unison. Ryan laughed at their antics as I buried my face in his chest.

I introduced Ryan to the rest of my family and then tried to pull him out to the back deck where Dad was firing up the grill, but my mom and sisters insisted he stay inside with them so they could get to know him better. I gave Ryan a worried look, but he shrugged his shoulders and gave me a quick peck on the lips. I watched as he picked up a knife and began chopping the vegetables that Mom had been working on when we arrived.

I turned to my sisters in resignation and gave them a mock glare. "Can you guys try not to embarrass me, please?"

"Not on your life!" Michelle said, arching her brow at me. "You showed no mercy when I brought Jason home the first time. In fact, I seem to remember somebody showing him my hideous junior high pictures and asking him if he really knew what he was getting himself into."

"The first time you met Mark, you told him that during every full moon I like to get naked and howl at the moon," Emma added. "The way I see it; you deserve anything that happens to you tonight."

I started to object, but Mom's sweet voice cut me off. "I love you, son, but they're right. You weren't gentle with them when they brought that important person home for the first time. Now it's your turn. You might as well take it like a man."

They all started laughing, including Ryan, so I headed outside, grumbling the whole way about how mothers were supposed to protect their children, not gang up on them. To be honest, I was just thrilled with how comfortable Ryan seemed to have become around my family in such a short amount of time.

I made my way out to where my dad and brothers were gathered around talking about baseball and grabbed a beer out of the cooler. I took a drink as Caleb moved over to stand by me. "You and Ryan look really happy. Does that mean that telling him about the tour went well?"

I nodded my head. "I told him all the things that worried me about leaving and he told me his own concerns. We agreed that we trust each other and that no matter what, we want to see where this thing is going between us."

Caleb cocked his head as he studied my face. "You're different."

"What do you mean?" I asked, scrunching up my face in confusion.

"It's true. I can feel it." He lowered his voice so the others wouldn't hear and I leaned in towards him. "I was really worried about you. You spent so long jumping from one guy to the next, like you could never quite find what you were looking for. I was scared for you."

"I *always* practiced safe sex. Have you forgotten that it was me who provided you with a condom for your first one-night stand?" I asked him defensively.

I immediately regretted my choice of words as Caleb glared at me. He hadn't appreciated the obnoxious yellow smiley face condom as much as I thought he would. "No, I have not forgotten the wonderful condom you gave me that could have ruined a very intimate moment," he replied sarcastically. I couldn't help but laugh, which earned me an eye roll from my twin. "I'm trying to be serious here," he pretended to scold me, but he couldn't hide the grin that tugged at the corners of his mouth.

I wiped the smile from my face and gave him a nod to continue. "I wasn't worried about *that* so much. I knew you practiced safe sex. I was worried about what was happening to your heart. With each meaningless sexual encounter, I felt you closing yourself off more and more. It was like you were shielding yourself from letting anyone get too close."

Caleb looked at me, waiting for me to deny it, but I couldn't. I had been headed down a destructive path. I don't know how or why it had started, but I had managed to shut out every man I was with. I convinced myself that they only wanted to be with me because I was in a band and that none of them would want to get to know the real me. So I kept them at arm's length, never being with anyone more than once and never exchanging any personal information.

"You're different now and I can only assume the difference is Ryan. You're happier, more settled. Like you've finally found that missing piece of yourself. Am I right?"

I glanced to the door, where Ryan had just stepped out. He saw me looking at him and winked at me before bending over to get a beer out of the cooler. I felt warm all over and every part of me vibrated with the need to be near him. Without taking my eyes off of Ryan, I answered my brother. "You're absolutely right."

165

Caleb squeezed my hand. "That's what I've always wanted for you. You deserve to find your soul mate just like I found mine, in Gio. Ryan's a good man, but so are you. I just wanted you to know how happy I am for you. It's *your* turn."

I pulled my gaze away from Ryan long enough to smile at Caleb. Ever since Caleb had met Giovanni and I witnessed the connection the two of them shared, I had felt like there was something missing in my life. I wanted to find what my brother had found: his soul mate. I just never thought it was a possibility for me until Ryan walked into my life, quite literally picking up my broken pieces and saving me.

"Thanks, Bubby." His smile grew as I used our childhood nickname for each other. I hugged him quickly and then walked over to Ryan.

"Well, have the women in my life scared you away with all of the terrible stories I'm sure they told you about me?" I joked.

Ryan's warm chuckle went straight to my cock and I wondered if anyone would notice if I dragged him around the side of the house and had my wicked way with him in the bushes. Thinking of how I might get away with that plan, I looked up at him through my lashes, biting my lower lip. He leaned down to whisper in my ear and his warm breath ghosted across my skin, sending delicious shivers down my spine.

"Nothing can scare me away, but if you keep looking at me like that, I'm going to have to drag you away from here and bury myself inside of you so deep that you won't know where I end and you begin."

A rather unmanly whimper escaped my lips before I could stop it and Ryan smirked at me. *Smug, sexy bastard knows exactly what he does to me, but two can play at that game.* I pulled him towards me and wrapped my arms around his waist, making sure to let my hard cock graze his leg. To my family it probably looked like I was giving my boyfriend a simple embrace, but I ran the tip of my tongue around the shell of his ear as I leaned up to whisper to him. "Maybe

I'll be the one buried balls deep in *your* tight ass. I know how much you love it when the fat head of my cock hits that special place inside you just right."

Ryan let out a quiet moan and let his head drop onto my shoulder in defeat. "You win, I call truce."

I laughed as I nuzzled his cheek. "Truce," I agreed. "Now I have to figure out how to get rid of the rod that's trying to fight its way out of my pants, before I turn and face my family."

"Oh, I have to show you guys the vase your dad and I made together," I heard my mom's voice ring out. Suddenly, I remembered my dad's comment about recreating the scene from Ghost and an altogether different shiver racked my body.

"Well, *that* did it," I said, my cock no longer pressing against my zipper. Ryan gave me a questioning look, but I just waved him off. "Trust me, you don't want to know."

After we had stuffed ourselves with the delicious food Mom had made, we sat around the long table out on the deck, enjoying the beautiful warm night air and catching up with each other. Ryan had his arm around the back of my chair and I was curled up into his side.

"I'd like to propose a toast," Dad said as he rose from his chair to stand at the head of the table. We all looked up at him in surprise and then raised our glasses. "First, to Ryan. Without you, we would no longer be the happy, complete family we are. We thank you for your bravery and welcome you to our family." I tilted my head up to Ryan who looked as if he were fighting back emotion. I squeezed his hand as he nodded his head in acknowledgement to my dad.

"And another toast to Carter." I swiveled my head back to my dad who looked at me with a mixture of love and pride. "You have an amazing gift when it comes to music, but you have also worked your fingers to the bone to get where you are and now it's your turn to be recognized for all of that hard work. I think I can speak for everyone here when I say that we are all so proud of you and we know that this tour is just the start of all of the amazing things you will experience in your life. We love you, son."

I swallowed past the lump in my throat as I stood to hug both of my parents. "Promise you will always stay true to yourself and never forget where your home is," Mom whispered in my ear as she hugged me tightly.

"I promise, Mom." I hugged her back just as fiercely and then stepped back, wiping the tears from my eyes. "I couldn't have done it without all of your support, especially Landon who made all of this possible." I looked around at the smiling faces of everyone I loved most in the world. "I'm going to miss all of you so much."

"You're not going to miss me," Landon announced and everybody turned to look at him. "I've decided to go with you on the tour."

I looked at him in surprise. "You are? What about your other clients?"

Landon shrugged his shoulders. "I can still work with them through video conferences and Skype. Anything else can be handled by the other managers I hired. I think it's important that I oversee things your first time out on the road and to make sure everything is handled properly."

I eyed my older brother suspiciously. Landon was one of the best business managers in the industry and he was also a bit of a control freak. He never trusted anyone else to do the job as well as he could, so it shocked the hell out of me that he was willing to place his clients in the hands of others just so he could oversee my band. Something wasn't adding up. I forced a smile on my face so Mom wouldn't worry, but I made a mental note to ask him about it later. "It'll be good to have you with me." I hugged him and then sat back down next to Ryan.

"Well, since tonight is a night of celebrations and announcements, Jason and I have something exciting to tell you," Michelle said. Mom gasped loudly and she looked at my sister hopefully. Michelle grinned widely and nodded her head at Mom who screamed at the top of her lungs, scaring the rest of us who were looking at each other for answers.

Mom jumped out of her seat and started dancing around the table like a loon. When she stopped she looked at the rest of us like *we* were the ones who were crazy. "Don't just sit there, dance with me! I'm finally going to be a grandma!" She shrieked. As her words sank in we all jumped from the table and started hugging each other. Michelle didn't have the slightest bump yet, but we all took turns touching her belly and talking to the baby growing inside.

"Well shoot! There goes *my* big news." Every head turned to look at Emma who was cradling her stomach and wearing a toothy grin. Mark laughed out loud at the shocked expressions on our faces. Suddenly everyone moved over to Emma to show her the same treatment as Michelle. I couldn't believe both of my sisters were pregnant at the same time.

Mom sank down in a chair and Dad knelt in front of her. He cradled her face in his hands reverently and they whispered something to each other before he leaned in for a kiss. I felt someone squeeze my shoulders and I looked back to see Ryan watching my parents with a look of awe on his face. He glanced down at me and his eyes softened as he tilted his head to brush his lips across mine.

"Did you two know about each other?" Caleb asked.

My sisters grinned at each other. "Yep. We found out last week and decided to surprise you when everyone was together."

"Well, you certainly surprised us all. I can't believe both of my little girls are going to be mothers now," Dad said, sounding choked up. He put an arm around each of them and hugged them closely.

After we had helped clean up the dishes, everyone headed home. It had been an exciting and eventful day. Caleb and Giovanni were one of the last to leave and they followed us out to the driveway.

"Hey, don't go just yet," Giovanni said. He popped the trunk of his sleek Mustang and pulled out a large package which was wrapped in colorful wrapping paper with little kissing turtles all over it. A bright red ribbon graced the top of the present. He smiled as he handed it to me and I looked at him in confusion.

"What's this for? I'm sure you know it's not my birthday yet."

"I'm well aware of when your birthday is, brat." Giovanni laughed.

"That's actually a gift for both of you," Caleb said. I arched my brow at the innocent look he gave me, not buying it for a second.

"You were so helpful when we first got together, we felt it was only right to return the favor." Giovanni smiled at me sweetly which only made my suspicions grow.

"Aww, you got your brother a gift? That's so thoughtful. Open it up so we all can see, Carter." My eyes widened at the sound of my mom's voice and I turned to see my parents walking towards us.

Giovanni coughed into his fist, but I could hear the laugh behind it and Caleb pressed his lips against his husband's shoulder to keep his laughter from bursting out. I glared at them both as my feeling of dread grew. I knew that wasn't going to end well.

"Babe, you want to do the honors?" I asked, holding the box out to Ryan. Caleb shook his head emphatically at Ryan who quickly pushed it back into my hands.

"No, sweetheart. It's from your family so you should open it." He gave me a toothy grin.

"Maybe we should wait until we get home."

"Don't be rude, Carter. There will be plenty of time to make out with Ryan later. Your brother went to the trouble of picking out a gift for you, the least you can do is open it," Mom insisted.

Resigning myself to the fact that there was no way I would be able to leave without opening the box, I began pulling the tape off of the ends. I took so long opening it, you would have thought it contained a bomb. Although, if it was a bomb and blew up as soon as I opened it, maybe it would save me from the humiliation of having my mother see whatever was inside.

When I finally pulled the paper away it was worse than I had imagined. Caleb and Giovanni gave up their pretense and began howling with laughter as I stared down at the vivid images that showed the many uses of the sex swing within.

"Oh my!" I heard Mom say over the sound of blood rushing through my ears.

I looked up at Ryan out of the corner of my eye. His eyes were as wide as saucers and his mouth hung open. I scowled at Caleb and Giovanni who clung to each other as fits of laughter took over, each of them with tears rolling down their faces. *Well played, assholes.*

Dad leaned in closer to get a better look at the box. His eyes roamed over the images that were strategically placed around the box showing couples in different sexual positions. He looked questioningly at my mom. "Is this the same one we bought, dear?"

"No, ours is that racing red color remember? What ever happened to that thing anyway?" she asked him.

All laughter stopped as we stared at my parents in shock. I looked around at each person as if in slow motion. My brother looked like he had swallowed a bug and Giovanni pulled Caleb behind his body as if he were protecting his husband from a physical attack. Ryan wore a grimace on his handsome face and I would almost swear I felt blood dripping from my ears.

Unaware of our anguish, Dad answered her. "Don't you remember? We had to put it up in the attic when your sister came for a visit. It's somewhere behind the Christmas decorations."

"Gotta ugh…go…something," I managed to say as I dove inside Ryan's truck. I loved Ryan with all of my heart, but he would soon learn that when faced with my parents' sex talk, it was every man for himself.

Luckily, my man was used to getting himself out of dangerous situations and he was soon slamming his door behind him and peeling out of the driveway, followed closely by the two idiots who had brought this wrath upon us. *I hoped on their way home they got a flat tire, had to call Dad for help, and he was still feeling chatty.*

After a few miles, Ryan's voice pulled me from my stupor. "Well, that was…ummm…"

I reached for his hand and shook my head. "Let's not *ever* talk about that again, okay?"

Ryan simply nodded his head.

CHAPTER
Thirteen

Carter

"GOOD JOB, GUYS, I THINK WE'RE DONE FOR THE DAY."

"Oh, thank God!... My fingers are about to fall off... Finally!" I couldn't help but agree as I heard the responses of my bandmates. The last week had been complete chaos as we rushed to get everything ready for the tour. I had been pushing them extremely hard, but they never complained. Now, after hours spent in meetings and practices, we were finally ready.

We had just a few days to ourselves before we had to leave and I planned on spending as much of that time as I could with Ryan. My stomach still tensed whenever I thought about having to be away from him for so long, but I clung to the belief that we were meant to be together and nothing would change that.

"Who's ready to hit the bars?" Rocko asked as he stood from his drum set. I looked up from putting my guitar in its case and caught Steve's eye. His mouth was set in a firm line as he moved his gaze over to Rocko.

"You really think that's a good idea, man?" Steve asked him.

We all knew what Steve meant. The day Landon had come to tell us about the tour, Steve had gone looking for an absent Rocko. After searching his usual party spots, Steve had finally tracked him down in a seedy bar. What he found had us all concerned.

A large man had him pinned in the corner of a dark hallway and Steve said Rocko looked almost frightened as the man reached his hands down our friend's pants. Rocko tried to fight off the guy's advances, but he was so drunk he only managed a feeble swat at the man's hands.

Luckily, Steve was able to intervene and got Rocko home safely, but we all knew that the consequences could have been much worse if Steve hadn't been there. Rocko seemed to be getting more and more out of control, but he refused to admit that anything was wrong.

Rocko was one of my best friends and I knew that pushing him to open up would only result in him shutting us out completely. The only thing we could do at this point was to keep a close eye on him and be there if he ever decided to confide in us.

At Rocko's angry scowl, Steve held his hand up to placate him. "I only meant that we're all exhausted from this crazy week. I just want to go home and curl up on the couch and watch mindless TV for the next few days. Why don't you come with me? You can keep me company and I'll even pay for the pizza." Steve gave Rocko his most endearing smile and I watched Rocko's defensive posture relax.

"Okay, but I get to pick the toppings this time."

Steve wrinkled his nose and grumbled. "Fine! I guess I'll just pick the anchovies off."

"Meet you there," Rocko said over his shoulder as he strode out of the room.

"I thought Rocko hated anchovies," Tyler said.

"Yeah, but he likes pissing me off more than he hates them," Steve answered with a shrug.

We said goodbye to Kalia and Tyler then I turned to Steve. "Do you want me to come too? I don't know what's going on with him, but you shouldn't have to deal with Rocko's problems all by yourself."

Steve patted my shoulder as he dug his keys out of his pocket. "It's all good, man. Rocko and I get along just fine and I really didn't have any other plans."

"No big date?" I teased.

Steve blushed. "Not tonight. She had to work. I'll spend some time with her tomorrow though."

"So there *is* someone in particular?" I arched my brow at him. Steve had always been very private about his love life, so of course we all tried mercilessly to pump him for information any chance we got.

"You'll never know," he retorted with a devious grin.

"I guess I'll just have to wait for the wedding invitation."

"At the rate you and your man are going, we'll be getting your invitation before mine." I shoved him out the door with a laugh and locked up the studio doors.

"See you in a few days. Call if you need any help with the kid," I said, referring to Rocko.

"Ugh! Hopefully he behaves," Steve replied with an eye roll.

As I drove to Ryan's place, the issues with the band ran through my mind on a loop. We were finally so close to reaching our dream, I just hoped that Rocko could pull himself together and make it through the tour. Mostly though, I worried about my friend. Rocko had been running from his demons, whatever they were, since I met him. Outwardly, he seemed like he didn't have a care in the world, partying all the time and sleeping with pretty much anything with a pulse, but once in a while, he showed another more vulnerable side to himself. That side seemed more like a lost little boy and I wondered if he'd ever let anyone in enough to see exactly how much pain he was in.

I shook off my worries as I parked in front of Ryan's home. Steve would keep an eye on our friend and I only had a few days left to spend with Ryan. *Time to focus on my man.*

I grabbed the bag I had packed and my guitar case out of the back seat of my car and then let myself into the old warehouse. Ryan had recently given me a copy of his house key, telling me I was welcome any time and I was thrilled with the new step in our relationship.

I kicked my shoes off at the door, then called out to let Ryan know I was there. I frowned when I got no response. It was quiet in the house, but I knew Ryan was home because his truck was parked outside. I made my way up the spiral staircase and then stopped. My jaw dropped at the sight that greeted me.

I barely noticed as the items I had been carrying fell to the floor with a thud, including my beloved guitar. All I could focus on was the gorgeous man who stood in the middle of the room, regarding me with a sexy smirk.

I took my time studying him, starting with the black boots then moving up to the uniformed fire pants. My mouth watered as I got to the red suspenders that were looped over his wide shoulders. His bare chest revealed rounded pecs covered in a smattering of blond hair which continued downward over rippled abs and ended in a single line that pointed like an arrow to what I knew was a rather well-endowed cock.

My eyes travelled up the pillar of his neck to his strong, stubbled jaw and I longed to rub my cheek against it, just to feel it's delicious scratch against my skin. His plump lips begged to be kissed and his hooded eyes had turned a dark, stormy gray. I swallowed around the lump in my throat.

"What's going on?" I choked out in a hoarse voice.

"I decided I wanted to play tonight. Is that okay?" Ryan's husky voice sent chills down my spine and I nodded my head in agreement. Every gay man I had ever known, and probably most women for that matter, had fantasies about hot firemen. There he was, my very own wet dream in the flesh and I couldn't wait to get my hands and mouth on him. *This must be what Heaven's like.*

"Sounds perfect. What exactly did you have in mind?"

"This." Ryan moved to the side and it was then that I noticed the sex swing hanging from the large wooden ceiling beam.

"Fuuuuccckkk!" I whimpered. I reached my hand down and pressed it against my groin, afraid I was about to embarrass myself.

Ryan's chuckle was deep and did nothing to help my current situation. "You have way too many clothes on. You want me to help you lose some of them?"

"Uhh…yeah…" I responded eloquently.

Ryan held my gaze as he neared me and gripped the bottom of my shirt in his hands. He slowly pulled it over my head and leaned towards me. I tilted my head, waiting for the slide of his lips on mine, but he bypassed my mouth and began laying gentle kisses along my neck and shoulder. He stopped at the juncture there and breathed me in.

"You smell so damn good," he said with a groan and I felt my knees go weak. Ryan trailed his fingertips over my collarbone and across my pecs, circling my nipples. The gentle scrape of his fingernails over the nubs had my nipples standing at attention and I cried out as he pinched them between his fingers. The sudden switch from gentle to rough had my cock dripping in anticipation.

I watched in silent awe as he dropped to his knees and popped the button of my pants. The sounds of my zipper being lowered and my ragged breathing were all that could be heard. Ryan looked up at me and I let my tongue sweep over my lower lip. He growled and reached his hand behind my neck, pulling me down to meet him in a ravishing kiss. He nibbled my bottom lip and then sucked it into his warm mouth. My tongue darted in, savoring the familiar taste of him.

He pulled away much sooner than I would have preferred to resume his job of undressing me. He lowered my pants to just under my butt and stopped. His eyes darted wildly to mine and then back as he got his first glimpse of the bright blue Andrew Christian jock strap I wore.

"You're not the only one with some tricks up his sleeve," I said saucily.

Ryan swallowed hard and I was thrilled that he found it so appealing. "I think these need to stay on for a while."

"You're running this show tonight. I'll do anything you want."

Ryan's control seemed to falter at my words and he picked up the pace a bit as he hurried to remove my pants and socks. He leaned forward and I felt the wet heat of his mouth as he licked my rigid shaft through the material.

I ran my fingers through his hair as he continued to worship my cock. His hands trailed behind me and he squeezed my bare ass. I jumped in surprise when the palm of one hand landed on my right ass cheek with a loud smack. The sting that was left behind walked the perfect line between pleasure and pain and I whimpered at the thought of the handprint that was surely visible on my smooth flesh.

"Get in the swing." Ryan's voice sounded strained as he stood. I couldn't help snapping one of his suspenders as I walked past him and crawled into the hanging contraption. "Brat!" he said with a quiet chuckle.

"What exactly are you going to do to me, Lieutenant Marshall?" I asked playfully as he helped secure my feet into the stirrups.

When I was completely immobile with the exception of my hands, he leaned his strong body over mine. "I'm going to take my time feasting on your delectable ass and then I'm going to fuck you into oblivion." His eyes held so much heat, I thought we would both burst into flames and a burst of pre-cum leaked out the slit of my cock.

"You better hurry up then. I don't know how much longer I'll last," I said through gritted teeth.

Ryan knelt down in front of me and I felt more vulnerable than I ever had in my entire life, with my legs spread wide and the most private parts of me exposed to him. Not that he hadn't seen it all before, but there was something about being strapped down, completely at his mercy that was worrisome as much as it was exciting. The two warring emotions made the whole experience hotter than hell and I felt my entire body flush with anticipation of his touch.

The first flick of his tongue over my hole had me crying out. I threw my head back in complete abandon as he stayed true to his word and began feasting on my hole like he was a starving man. He used his mouth to suck at my entrance, gently nibbling the delicate skin and teasing it, then he speared me with his tongue, wiggling it deep inside my ass as he worked me open.

I looked down the length of my body and the sight of his head nestled at the juncture of my legs and the feel of his tongue inside my ass, brought on the telltale burning sensation at the base of my spine.

"I'm close, Ryan. Really, really close." I expected him to stop with my warning, but he surprised me when he quickly leaned forward, pulled my underwear down until my cock sprung free and swallowed it whole. "Ahhh...Ryan....FUCK!" I gripped the chains of the swing because I needed to hold onto something as my orgasm raced through me with ferocity.

Cum streamed from my cock over and over in thick spurts which Ryan drank down greedily. He licked my cock until it was clean and then tucked it back into my jockstrap. I felt boneless as I collapsed back into the swing.

Ryan looked up at me with a smug look. "Good?"

"Amazing!" I sighed. The swing swayed as Ryan moved to a standing position between my legs. He grabbed the chains on each side of me and pulled me towards him.

"Yes, *you* are amazing," he said before sweeping his tongue into my mouth, sharing the salty flavor of my seed with me.

I gripped his head between my hands and stared into his eyes. "I need you to fuck me now. I want to feel you moving inside my body." Ryan shivered violently, then stood and unsnapped the button of his pants and started to remove them. "Uh uh, those stay on Big Guy," I commanded.

"I thought I was the one in control tonight," he teased.

"You love it when I'm a bossy bottom and you know it," I said with a sly grin.

Ryan gave me an answering smile and pulled a condom out of his pocket. I reached for his hand before he could rip it open and he looked at me questioningly.

"I've been thinking a lot about this and I just had a full workup of tests for the tour and I know you are tested regularly as part of your job, so..." My words tapered off as I saw Ryan's eyes widen in shock. I bit my lip, suddenly feeling nervous. "You know what, never mind. We don't need to rush into..."

Ryan cut me off as his mouth slammed into mine, stealing the breath from my lungs. When he pulled back, each of us gasping for air, he wore a huge smile on his face. "I wanted to ask you the same thing, but I was afraid you weren't ready yet. I didn't want to put any pressure on you."

"I'm committed to you and *only* you, Ryan. Of course I'm ready for this. I want to feel you with nothing between us." I kissed his lips again.

"I love you so much, baby," he whispered and then he devoured my mouth once again. The flames of lust raced through me, bringing my cock back to life.

"I love you too. Now hurry up and fuck me."

Ryan threw his head back with a laugh. "So bossy." He grabbed a bottle of lube and slicked his length and then poured some onto my waiting hole. I jumped as the cold liquid hit my skin, but it was soon forgotten as Ryan worked two of his long fingers inside me, twisting his wrist and stretching me.

"You look so fucking good hanging there. Are you ready?"

"Yes!" I growled impatiently.

Ryan held my gaze as the head of his cock breached my hole and he slowly slid inside, bare skin to bare skin. My breath caught in my throat at the tender emotions I saw in his eyes. The connection between us at that moment was unlike anything I had ever experienced before. There was a bond between us that went deeper than even the one I shared with my twin and I knew that I could never live without this man in my life.

"God, baby! You feel so good. I want to crawl inside of you and live there forever," he whispered reverently.

"I need you." No other words were necessary. Ryan knew what my body needed and he was more than happy to oblige.

I gasped loudly as he gripped the swing and pulled almost all the way out and then yanked me towards him, impaling me onto his thick shaft. He did this several times, letting the forward momentum of the swing aide him in his thrusts.

Ryan adjusted his hips so that his cock rubbed against my prostate with each glide in and out of me. Sweat ran down the side of his face and landed on my stomach as he worked feverishly to bring us both to the height of pleasure.

I felt myself nearing the end so I reached for my cock and began working my hand over it. I couldn't breathe and my eyes rolled back in my head as fire raced up my spine and my balls drew up tight against my body.

"Ryan!" I screamed as white ribbons of cum landed on my chest. My internal walls squeezed tightly around his cock, not wanting to let him go and he let out an animalistic growl as he came. I could feel his hot cum filling me and my eyes burned with the sudden urge to cry. He slumped over me, leaning his forehead against mine as we tried to catch our breath.

"I love you," I said between gasps.

"I love you more," he whispered back. I wasn't sure that was possible and I was about to argue with him, when I lost the ability to speak. Ryan had pulled back from me and lowered himself to his knees once more and ran a flattened tongue up my crease, tasting himself as he spilled out of me. The kinkiness, yet complete possessiveness, of the act left my mind blown and rendered me totally speechless. If I had had anything left in me at all, I would have been rock hard, but after two overwhelming orgasms, I was completely spent.

When he stood, I reached up with shaky hands and grabbed him by his suspenders, pulling him down so I could kiss him. I moaned as a mixture of sweat and his cum coated my tongue.

Ryan carefully helped me out of the swing and when my legs buckled weakly under me, he lifted me in his strong arms and carried me to his bed. He quickly got undressed and grabbed a warm washcloth to gently clean the cum from my chest and crease. I was already starting to drift off as he turned out the lights and climbed into bed behind me, pulling me up against his strong body.

"Good night, sweetheart," he whispered. I felt his soft lips kiss my shoulder.

"Good night, Superman."

CHAPTER
Fourteen

Ryan

"WHO WANTS ANOTHER BEER?" CARTER'S MUFFLED voice called from the inside of the fridge. I tilted my head, appreciating the view as he bent over. I could just make out the waistband of his underwear peeking out of the top of his low slung jeans and my eyes widened as I wondered if he was wearing a jockstrap again. The guy seriously owned the sexiest underwear.

A set of fingers snapping in front of my face pulled me from the dirty fantasy my mind was creating. "Dude, where the hell did you go? You haven't heard a word I've said." I turned to Joe who was scowling at me.

Beside him, Suzy waggled her brows at me. "I'm pretty sure I know where his mind was and it had nothing to do with baseball."

She rolled her eyes skyward as Joe looked back and forth between us, his forehead scrunched in confusion. "He was ogling his boyfriend, honey. Remember what that was like when we first got together and you couldn't keep your eyes off of me?"

Joe stared at his wife in disbelief. "What are you talking about? I still can't keep my eyes off of you. Take now for instance, you're the prettiest girl in the whole room."

Suzy poked a finger into his side, making him jerk as he laughed at his own joke. "Thanks, jerk. I'm the *only* girl in the room."

"Yeah, but you're still the prettiest," Joe said sweetly. He pulled her close to him and kissed her on the lips until she sank into him. I laughed at their antics. Joe and Suzy liked to tease each other, but they had one of the most solid marriages I had ever seen. Suzy still looked at Joe like he hung the moon and I knew my best friend thought his wife walked on water.

I glanced at Carter as he walked towards me, a couple of cold beers in his hand. He smiled at me warmly and popped the cap off of a bottle before handing it to me. I raised my arm so he could snuggle up against me on the couch and kissed the top of his head, breathing in the fresh, clean scent of the shampoo he used.

"So, Carter, tell us more about the tour. Have you had a chance to meet Maximum Mayhem yet?" Suzy asked excitedly.

I had wanted Carter to get to know my best friends before he had to leave, so I had invited them over for dinner. Suzy and Carter had hit it off from the very beginning, bonding over the pros and cons of being involved with a firefighter. They had a surprising amount in common and shared the same sarcastic sense of humor. Joe and I had looked at each other several times that night, wondering if it might have been a mistake to put the two of them together.

"No, we won't meet them until the tour kicks off, but I've heard they're all really nice and easy to get along with." Carter reached for my hand and held it between us on the couch. As he talked he began rubbing small circles on the palm of my hand and my cock jerked in response. I looked at him out of the corner of my eye, wondering if he was doing it on purpose, but he continued on as if nothing were happening.

"I think it's all very exciting. Where does the tour kick off?" Suzy asked.

As Carter proceeded to give her a rundown of their schedule, he scraped his fingernail against my palm and my cock began to plump as all the blood rushed below my waist. I crossed an ankle over my knee to hide my predicament from my friends and narrowed my eyes at Carter. He had to know what he was doing to me, but I couldn't be sure because he seemed completely caught up in his conversation with Suzy.

As they talked about the size of the venues he would play at, he made his fingers into a circle around my finger and began discreetly rubbing it up and down as if my finger were a cock thrusting into a hole. The little shit was definitely up to no good, but he was great at covering it up. The slightest twitch of his lips as he responded to Joe's question was the only indication that something was amiss.

Suzy excused herself to use the restroom and Joe moved to the kitchen to grab another beer. I used my torso to pin him to the back of the couch and glared at him. "What the hell are you doing to me? You want me to embarrass myself in front of my friends?"

Carter couldn't contain his laughter. "I'm sorry. It's just so much fun to get you all worked up."

"Yeah? Well now I'm going to be sitting here with blue balls the rest of the night." I pretended to pout until Carter sucked my bottom lip into his mouth. I moaned as his tongue licked across the roof of my mouth.

He kissed his way across my jaw and whispered into my ear. "Would it make it better if I kissed your blue balls later?"

I chuckled huskily. "You might need to do more than that. They're pretty upset with you right now."

Carter's eyes flared with heat. "I promise to make it up to them fully."

My response was interrupted by Joe who plopped himself back down in the chair, followed by Suzy.

"Unfortunately, I never got to hear your band play because I've been working a lot of night shifts, but Joe told me you're very talented. Is there any way you'd sing something here?"

"Don't put him on the spot, honey," Joe cut in.

"No, it's fine; I'd love to sing something. Let me just grab my guitar," Carter offered graciously.

As Carter played a few of his original songs, I watched him. When I saw him play at the bar, I had been blown away by his talent and stage presence, but watching him now as he sat hunched over his guitar, fingers caressing the strings, I realized that this was more than just a career for him. Music was truly a part of who Carter was as a person. His guitar seemed like an extension of the man himself and he used it to express his thoughts and feelings.

My chest grew tight with pride and admiration for the man I loved. The sky was the limit for Carter once the world got ahold of him. I had no doubt that he was about to explode into stardom. *I just hope I don't get left behind.* A cold chill swept over me at the thought, but I pasted a smile on my face as the song ended and he looked up at me. A small line appeared between his eyes as he studied me and I was pretty sure he could see right through me.

"That was amazing!" Suzy gushed. "Everyone's going to love you!"

"Yeah and just think, we'll be able to say we knew him before he was famous. You won't forget us little guys when you're playing in front of millions, will you?" They laughed at Joe's teasing, but all I could manage was a half-hearted chuckle as Joe's words hit a little too close to home.

Carter reached over and took my hand, giving it a reassuring squeeze. He gave an almost imperceptible shake of his head and winked at me. I should have realized that he would know my thoughts, after all, he knew me better than anyone else in the world.

We walked our friends to the door and Carter promised to send Suzy lots of pictures from the tour. I was happy to see them hug my boyfriend goodbye, just as they always did with me. They were more than just my friends, they were my family and it warmed my heart to see that they had accepted Carter into their fold.

I locked the door behind them and held Carter's hand as we climbed the stairs. I waved off his offer to help clean up the kitchen, assuring him that there were only a few pots and pans left to put away.

Carter settled into the couch and propped his feet up on the coffee table. He reached for his guitar and began strumming a melody with a faraway look in his eyes. I sighed happily. I loved having Carter in my space. He had a way of bringing it to life; of making it feel like a home.

I finished cleaning the counters and was washing my hands when I heard Carter's clear voice as he began singing. I whipped my head around to look at him as he sang the familiar words of Charlie Puth's "One Call Away" and my heart swelled with love for him. I knew that this was his way of reassuring me, of letting me know that he would always be there for me. Carter arched his brow at me as he sang about Superman, and I threw my head back with a laugh. *God, I love him!*

I tossed the towel I was holding over my shoulder and sauntered over to him. He looked into my eyes as he continued to sing the words to me. When he had finished the song, I reached for his guitar and took it from his hands, carefully laying it down on the cushions beside him. I threw a leg over his and placed my hands on the back of the couch, caging him in without touching him.

I bent down until there was only an inch between our lips. When he tilted his head up, searching for a kiss, I pulled back just out of his reach. He looked at me in surprise, but then his expression changed with understanding.

"What do you need?" he whispered and I shivered as his warm

breath blew over my face.

"I need you."

"What else, baby?" I sighed as he reached up to thread his fingers through my hair, rubbing his thumbs in sensual circles along the sides of my neck.

"I need you to fill me up until there's nothing else in the entire world but you and me." I hated how vulnerable and desperate I sounded, but I couldn't help it. Only he could block out all of the worries and uncertainty of what was to come and help me to forget everything but the connection between the two of us.

"I can do that." Carter pulled me into a kiss that was both blistering and tender and I felt the tension leave my body as the rest of the world faded away.

The next few days passed in a blur as Carter and I christened nearly every surface of my home. We savored the feel and taste of every inch of each other's bodies and committed them to memory. In between, we lazed around, watching movies, playing video games and having food delivered, neither one of us wanting to waste precious time with menial tasks such as grocery shopping or cooking.

All too soon, it was the day Carter had to leave. I woke while it was still dark out, the first few rays of sun just starting to break through. My heart felt heavy as I turned my head to look at him. My eyes lingered over his features, not wanting to miss anything.

He was lying on his back, one arm above his head. His messy hair went in all different directions and his unbelievably long lashes were fanned out over his cheeks. His lips were red and plump from sleep and the long hours we had spent kissing the night before.

Carter's chest rose and fell in a gentle rhythm with each steady breath and his nipples were pebbled from the cool morning air. The sleek muscles of his abdomen disappeared beneath the sheet that revealed a clear outline of his morning wood.

A smile spread across my face as I decided exactly how I wanted to wake my sleeping beauty. I carefully climbed from the bed, making sure he was still sleeping then lifted the sheet at his feet and slowly crawled up the bed between his bent legs. Luckily, he slept naked so there was nothing to stop me from reaching my prize.

I trailed my nose up the crease of his thigh and breathed in the warm, sleepy scent of him. A quiet sigh escaped his lips as he slept and his cock jerked in response to my nearness. My tongue trailed a wet line up the length of his shaft and I smiled as I heard his surprised gasp as he stuttered awake. I licked around his broad tip, then dipped my tongue into his leaking slit.

"Oh God, Ryan!" he yelled as I tightened my lips around him and took him down my throat. He tried to thrust his hips, but I used my arms to hold him firmly to the bed as I hollowed my cheeks and sucked hard, thrilled when I was rewarded with a burst of his seed on my tongue. I was unrelenting in my hunger for him as I continued to suck him, swirling my tongue along the tip before plunging back down again. I opened wide, allowing him to brush the back of my throat and then held there as I swallowed around him.

"I'm close, baby, so fucking close!" He writhed on the bed as I continued to devour him. I wanted to take everything he had to give me. I quickly wet a finger and circled his pink pucker a few times before pushing it in. I sucked him deep and then curled my finger until I found that perfect spot that would make him lose control.

"Ryan! Fuuuccckkk!" he screamed and arched up off the bed as his warm essence filled my mouth. My throat worked furiously to keep up with the amount of cum he was feeding me, not wanting to waste a single drop. When he was drained, he collapsed to the bed gasping for air. I crawled out from under the sheet and kissed my way up his body. I took the time to trail tender kisses along the jagged scar on the inside of his bicep before laying claim to his mouth.

His arms and legs wrapped around me and he held me like he never wanted to let go. *I hope you never do.*

"There's not much time before we need to leave. Why don't we get in the shower and I'll return the favor," he said in that scruffy, early morning voice I loved so much.

As hard as we tried, we were still late getting out the door. That was mostly my fault since what started out as a quick blow job in the shower, soon turned into an overwhelming need to be inside of him one more time.

I know it was stupid, but I needed to know that when he left, he would be carrying evidence of our love with him. While no one else would even know it was there, Carter would know and *that* was what mattered to me. Carter seemed to understand that need and he clung to me, his eyes never leaving mine as I filled him. More was said between us in that moment than in any other time we had spoken actual words and we stopped existing as two separate people: our souls merging into one.

As I pulled into a parking space near the tour bus, I saw Carter's family waiting for him. His mom scooped him into a vigorous hug as he climbed out of the truck and he curled his arms around her, whispering in her ear as she wept. I wanted to cry right along with her, but I managed to hold myself together, not wanting to make the goodbye any harder on him than it already was.

I waited patiently as Carter was passed around from one family member to another. Landon would be leaving the following day and meeting them on the road. He spoke quietly to his mother, assuring her that he would help keep an eye on his younger brother.

The rest of the band showed up and after shaking hands with everyone, climbed on the bus, dragging their heavy suitcases behind them. Tears rolled down Caleb's face as he stood before Carter. They stared at each other for a long moment, using their silent twin speak to communicate with each other. As they embraced I heard Caleb whisper, "I love you, Bubby." Carter nodded as he pinched his lips between his teeth. I knew he was struggling to hold himself together.

I swallowed hard as I realized the moment I had been dreading was finally here. Carter's eyes swam with tears and I dug my nails into the palms of my hands, fighting back my own surge of emotion. I would have time to lose control later when I was all alone, but while he was still here, I didn't want to miss a single second of seeing his perfect face by letting tears cloud my vision.

I bent down, meeting Carter halfway as he leaned up to wrap his arms around my neck. I buried my nose in his neck and breathed deeply, filling my lungs with the familiar scent of him and my hands fisted the bottom of his t-shirt. "How am I supposed to let you go?" I rasped.

"I'll be back, Superman. You've given me every reason to come home," he whispered. He kissed me hard, his lips trembling against mine, then turned and climbed on the bus without looking back.

I stood there watching until the bus disappeared from sight, feeling as if it had taken my heart with it. I turned and was surprised to see the Greenes still standing there with their arms around each other, offering comfort to one another. Somehow I had forgotten they were there.

Through his tears, Caleb reached his hand out to me. I shifted my focus to the ground and quickly walked away from him, but not before I saw the hurt my rejection had caused in his eyes. I hated it, but the fact of the matter was, I couldn't handle being around Caleb right then. When I looked at his face, identical to the one I wanted to see most in the world, I felt like I couldn't breathe. Besides, they were Carter's family, not mine. I just wanted to be left alone.

Somehow, I managed to hold myself together long enough to drive home. I locked the door behind me and slowly climbed the steps. I was so tired, my heart hurt and my head pounded out a painful rhythm. A nap sounded like a good idea so I started stripping my clothes off as I made my way to the bed, but stopped when something caught my eye on the floor. I bent down and picked it up, feeling the smooth edges of the guitar pick against my fingers. A sob burst from my chest and my tears spilled over as I slowly sank to the bed and pulled Carter's pillow close to my face, breathing in the scent that still lingered. I cried my heartache into his pillow for what seemed like hours, until finally I was forced to succumb to my exhaustion.

CHAPTER
Fifteen

Carter

I SPENT THE FIRST NIGHT ON THE BUS CURLED UP IN MY BUNK. MY friends seemed to understand that I needed some time to myself and so they left me alone to wallow in my misery. I missed Ryan so much it hurt and I was tempted several times to call the whole thing off and have the driver take me back home, but I knew that going on tour was something that I needed to do. Not only for myself, but for the rest of the band and for Landon. They had all worked just as hard as I had and they didn't deserve for me to back out, even though it felt like I had left my heart back in Chicago. Besides, what would it say about our relationship if Ryan and I couldn't handle being away from each other for a small amount of time.

The next morning, I sent Ryan a quick text telling him how much I loved him and that I would call him as soon as I could. Filled with a new resolve to get out there and do the best job I could, I grabbed my clothes and toiletry bag and made my way down the narrow hallway of the bus to the bathroom. It was quiet as I climbed beneath the spray of the tiny shower and quickly washed myself. The bus rocked back and forth, knocking me off balance as I toweled myself dry and struggled to get dressed in the tight confines of the bathroom.

When I emerged, fully dressed but with likely bruises, I found Kalia and Tyler snuggled on the couch together, drinking coffee and watching the morning news. I quickly tamped down the jealousy I felt that they got to travel with their loved one and smiled at them. I knew they weren't to blame for my heartache.

"Morning! How did you guys sleep?"

Kalia chuckled when Tyler glared at me. "Ignore him. Between Steve's snoring and Rocko's…whatever it was he was doing," she grimaced, "Tyler barely got any sleep."

"Remind me to pick up earplugs next time we stop," Tyler grumbled. I laughed as Kalia patted his chest in sympathy.

"I didn't hear any of that. I guess I was pretty out of it last night."

"I know you didn't want to leave Ryan. Are you sure you're up for this?" I stared at Kalia as I gave her question careful consideration. I saw the way they each held their breath as they waited for my reply. I knew that as disappointed as they would be, they were also my friends and they wanted me to be happy. They would understand if I needed to back out of the deal.

I took a deep breath and nodded at them. "Let's show the world what we've got."

I grabbed the towel that someone held out for me and used it to wipe the sweat that dripped from my face as I made my way behind the stage. I was tired, but adrenaline rushed through my veins.

We had been on tour for two weeks and had just finished another perfect show in front of a sold out crowd. The excitement that poured off of the audience as we sang, gave me a natural high and I could understand how musicians became addicted to being on stage.

So far, the crowds had welcomed us with open arms, often singing our songs along with us, which never grew old. Once in a while a fan would get out of hand, trying to cop a feel or asking me to sign something completely inappropriate, but for the most part they were respectful and fun to get to know.

Landon said that Lachlan Edwards had called him to say how happy he was with our performances. He reported that both our social media searches and merchandise sales were through the roof. Landon told me privately that Lachlan had been so pleased he had mentioned that if things continued as well as they were, he didn't see any reason why our contract wouldn't be extended at the end of the tour, but I didn't say anything to the others because I was afraid to get their hopes up in case it all fell through.

The guys from Maximum Mayhem were cool and had welcomed us with open arms. Sometimes after a particularly good show, when we were all too wired to sleep, the two bands would gather in one of our hotel rooms and play old classic songs until the wee hours of the morning. It was fun spending time with other people who shared the same love of music that we did.

Being on tour was everything I had ever dreamed of except one thing, I missed Ryan. I had lost count of how many times something incredible happened and I turned, wanting to share it with him, only to realize he wasn't there.

We were kept extremely busy from the moment we woke up, but it was the quiet moments as we waited to go on stage or I was getting my makeup done that it would hit me, just how much I missed him. We texted and called each other as much as possible, but it was sometimes difficult to line our schedules up together with him often going to bed just as I was getting up and vice versa. I missed everything about him. His warm smile, his strong arms, his infectious laugh.

The nights were the worst. Whether I was in a hotel room or curled up in my bunk on the bus, the nights dragged on and the loneliness that started out as an ache soon became a festering wound. It was at those times - when I found it difficult to breathe - that I would open my phone and stare at Ryan's picture, remembering our time together until my breathing evened out and my eyes grew heavy.

I made my way down the long corridor, stopping to sign autographs for a few fans that were waiting backstage. I smiled as the hum of the crowd morphed into a loud roar when Maximum Mayhem took the stage.

I showered quickly and then went down to the common area where a buffet style dinner was set out for the bands and road crew to enjoy. I grabbed a plate and filled it with fresh fruits and vegetables as well as brown rice and grilled chicken. I had learned quickly that I needed to eat healthy if I wanted to maintain my stamina while following such a grueling schedule. I took a bottle of water out of the cooler and made my way over to the round table where my friends sat.

"Great show tonight, guys," I said as I sat down.

"Hell, man, that was out of this world," Steve replied, the disbelief still evident in his tone. I supposed it would take a long time for all of it to quit feeling like a dream.

"Would have been better if Animal here could slow down enough for the rest of us to keep up," Tyler teased with a shake of his head.

"Fuck off! It's not my fault you guys play slower than an old lady driving on Sunday morning," Rocko said with a snort. We often referred to Rocko as Animal from The Muppets because he went wild whenever he got behind a set of drums. It was almost like he used the drums as an outlet to help deal with whatever demons were chasing him. So far, the mixture of the adrenaline from being on stage and constantly moving from one place to another seemed to suit Rocko perfectly and other than his usual method of fucking everything in sight, he had been behaving himself fairly well. The rest of us were thrilled to see our friend finally getting back to his crazy, loveable self.

We joked around for a while as we ate, then got down to the business of dissecting every second of our performance, discussing what changes needed to be made so we could keep improving. As we were wrapping up for the night, Landon walked in.

The rest of the guys took off, but I stayed behind to visit with my older brother. Other than a few moments here and there, I had hardly seen Landon, so I was taken by surprise with how drawn and pale he looked. I noticed he only grabbed an apple before sitting down across from me with a tired smile.

"You okay, man?"

He swallowed his bite of apple before answering me. "Yeah, I'm fine. Why?"

I studied him for a minute, taking in the dark circles under his eyes and the pinched look to his mouth along with the stiff set of his shoulders. "Seriously? You look like you haven't slept in days and you're tense as shit. What's wrong?"

Landon shrugged his shoulders. "I haven't been sleeping well. You know how it is, different bed every night, new sounds, new places. I'll get used to it soon enough and then I can relax. One good night of sleep will fix me right up." He gave me a pitiful excuse for a smile. I wasn't buying it, but I decided to give him a break and not push. The poor guy looked like he was about to fall over from exhaustion.

"Sounds to me like you need to get laid. A sweaty night between the sheets will have you sleeping like a baby and suck the stress right out of you, literally," I joked.

I had expected him to make some smart ass reply, but instead he got a faraway look to his eyes and I wondered if there was someone in particular he was thinking about.

Landon had always been very private about his love life so I never knew if he was seeing anyone or not. The last time I had met one of his boyfriends was when he was a freshman in college. He brought some guy home with him for Thanksgiving break to meet our family. Landon had seemed crazy about him, but their relationship didn't last long because by Christmas Landon came home alone. He had been a moody fucker that week and all he had said was it was over and he didn't want to talk about it. He'd never introduced us to anyone else since.

"Well damn! I'd like to meet whoever has you so lost in thought over there."

Landon looked startled as he turned to me. "Sorry, just zoned out for a minute."

I smirked at him knowingly. "Yeah, I noticed. So are you going to tell me his name?"

His shoulders slumped and he looked down at the apple he was spinning in his hands. "Doesn't matter anyway." He murmured before pushing away from the table and standing. "I'm going to bed. I'll catch you tomorrow."

I followed his movements as he weaved through the tables and chairs that were scattered around the room, tossing his uneaten apple in the trash before walking out the door. There was definitely something going on with my big brother. He obviously had something weighing on his mind and he hadn't denied that there might be someone in particular he was thinking about. I didn't like seeing him upset though. I was going to have to keep a closer eye on him in case he needed me.

I checked my watch and then scrambled to my feet as I noticed the time. Ryan was off work so we had set up a Skype date and I didn't want to be late. I hurried from the dining area and made my way to the rear of the building where several limos had been set up to take the band members back and forth safely. I hopped into the first available car and then sighed happily as it took off for the hotel.

I got to my room with just minutes to spare. I quickly stripped down to my briefs and climbed into bed. I propped several pillows behind my back and then opened my laptop and connected to Skype. My heart raced when I saw the notification that Ryan was connecting also. Seconds later, the most beautiful face in the world filled my screen and I felt like I could breathe for the first time since I left home.

Ryan smiled at me from where he lay in his bed and neither of us spoke as we took a moment to just drink each other in. His blue-gray eyes looked weary with dark smudges under them, but they were full of affection as he looked me over and I would have given anything to have been cuddled up next to him in that bed. "Hey, sweetheart," he whispered and a lump formed in my throat at the endearment.

"Hi, baby," I managed to rasp out. I cleared my throat and chuckled at myself as I wiped the moisture from my eyes. "God, I miss you." His finger reached forward as he traced my face on the screen. I shivered as if I could feel his gentle touch.

"I miss you too." He let out a long sigh then shook his head as if to clear it and gave me a genuine smile. "How was your show tonight?" he asked.

"It was great! The crowd was nuts, but in a good way. It's still surreal to have people chanting our names."

"I'd scream your name if I was there," Ryan said with a cocky grin that had my dick standing up to take notice.

"Would you now?" My voice sounded husky to my ears.

"Of course the screaming I'm talking about would be done in a more private setting." I watched as Ryan's arms jerked with a movement I couldn't see on screen. I had a pretty good idea what he was doing though and I decided it was time to play.

"I bet I can make you scream my name even if we're not in the same room." My tongue darted out to wet my bottom lip and I smiled to myself when I heard his sharp intake of breath.

"What do you have in mind?" he asked in a hoarse whisper.

"Are you up for a little game?"

Ryan quirked his eyebrow at me. "You mean like checkers?" he joked.

I laughed. "I was thinking more along the lines of 'Carter Says.' It's the adult version of 'Simon Says.' Same rules apply. You can only do what Carter says or you lose and the game is over. Sound good?"

"Hell yeah. But I think I should warn you, I was quite the champion of this game when I was a boy." He flashed a smug smile at me and I could almost picture him as a little boy.

"I sure hope you weren't playing this version of the game on the playground or you probably spent a lot of time in the principal's office." Ryan threw his head back with a laugh and the sound made my toes curl.

"Okay, before we start, you need to set your laptop down on the bed so I can see you better and because you're going to need the use of your hands." Ryan complied immediately and I instructed him on the placement of the laptop so I would have the best view.

"Now what?" he asked eagerly.

"Now open that drawer next to your bed and grab some lube and…pinky." I knew that would get to him and I wasn't disappointed as Ryan's hands stilled from where they were reaching for the drawer and he looked over his shoulder at me, his eyes wide. I tilted my head at him and threw out a challenge. "Carter Says…bring out pinky." I smiled as he reached into the drawer and pulled out a bottle of lube and the ten-inch pink dildo.

Ryan had been embarrassed when I had discovered his toy collection until I assured him that I had one of my own. We hadn't had a chance to use any of them when I was home, since we were more than happy to use the real thing instead, but I thought they would come in quite handy while we were apart.

Ryan's face was bright red as he carefully laid the supplies out on the bed. After everything we had already done, all the ways we had explored each other's bodies, I found his sudden shyness adorable. I never wanted him to feel uncomfortable with me though, so I quickly reached for my bag and pulled out my own dildo. Ryan watched me through hooded eyes, his earlier embarrassment replaced with a sizzling heat.

"Have you used that often since you've been gone?" The gravely quality to his voice gave away how much the thought turned him on.

"A few times," I answered honestly before giving him a command. "Carter Says lie back and stroke yourself."

Now fully committed to the game, he stretched out on the bed and I did the same. From the position of the camera, I had a perfect view of his chiseled body. My eyes shuttered at the sight of all that golden skin as it rippled over his lean muscles with every movement of his hand on his cock. My breath faltered as I saw a bead of clear fluid glistening on the tip of his wide head and I had the overwhelming urge to lick the screen to see if I could taste him.

"Carter Says play with your balls." Ryan reached between his legs with his long fingers and cupped his sac, squeezing and pulling on it gently. I reached down, fondling myself and gasped as arousal lit my body on fire. Ryan watched my every move and his chest rose and fell rapidly as his breathing increased.

"Carter Says wet your fingers and play with your greedy hole. I want to watch as you prepare yourself to take that cock." I fumbled to open my own bottle of lube as I watched Ryan drizzle the liquid over his fingers, rubbing them together to warm them.

I forgot what I had been doing as he leaned back against his pillows, pulled his legs against his chest and began circling his pink hole with his finger, letting the tip dip inside every so often. I couldn't help the tortured groan that escaped my throat at the sight of him pleasuring himself.

His eyes darted to mine and then back down to my weeping cock. He licked his lips as he added another finger inside his tight opening. "You do it too," he growled and I had to squeeze my eyes shut and concentrate on my breathing as I struggled to fight back my looming orgasm. A moment later, I was able to follow his command

and had soon worked two fingers inside, groaning at the delicious-ness of the burn as I opened myself for the large dildo.

"Carter Says use the cock instead of your fingers." He gave me a grateful look as he spread lube up the length of the toy then steadied it against his opening. He held his breath as it breached the first ring of muscle and sweat trickled down his temple as he struggled to ac-commodate its girth. "That's it, baby, close your eyes and imagine it's my cock sliding into you." My words must have worked because with a loud curse he slid it in the rest of the way.

"Holy fuck!" He began working the phallic toy in and out of himself while his other hand continued fisting his cock.

I hurried to catch up and had soon joined him in writhing ecsta-sy. The silicone dick was nowhere near as good as having Ryan's cock fucking me, but sharing this experience together was the next best thing given the distance between us.

The sounds of our hands rubbing over slicked skin and our whis-pered words to each other soon had me right on the edge. "Come!" I told him through clenched teeth.

"You've got to say it," he choked out.

"Oh, for fuck's sake! Carter. Says. Come!" Ryan shouted my name as he found his release and I barely bit back a scream as my cock erupted like a geyser, spewing hot cum all over my chest and up my neck.

We lay there, each of us fully sated and exhausted. I carefully let the cock slide from between my cheeks. I rolled on my side to face him and pulled my laptop closer to me, smiling when Ryan did the same. He pulled the covers over his cooling skin and rested his head on his pillow as he gazed at me with adoration.

"Carter Says…never stop loving me," I whispered sleepily.

"I promise, I never will," he whispered back as my eyes drifted shut.

CHAPTER
Sixteen

Ryan

I HAD ALWAYS BEEN USED TO A QUIET HOME. GRANDPA WAS A highly intelligent man who often got lost in his thoughts as he tried to work out some problem in his mind. I usually had my nose stuck in a book or working on some project around the house, so it wasn't unusual for whole days to go by without either of us uttering a word. Once Grandpa passed away and I moved into the warehouse, the only sounds in the house were mine. I enjoyed the stillness and being alone with my thoughts because it was all I had ever known.

Then Carter entered my world and brought to it a life that I hadn't known was missing. He filled my home with color and light and music. His personality oozed energy and happiness. That was what drew me to him and made me fall in love.

I lay in bed, willing myself to get up and do something productive with my day off, but my heart felt heavy and I had no motivation to drag myself out from beneath my covers. Carter had been gone a month and the house was so silent, I felt like I was going to lose my mind. Rick Greene had called to invite me over for dinner, but I had turned him down. I appreciated the gesture, but I didn't feel like I belonged there without Carter by my side.

I had tried playing music to fill the house with sound, but every song reminded me of Carter and made the ache in my chest worse. Missing Carter was like having an itch I couldn't scratch; it ate away at me until I just wanted to pull my hair out. *How in the hell am I going to make it through another two months?*

With a frustrated sigh, I dragged myself out of bed and made a cup of coffee. I decided to sit on the rooftop patio as I drank the hot brew, letting the caffeine clear the sleep from my head. I needed to find something to do to occupy my mind. It was a gorgeous day to spend outdoors. The temperature was a perfect seventy-eight degrees and the sky was bright blue with big, fluffy white clouds.

As I looked around, I noticed the pile of bricks, stacked neatly in a corner. I had been so caught up in Carter that I hadn't had a chance to finish the outdoor kitchen project I had been planning. Happy to have found something to occupy my time, I made of list of the supplies I would need and then jumped in the shower before heading down to the local home improvement warehouse.

I worked tirelessly for several hours, stacking the bricks precisely and smoothing out the layers of mortar that would hold them together. It felt good to do something productive and my muscles felt warm and relaxed for the first time in a month. I finished laying the final brick and stepped back to survey my work. After it had time to set, I would install the countertop and sink and then hook up the new grill and refrigerator I had purchased. It was going to look incredible once I was done.

I smiled, feeling good about all I had accomplished when I heard a car pull up near my building. Figuring it was probably Joe or Suzy, I yelled out for them to come on up. I gathered my tools and put them away neatly then made my way downstairs to wash my hands.

"Hey! You need to check out my latest project. I just got done…" My words tapered off as I realized that instead of Joe or Suzy, it was Kathy Greene who stood in my kitchen. She smiled at me, holding a pot of something in her hands and the delicious smell wafting from it made my mouth water. I stood there stupidly, just looking at her.

"Hi, Ryan! I figured you probably hadn't been eating properly so I made you a little something. Looks like I was right too. You've lost weight, sweetie." With a shake of her head she set the pot down on the stove and then started moving around my kitchen as if she'd always been there. She grabbed two plates out of the cabinet and began dishing up what appeared to be chicken and dumplings. My stomach growled embarrassingly, but Kathy ignored it and arched a brow at me.

"Well, are you going to just stand there or are you going to wash up?" That snapped me out of my stupor and I rushed to the sink to scrub the dust from my fingers. I poured us each a glass of iced tea and then sat at the table. Kathy placed a steaming plate in front of me then sat down with her own food.

"This looks great. Thank you," I managed to say. My mind was still reeling at the fact that she was in my home and she had cooked for me. Grandpa had never been much of a cook so as I got older, I taught myself how to cook and took over the responsibility for both of us. Other than Suzy, no one ever cooked for me and the fact that Kathy had cared enough about me to plan out a meal and prepare it for me had me swallowing a lump in my throat.

"You're welcome, sugar, now eat up before it gets cold." I bit back a grin at her bossy nature. I figured that was just the mother in her coming out, not that I would have a clue what that was like. I supposed as a mother of five children, she was required to act like a drill sergeant at times, just to keep them in line; *especially Carter*, I mused.

I scooped a spoonful into my mouth and groaned as the flavors burst on my tongue. "Wow, Kathy! This is incredible." I quickly ate several more bites, not realizing how hungry I had been. When my plate was nearly empty, she brought the pan over to the table and served me another helping. I smiled at her gratefully.

"So, do you want to tell me why you've been avoiding us lately?" I looked up from my plate to see her staring at me with a pointed look.

"I haven't been avoiding you, I've just been working a lot." I tried to look away from her, but I was almost mesmerized by her "mom look" and I wondered if any of her kids had ever been able to stand up to that knowing stare. I found myself wilting back in my chair.

"Don't lie to me, Ryan." She held a hand up to stop my protest. "I'm sure you've been working a lot and I commend you for it, but I'm also sure you've worked as much as possible to avoid being alone in this big place. Am I right?"

"Yes, ma'am," I mumbled.

Kathy reached across the table and covered my hand with her own. Her eyes were compassionate as she talked to me. "I know you miss him; I miss both of my boys. It's hard being the one left behind. Things here are the same old same old, so you notice the time creeping by slowly and it feels like he'll never come home."

I nodded my head as she spoke my thoughts aloud. "You know what helps though?" she continued. "Being around people who can help share the pain of missing him so you aren't doing it all by yourself. People who love you. And, Ryan, we *do* love you. Like it or not, you're a part of our family now."

I looked down at my hands, blinking back the tears that threatened to spill. Could I really have found a family in the Greenes? They were an amazing group of people, but I had never been part of a big family before.

Kathy stood and came around the table. I felt her warm hand as she cupped my cheek. "I know this is all new to you. Carter told me it had always been just you and your grandpa, but perhaps now is a good time to let more people in your life that can love you. We're here whenever you're ready." With that, she kissed the top of my head and headed towards the door.

She looked back at me and I gave her a wobbly smile, still too emotional to speak. She winked at me in understanding and then walked out the door. When she had left, I let the tears flow freely. I cried for the lonely boy I had been and for the love that Carter and his family were bringing into my life. Grandpa had loved me and raised me the best he could, but I had never known the love of a mother or father. I had never experienced the trusted closeness between siblings. Maybe Kathy was right, maybe I could have all of that now with Carter's family.

I wiped the tears from my eyes, somehow feeling lighter than I had since Carter got on that bus. I needed to quit moping around and living like a hermit. Other than work and my quick run to the hardware store, I hadn't been around any other people. Joe had asked me to go out on several occasions, but I had pushed him away, preferring to wallow in my own misery. I needed to change that.

I grabbed my phone and quickly punched in Joe's number. He sounded surprised to hear from me and I couldn't help the stab of guilt that hit me. I had been acting like a selfish ass. We made arrangements to meet up at a bar later and I even went so far as to suggest calling some of the other guys from work to see if they wanted to grab a couple of beers with us. Joe sounded happy that I had called and I had to admit it felt good to be doing something I normally would have done before I met Carter.

"So she goes completely nuts and starts kicking me and clawing at my back and I'm trying to carry her down a sixteen-foot ladder. I was so pissed off by the time I got to the ground that I plopped her down and screamed at her that I didn't care if her six cats made it out alive or not." We all started laughing at Paul's story about a run he went out on that day.

"Did the cats make it out alive?" Kevin asked.

Paul rolled his eyes and let out a long-suffering sigh. "Yeah, I went back and got them out. It's not their fault that their owner's crazy. The worst part will be later when I have to explain to my girlfriend why I have claw marks down my back that she didn't put there." We all roared with laughter and I ordered another round of beers for everyone.

It felt good being out with the guys and even though Dan had shown up uninvited, I really appreciated the time with my friends. I hadn't realized how closed off I'd been, even at work, until I saw the shocked looks on their faces when I arrived. They ribbed me about finally joining the living again, but in a way that's exactly how it felt.

The waitress arrived with our drinks and I grabbed an icy mug, enjoying the slightly bitter taste of the beer. As I set my drink back down on the table, I noticed a group of young women sitting at a table near ours. They looked like they were probably college students and they were laughing and whispering about something while their eyes continued to dart in our direction. I turned my attention back to my friends, but their conversation suddenly stopped.

I looked to see what had caught their attention and saw a pretty redhead with freckles across her nose, making her way towards us. She nervously glanced over her shoulder at her friends who all waved her on and smiled at her encouragingly. She threw back her shoulders with an air of confidence and walked towards us and I wondered idly which of my buddies she was trying to pick up.

I snickered at several of the guys who were practically drooling. I looked the woman over again, I supposed if I had been into women I would have found her attractive. She had long wavy red hair and a petite frame along with curves that seemed like they were in the proper places. The whole female form was completely lost on me however, so I sat back and crossed my arms, content to enjoy the show as my single friends tried to win her over.

"Hi!" she said breathlessly as she stopped at our table.

"Hey, gorgeous!" Todd said in a southern drawl that didn't match his usual Chicago born dialect. It must have worked on her though because her face turned a bright shade of pink and she giggled.

"Um…I saw you over here and I was wondering if you'd sign my calendar," she said in one breath. I fought back a laugh as she pulled the firemen's calendar from behind her back. I hadn't realized the thing was even finished yet. It suddenly made sense why she and her friends were whispering about us now.

"Sure thing, babe. We can sign anything you want. I'm Paul, but you can call me Mr. April if you want to." I fought back a laugh as I wondered if this cheesiness worked on all women.

"Oh, um…I was actually talking to him, but yeah, the rest of you can sign it too, if you want." She looked around the table apologetically and I was shocked when she shoved the calendar in front of me and handed me a permanent marker.

"Oh yeah, my boys got game, y'all," Joe yelled out as he burst into raucous laughter. The other guys slumped in their seats, scowling in my direction.

I shrugged my shoulders at them, but I couldn't wipe the smirk off my face as I popped the cap off the marker and searched through the calendar for the month with my picture. When I found it, I couldn't help but smile wider at how good it had turned out. It seemed my boyfriend was very talented in the art of photography as well as music.

"Would you mind putting your phone number on there too?" the woman asked as she lay a perfectly manicured hand on my shoulder. She was obviously feeling bolder now that she had made it that far.

I smiled at her kindly as I handed the calendar back to her sans phone number. "I'm really flattered, but I'm actually seeing someone." Her shoulders slumped and I almost said something to make her feel better, but the sound of Dan's obnoxious voice filled the air, grabbing my attention along with everyone else around us.

"Oh don't take it personally, little girl. You just don't have the right parts for this one here. You see, Mr. October," he said with a sneer, "is a queer. He's too busy taking it up the ass to know what to do with a pretty young thing like you."

I stood up so fast my chair crashed to the floor. Joe tried to squeeze his way in between us as I got in Dan's face. "What's your fucking problem, man?" I roared. I had never been so angry in my life, but the guy had pushed and pushed until I had finally had enough. I barely noticed Joe as he shoved at our chests which were practically pressed together. We were each breathing heavily and I had my hands balled into fists at my sides.

"You and all the other fairies of the world. You're everybody's problem. You think you can just go against nature and everyone's supposed to be fine with it. You fucking disgust me," he spat out, his face contorted with rage.

"Listen, you ignorant homophobe," I growled. "There is nothing about loving someone else, no matter what sex they are, that goes against nature. It's exactly what God created us to do, but I'm not here to try to change your narrow mind; I doubt I ever could. Unfortunately, we have to work together and it would be nice if you could lay off the shit and try to act civilized when we're around each other. You think you can manage that?" I held my breath as I waited for his response. The guy didn't have to like me, I couldn't stand *him* to be honest, but I wasn't going to continue to let him harass me.

"Dan, lay off, man, we're all just trying to have a good time," Paul spoke up.

Dan swung his head around to look at the other guys, almost like he had forgotten they were there. He held his hands up in surrender. "You're right. I think I've just had too much to drink and I said some things I didn't mean. I apologize." He held his hand out for me to shake and Joe stepped aside, seemingly satisfied that the moment wasn't going to erupt into violence. I eyed Dan warily as I placed my hand in his.

To the others it probably appeared that he was making amends, but I felt his hand grip mine roughly as he pulled me forward. He leaned in and spoke in a low voice so no one else could hear and his words sent cold chills down my spine. "You don't deserve to breathe air. If we're lucky that may not be a problem for long." He bumped my shoulder hard with his as he stormed passed me. Our group was quiet for a long minute after he left as everyone sat in stunned silence.

"I don't know about the rest of you, but I'm sick of that asshole," Kevin said angrily. The others nodded their agreement.

"Hey, are you okay?" Joe asked as he placed his hands on my shoulders.

"Yeah, I'm fine," I assured him. "My head's starting to hurt though. I think I'm just going to call it a night."

"Okay. I'll give you a call tomorrow."

After saying goodbye to the rest of the guys, I made my way out to the parking lot. I couldn't help but breathe a sigh of relief when there was no sign of Dan. Alone in the cab of my truck, I could admit that his words had shaken me. I knew there was a lot of stupid people out there who liked to spread their vile hatred towards members of the LGBTQ community, but I had never been exposed to such a blatant threat against me.

I walked in the door of my empty house and felt the weight of the silence that surrounded me. I knew Carter had a bunch of interviews scheduled after his concert and a meet and greet with some of the fans, but I needed him. My encounter with Dan had left me feeling cold and I missed Carter so much that it had become a physical ache.

I climbed into bed with only the bedside table lamp on and decided to try to get ahold of him. With any luck he'd be done with his responsibilities and would have a few minutes to talk. A few minutes was all I needed. Just long enough to hear his voice and feel the connection between us. I sent out a quick text asking him if he could talk yet and then sat there, drumming my fingers on my crossed legs as I waited for his reply. I didn't have to wait long because my phone rang almost immediately.

"Hey! I hope I didn't pull you away from anything. I wasn't sure if you'd be done for the night or not."

"I was just doing the meet and greet, but the others can handle it. How are you, baby?" Tears swam in my eyes at the comforting sound of his voice and I struggled to answer him around the lump in my throat.

"I'm okay."

"You don't sound okay," he said and I hated that I had worried him. "Look, give me five minutes to get back to the bus and then we can Skype. I need to see your face. Can you give me five minutes? Will you be alright?"

I chuckled through my tears. "I'll be fine. I'll see you in a few minutes."

"I'm walking out to the bus now. I love you."

"I love you too," I whispered.

The wait was torture, five minutes seemed like an hour. I hated worrying him and I didn't want to come across as some clingy boyfriend, it had just been a really emotional day and I'd reached my breaking point. Only time spent with the man I loved would help put me back together again, even if it was only through a computer.

Finally, we were connecting and I held my breath until his face appeared on the screen. He pulled the beanie off that he liked to wear when he performed and smiled at me tiredly. His hair had gotten longer and was sloppily hanging down over one eye. The sides were slick with sweat from his performance and he had dark smudges under his eyes, but he was still the most magnificent creature I had ever seen. My shoulders slumped in relief that we were finally together.

"I didn't mean to pull you away from your fans. Will you be in trouble for leaving early?"

He swept the hair out of his eyes, but it stubbornly flopped right back down. "None of that matters. Everyone here knows that you come first and that if you need me, I'll drop anything I'm doing to take care of you. Now tell me what's wrong." He looked at me intently, worry etched on his face.

My heart swelled with the knowledge that he had talked about me with the people he worked with and that they knew that I was an important fixture in his life. Somehow it helped to validate my place in his world and that made me feel better. I had been feeling cut off from that part of his life, but I should have known Carter would have picked up on my feelings and found a way to fix it.

"It's just been a really rough day and I wanted to hear your voice, see your beautiful face." He smiled at me so wide his dimples popped on each of his cheeks.

"I hardly think I look beautiful right now. I'm a sweaty mess."

"Some of my favorite times with you have been spent with us turning into sweaty messes. I like that look on you." I winked at him, feeling much lighter than I had mere minutes before.

Carter groaned. "Oh God, don't start. You don't know how badly I need you. My balls are so blue; I think they're going to fall off." I laughed as he stuck his bottom lip out in a perfect pout.

"Believe me, I feel the same way. When we finally get in a room alone together, we may spontaneously combust."

"I just hope I don't come as soon as I see you, like some randy teenage boy," he joked back.

When we had stopped laughing he ran his eyes over my face lovingly. "Talk to me, Ryan. Why was it a rough day?"

I sighed. I knew that he would be upset about the altercation with Dan and I was right. He listened quietly as I told him everything, but I could see the tension in his posture and the slight tightening of the skin around his eyes.

"God, I want to kick that fucker's ass! Seriously, what the hell?" he exploded as soon as I had finished. I had never seen Carter so angry and while I was by no means a damsel in distress, I had to admit it did strange things to me to see him jumping to my defense.

"Easy there, Rocky," I said, hoping my teasing would calm him down. I didn't want him stressing about this when he was too far away to do anything about it. He calmed down when he saw my grin, but only marginally. "I'm sure he was just talking out of his ass. He's a typical bully, all bark but no bite."

Carter looked at me seriously. "How is that guy even still allowed to work there? I thought there was a no tolerance policy at your station for violent threats."

I rubbed my hand along my jaw then shrugged my shoulders. "There is, and he's been written up, but this time he was just sneaky enough to make sure no one else heard what he said. If I filed a complaint, it would be my word against his."

He slumped back in his seat and ran his hands through his hair in frustration then he looked at me. "So what are we going to do?"

I couldn't help but notice he used the word "we." The fact that he saw this as *our* problem, something we would deal with together, made me fall in love with him all over again. I truly wasn't alone any more.

"Now, we wait for him to either give up or slip up and say something stupid in front of other people. I'm sure I won't have to wait long for him to make a mistake. He's a hot head, quick to get angry and quick to explode. That type of person can't control themselves enough to be cautious all the time. When that time comes, he'll be fired and I'll be free of his hateful slurs."

Carter let out a long sigh. "Promise me you'll be careful and watch your back."

"I promise, sweetheart."

"You better, because I'm very fond of that back and all the other parts that go with it." Carter gave me a devilish smile and I was

214

relieved to move on from such a heavy topic.

"You are, are you?" I grinned at him.

"Yeah, in fact, I love them." His words warmed me.

"I love you too," I whispered. "So, how was your concert tonight?"

"It was amazing. You should see it sometime. I don't think I'll ever get used to people screaming my name and wearing t-shirts with my face on them. It still feels like a dream most of the time. The only thing that would be better is if you were here."

"It sounds awesome. I'm so happy for you and I really believe this is only the beginning," I said sincerely. "I can see it now, you guys will be headlining your own show before you know it, travelling all around the globe, rubbing elbows with movie stars and I'll be put on some reality show for rock star spouses." I laughed at my own joke, but then I noticed that Carter wasn't laughing with me. I replayed my words in my head and understanding dawned on me that I had probably freaked him out by referring to myself as his spouse.

"I was just joking about the rock star spouse thing; I didn't mean to freak you out."

"No, I'm not...freaked out," he said slowly as he stared at me intently. His lips turned up into a beautiful smile. "In fact, I really like the sound of that."

Something fizzled in my stomach and it was suddenly hard to breathe. We had never really talked about the future before. "Me too," I admitted quietly.

We talked for another hour. Carter thought it was well deserved that I had been asked to sign an autograph for my calendar picture. He admitted that he'd had Caleb send him a copy of the calendar and it was currently hanging on the wall of his bunk, open to my month of course. He talked about his concern for Landon and I told him about my lunch with his mom.

When we couldn't keep our eyes open any more, we finally said goodnight. As I drifted off to sleep, I smiled, thankful to have such an amazing man in my life.

CHAPTER
Seventeen

Carter

"HEY, MAN! WHAT'S UP?" I SETTLED BACK ON MY BUNK to talk to my brother. The bus rocked as it travelled down the stretch of highway. We had another hour before we would stop for the next gig. I could hear the sounds of my bandmates where they were gathered towards the front of the bus. Steve and Rocko were having a video game battle of some sort and kept screaming obscenities at each other. Tyler was strumming his guitar, trying to work out a difficult riff. I don't know what Kalia was up to, but I wanted to kiss her for being quiet. My friends were great, but it was difficult being cooped up for hours on end with the same people.

That's why I had escaped to my bunk and pulled the curtain closed. I wanted just a few minutes to touch base with Caleb before I faced another crazy night of fans. He had called and left a voicemail asking me to call him, but we were travelling through the mountains and my phone had just recently picked up signal.

"Carter! Hang on a minute," he said excitedly. I could hear pots and pans clanking in the background, then a shuffling sound as he moved further away from the noise. "Sorry about that, the kitchen is so loud, I couldn't hear you. I'm in the office now. How are you? Do you still love being on tour? I miss you so much." I smiled at the familiar way my twin ran all of his words together when he was excited.

"I miss you too. I'm doing good. It's still a trip playing in front of such large crowds so that part's fun, but then we have long periods of time where we're travelling from one city to another and that gets old pretty quick. I can't wait to get home again."

"I understand," he said sympathetically and I knew that he really did. Caleb had left home soon after high school to study the culinary arts around Europe and the Mediterranean. It had been difficult for him to be away from our close-knit family, so as soon as he had completed his education, he headed home to find a job in our hometown of Chicago. It seemed as if I had just gotten him back and then I was the one leaving.

"Catch me up on everything going on there. How's that sexy husband of yours? Still pining away for me?" I teased. Giovanni was a gorgeous specimen of a man, no doubt about it, but all you had to do was watch his face when Caleb entered a room and you'd know that my brother was his whole world.

"You wish." He chuckled. "So, I was trying to get ahold of you. I wanted to tell you in person, but I can't wait that long."

"What is it? Is everything okay?" Picking up on his seriousness, I sat up and threw my legs over the side of the bunk.

"Everything's fine…great, in fact. I just wanted to tell you that Gio and I have started the adoption process for a little girl." He paused, letting his news sink in.

"Oh my God, Bubby. You're going to be a daddy?" I whispered.

Tears sprung to my eyes and I laughed as I wiped them away. I knew that Caleb had always wanted a house full of kids and that he and Giovanni would make the best dads on the planet.

"Yeah, I am." The awe was evident in his voice as he told me about the four-year-old girl named Sarah who had been shuffled around within the foster care system ever since she was abandoned by her parents at the hospital. It had been difficult to find a family willing to take on the responsibility of caring for a child with down syndrome, but as I listened to Caleb describe their first meeting with her, it was clear to me that he already loved his daughter unconditionally.

"I am so happy for you guys. I know you both will be incredible parents. When will she come home with you?" My cheeks hurt from smiling so much.

"It will take a while longer for everything to go through the courts, but fortunately she's staying with a really kind, older woman right now and we get to visit her every day. Hopefully you'll be finished touring when we have the big adoption ceremony."

"Like that matters at all. You give me a date and time and I'll be there, whether the tour's over or not. Nothing's going to keep me from celebrating my new niece," I said sincerely.

"Thanks, Carter. I can't wait for you to meet her. She's the most beautiful girl in the world," he said with a happy sigh.

"I can't wait either. I bet Giovanni's over the moon, isn't he?"

Caleb groaned. "Oh man, you should see him. He's running around the condo making sure everything is completely childproof."

"That's a good thing, isn't it?" I asked.

"Don't get me wrong, I want things to be as safe as possible for Sarah, but Gio's going overboard. He's put safety locks on absolutely everything. The other day, I had to run down to the corner store and beg them to let me use their restroom because I couldn't figure out how to unhook the safety latch on the toilet." I howled with laughter as he continued to describe the steps needed to get into the refrigerator. "I'm telling you, we haven't even brought her home yet and the man has lost his mind."

"He'll calm down, you know that," I reassured him. "There's just nothing more important in his life than you and your little girl. He has to do everything he can to make sure you're both kept safe."

Caleb sighed happily. "Yeah, I know you're right. He and Sarah mean everything to me too. Hey, do me a favor, don't say anything to Landon. I want to be the one to tell him, but I haven't been able to get ahold of him yet."

"I won't. Tell Giovanni I said congratulations. Oh, and send me pictures of my niece."

"I will. Love you, Bub. Be safe."

"Love you too." I was so happy for Caleb and Giovanni that they were starting a family. Any child would be lucky to have them as parents. I smiled as I pictured Caleb with a child on his lap, reading her a bedtime story. The image soon changed into one of me with the little girl and Ryan joining me to help tuck her in.

Warmth flowed through my veins as I imagined a future I had never really considered before. I had always assumed I would have a family someday, but it always seemed more abstract than a real possibility. Music had been my sole focus for as long as I could remember, but ever since I had met Ryan, I could feel subtle shifts in my priorities. I still wanted a career in music and to spend time touring, but now I could see a future beyond all of that. One that included Ryan and hopefully a kid or two. As I got up to change my clothes, I wondered if Ryan saw the same future in his mind.

I glanced down at my phone and slid it back in my pocket with a sigh. I had texted Ryan a few times throughout the day, but hadn't gotten any response from him. We both had very demanding jobs and while I knew it wasn't unusual for him to not be able to text me back if things were crazy at work, the whole mess with Dan had me on edge.

I already worried about Ryan's safety because of the line of work he was in, but there was the added threat that one of his coworkers might want to hurt him. He had tried to assure me that he was perfectly safe, but I wasn't convinced. I may have joked that he was a super hero, but he was really just a man; made of flesh and bone and just as easily broken as the rest of us.

"Yo, Carter! You ready, man?" Rocko eyed me from behind his drum set, waiting for me to give him the signal to start.

"Sorry. Yeah, I'm ready." I gave him a nod and he raised his sticks above his head, hitting them together to count out the beat while I waited for my intro.

As we went through the routine sound check, I let my mind wander back to the dinner I had just had. Nathan, the lead singer from Maximum Mayhem had invited me out so we could talk. We had bonded over our love of music and become close friends. We had similar musical styles and had helped pass the long hours between gigs with impromptu jam sessions.

Nathan and I respected each other's talents, but he still took me by surprise when he told me over dinner that he knew I was going to go far and he was willing to help me any way he could. Apparently he wasn't just saying that, because he had already put a call into the executives at Golden Entertainment Studios, letting them know that they would be fools not to give us a full contract.

I couldn't thank him enough. There were a lot of truly talented musicians in the world who never got noticed because they didn't have the right connections. As much as I wished I could rely on my talents alone to get ahead in this business, it often came down to who you knew. Nathan had given us a foot in the door, but the rest was up to us and I knew we were up to the challenge.

We ran through our set of songs, making necessary sound and lighting changes. When we were satisfied that it was perfect, we filed off the stage so that Maximum Mayhem could do their thing.

I got something to eat and changed quickly then made my way to the meet and greet room where fan club members and radio contest winners were waiting to meet the two bands. There were about fifty people waiting in line to be let in the room and I quickly walked passed them and entered the room where my bandmates were gathered. I grabbed a water bottle from the mini-fridge and took a seat next to Rocko on the couch.

Over the next couple of hours, security let a few people in at a time to meet us. Most were polite and asked us to sign some of their memorabilia. A couple of girls used their time to try to hook up with us though, blatantly showing their tits and sitting on Steve and Rocko's laps. I laughed off their advances, telling them I was very happily taken, but I didn't miss the fact that Rocko slipped them his number before they were escorted out.

I shook my head at him. "Dude, you know they only want a story to tell, right?"

"I'll give them a story they won't ever forget," Rocko said with a lecherous smile.

"You're disgusting," Kalia jumped in. "How has your dick not fallen off yet?"

"I don't know; you want to check it for me?" Rocko snapped back. Tyler jumped up from his chair, his hands balled up at his sides and I decided it was time to break things up.

"That's enough, guys, everybody back to their corners. We're all just getting on each other's nerves because we've been cooped up together on that bus, but after tonight, we have a couple of days before we hit the road again. So let's take a breath and get through this show. Then we can all take off to our own hotel rooms and forget each other exists for a while." I let my eyes roam over each of them until they gave me nods of agreement.

Crisis averted, I pulled my phone out of my pocket. Still nothing from Ryan. I tried calling him one more time. When his voicemail picked up, I left him a message.

"Hey, I've been trying to get ahold of you all day and I'm starting to get worried. I'm getting ready to go on stage, but call me whenever you get this message and I'll call you back as soon as I'm done. I hope you're alright. I love you." I studied my phone for another minute before sliding it back in my pocket. *If he hasn't called back by the time the show's over, I'm chartering a plane and going home.*

I nodded to Rocko who raised his drum sticks in the air. I turned to face the audience as the lights went up and the noise from the crowd became deafening. I could already tell an increase in their response towards us from the beginning of the tour to a month and a half later. At first, people came just to see Maximum Mayhem, but as time went on we had begun building a name for ourselves. Radio stations had begun playing our songs on a regular basis which helped us to grow a stronger fan base.

I stepped up to the mic, the excitement from the crowd helping to ratchet up my own energy and began singing a song that was sure to get them on their feet. In between songs, I introduced the other members of the band and talked to the audience, forming a connection between us. I had never been shy on stage and that time was no different. I teased them and bent down to sing in their upturned faces and soon they were eating out of the palm of my hand. It was what I had always been working towards and I loved every minute of it.

As we neared the end of our set, the lights were lowered and a stool was brought out and placed in the middle of the stage. Rocko kept a steady, pulsating beat going while Kalia, Tyler, and Steve played the intro to the next song on a gentle loop. The crowd quieted as I sat down and pulled the mic closer to me. My voice was scratchy from use.

"Hey, Atlanta! How's it going? You all enjoying yourselves tonight?" I smiled as a large roar filled the air. When they had settled down, I continued. "We have one more song we want to play for you before we go. It's a new one I wrote." Another cheer filled the air. "I wrote it for someone that I love more than life itself and even though he's not here, I want to dedicate this song to him. It's called, *You're my home*."

I bent over my guitar and let myself get lost in the song that I had written the morning after Ryan and I had admitted we loved each other for the first time. I closed my eyes and for a few minutes, I was able to block out everything around me. Scenes from my time spent with Ryan flitted through my mind like a movie playing and I felt like I was home again.

As I played the last note, I was pulled back to the present by the sounds of cheering and screaming. I gave a small smile, and thanked them for listening before making my way off stage. It always hurt to get lost in my own head, only to have it ripped away with the reminder that I was hundreds of miles away from the man I loved. It was worth it however to spend that little bit of time with Ryan, even if it was all imagined.

Kalia gave me a sympathetic hug. She knew how much I missed Ryan. "We're halfway done. You'll be home with him before you know it." I pasted a smile on my face, knowing she meant for her words to comfort me, but inside I felt like screaming. *Only halfway done? It's already felt like years since I'd held Ryan in my arms or felt his lips on mine.*

Without bothering to change first, I jumped in the nearest limo which sped off to the hotel Landon had booked for us. I was grateful to have the next few days off. I needed to get out of my slump if I was going to make it through the last leg of the tour.

If I could talk to Ryan, I knew it would go a long way towards making me feel better. With that thought in mind, I pulled my phone from my pocket only to feel crushing disappointment when there was no call from him. *Looks like I might need to charter that flight after all.* I decided to go to the hotel and change and then see if Landon could hook me up with a flight home. Something was going on with Ryan and I needed to find out what it was.

Back in my room, I paced back and forth in agitation. I couldn't get ahold of Landon and everyone else I called said they hadn't seen him since we took the stage. *Screw it, I'll just call the airline and take the quickest flight home.* That wouldn't be as fast as a chartered flight, but at least I'd still get there.

I pulled my credit card out of my wallet and called the airline. I was on hold when there was a knock at my door. I knew it had to be someone with our group because Landon had reserved the entire floor just for us. I opened the door and my phone which had been shoved between my shoulder and my ear landed at my feet with a thud. My mouth hung open at the sight that greeted me.

Ryan was leaning against the wall, a shy smile tilting the corners of his mouth. His hands were shoved in the pockets of his tight black jeans and he wore a Carter's Creed t-shirt that stretched enticingly across his broad chest.

I couldn't form a coherent thought as I stood gaping at him in shock. Finally, he stepped forward and placed his hands on my hips, pulling me towards him until his head rested on mine. "Hi, baby," he whispered and I felt a tear roll down my face.

I lunged at him, wrapping my arms around his neck and pulling him down so his lips covered mine. Our kiss was passionate, a reunion of our souls. We poured every bit of frustration and loneliness and love that we had been feeling for the past month and a half into that kiss until we were forced to break part long enough to catch our breath.

"What…how…?" I managed to get out, but then I pulled him back in for another earth shattering kiss before he could respond. Ryan lifted me and I wrapped my legs around him as he carried me back into the room, using his foot to slam the door behind us.

He carried me into the bedroom and gently lowered me down onto the mattress. His voice sounded husky when he spoke and it sent a delicious shiver down my spine. "I promise we'll talk, but I've waited forty-five days, six hours and approximately 32 minutes to be inside of you and I can't wait one second more." I couldn't do anything but nod.

Ryan made quick work of undressing us and slicking himself with lube, then he was leaning over me, his arms straining as he held himself poised above me. He stared into my eyes for a brief moment and then he slid into me. He went slowly, studying me closely for any signs of discomfort until finally his hips rested snuggly against me. We were as close as two humans could possibly be and yet I still craved more. I wrapped my arms around his muscled back and slid them down until I was cupping his ass in my firm grasp.

"We can go slow later, right now, I need to feel you, baby. Prove to me this isn't just a dream." Ryan gazed down at me and I could feel the tension in his body from restraining himself. He nodded at me and then crushed his mouth to mine.

His hips drew back slowly and then he slammed into me, giving me everything I had asked for. He swallowed my screams as he continued to drive his cock into me and I dug my heels into his ass, pulling him back into my depths every time he would retreat. It was rough, animalistic, and absolutely perfect.

It didn't take long for either of us to find our release and I nearly wept as I felt his warmth flooding me, becoming a part of me. He collapsed onto me and I ran my fingers over the slick muscles of his back.

After a few minutes, Ryan leaned up, his forearms resting on either side of my head. "I've missed you," he whispered and I could feel his warm breath fan across my face.

"How are you here? I've been trying to call you all day. I was so worried that something…" My words were cut off as he stole another kiss from me.

"When we talked the last time, you said that I should see your show sometime. I couldn't stop thinking about that, so here I am." He looked at me through his lashes. "To be honest, I just couldn't make it through one more day without seeing you."

"I'm so glad you're here. I was actually calling the airport when you knocked on the door. I was trying to get a flight to Chicago so I could see you," I admitted.

Ryan smirked at me. "I don't think Landon would have let you do that."

I narrowed my eyes at him. "Landon's my manager, not my boss. If I want to come see you, I will."

"Easy there, tiger," he said with a chuckle. "All I meant was Landon's the one who helped me set all of this up. He arranged my flight and got me a ticket to the concert."

Definitely giving my big brother a raise for this one. "So you saw the show?" I asked.

Ryan's face became animated as he answered me. "Yes! Oh my God, Carter, I thought you were incredible when I saw you playing in the bar at home, but seeing you up on that huge stage, with all the lights...Wow! You were mesmerizing. Your songs are better than anything else on the radio and then..." His words trailed off as he looked at me. "The song at the end, that you wrote for me..." He shook his head in awe.

"I wrote that the day after we said we loved each other. I meant every word of it too. It doesn't matter if we're in your bed in Chicago or this hotel in Atlanta, whenever I'm with you, I'm home."

We shared another lingering kiss and then he rolled off of the bed and stretched his hand out to me. "Let's take a long hot bath together and then I can make you all dirty again."

I placed my hand in his and let him pull me up then followed him into the bathroom. He bent down to start the water running and then wrapped his arms around my waist and pulled me close. He nuzzled my neck, breathing deeply and I lay my head on his chest, letting my fingers sift through the soft hairs there. I could feel his heart beat against my cheek and I closed my eyes, wishing the moment never had to end.

Ryan flipped on the radio that sat on the wide ledge that rimmed the sunken tub and then climbed in to sit in the warm water, helping me in next so that I sat straddling his hips.

"What's this? Did you get a new tattoo?" Ryan said as he noticed the colors underneath my arm for the first time. I couldn't really blame him; we had been pretty distracted earlier. I sat quietly as he lifted my arm to get a better view and I heard his sharp intake of air.

"I did it to symbolize the two of us," I whispered. His fingers trembled as they followed the lines created by the artist. Along the scars left behind from the fire, I had flames that morphed into a line of musical notes; the first few notes of the song I wrote for him to be exact, followed by a tiny guitar with the Superman logo as its skin.

Ryan leaned in and placed gentle kisses along the length of my tattoo. "That's permanent," he said in awe.

"So is my love for you." I reached for the soap and worked it into a lather between my palms, then let them slide over the smooth planes of his chest, my fingers circling his erect nipples. My hands continued their journey south over his washboard stomach until they finally landed on his straining erection. My fingers curled around his thick shaft and squeezed.

He was stunning with his head thrown back and his eyes shut. He groaned his pleasure and I felt it all the way down to the tips of my toes. I leaned down, and grazed my teeth along his Adam's apple, licking a line along his jaw.

His eyes flew open and he held my gaze as I lifted up onto my knees and lined the head of his cock up with my opening. I felt every ridge of his thick shaft as I slid down his length. The stretch burned my tender skin, but I welcomed the pain, wanting to feel him even after he was gone. I didn't know how long he would be there, but I was going to make the most of the time we had together. I heard

"Satellite" by Nickleback playing on the radio and I thought it fit the moment perfectly. The words described exactly how I felt, wanting to lock out the rest of the world and have this night just for the two of us.

I sat nestled against his groin and rested my head on his shoulder, savoring the moment. When the urge to move became too great, I lifted myself up and then lowered myself back down, circling my hips in a slow grind which issued a curse from Ryan. I was soon lost to everything but the electricity he was causing to spark throughout my body as he found my gland and hit it over and over again.

I reached between us for my cock, but he swatted me away and began fisting his own hand around my length. All too soon, I spilled over him, my internal walls clamping down on him tightly. With a loud gasp, Ryan came inside me. I watched as he brought his hand to his mouth and licked my cum from each finger. We stayed wrapped around each other until the water cooled then we dried off and climbed beneath the sheets together.

I reached for him and he pulled me up against his body, my head nestled beneath his chin. "I love you," he whispered as his eyes drifted shut.

"I love you too," I whispered back. I lay in the dark, listening to the sounds of his even breathing and thanked God for the perfect night we had together.

CHAPTER
Eighteen

Ryan

I CLIMBED OUT OF MY TRUCK FEELING HAPPIER THAN I HAD IN A long time. My time with Carter had been just what I needed. We had locked ourselves in the room for two whole days, doing nothing but talking and making love. We turned our phones off and other than having room service delivered out of necessity, we cut off all communications with the outside world.

I had expected to feel devastated when it came time to say good-bye, but instead I felt reassured that our relationship could withstand anything. Seeing him again had proved to me that no matter the amount of time or space between us, we would always be able to connect with each other because he was more than just the man I loved, he was my soul mate.

I had a lot of time to think on the flight home and I had come to the conclusion that Carter was my family, but so were the rest of the Greenes. I knew Kathy meant it when she said that they loved me and I already loved them back. If I was going to build a life with Carter, I had to quit shutting them out. It was time to show them that I was ready to let them in and what better place to start than with the person most like Carter: Caleb. *I just hope he forgives me for pushing him away.* Gripping the wrapped box in my hand, I took a deep breath and opened the door, smiling when the rich scent of garlic and tomatoes filled my nose.

A beautiful woman walked up to me with a smile and I quickly remembered that Carter had said her name was Lauren. "Hi! Ryan, right?"

I nodded at her. "Yes. Hi, Lauren. Is Caleb working tonight by any chance?"

"Yeah, he and G are in the office. Come on, I'll show you back there." I followed her through the busy restaurant and into the kitchen. A big bear of a man rushed up to Lauren with a question about a food delivery so she pointed me down a long hall to the office that Giovanni and Caleb shared. I could hear voices on the other side of the door and I swallowed my nerves as I knocked.

"It's open," I heard Giovanni's deep baritone call out.

They both turned their heads to me and Caleb gave me a dazzling smile when he saw who it was. I felt a tinge of sadness when his dimples appeared because they weren't the dimples I wanted to see in front of me, but I pushed the feeling aside as I smiled back at him. "I'm sorry to interrupt, but I was wondering if I could talk to you guys for a minute."

Caleb shared a look with his husband and then ushered me inside to take a seat. "Don't be silly, you're never interrupting. How have you been?"

"I'm good. Really good actually," I said with a smile. "I just got back from seeing Carter."

"Oh, I'm so jealous. How's he doing?" Caleb looked at me with longing and it hit me that he had been missing his brother almost as much as I had, but instead of helping him through it, I had selfishly only thought about my own loss.

I cleared the lump from my throat. "He's doing great. Gaining more fans each day and creating amazing music. I got to see his concert and he is absolutely doing what he was made to do. He misses home, but he's happy."

Caleb leaned back in his chair and his shoulders slumped in relief. I hadn't realized how much he had needed to hear that; to know that his twin was happy with the choices he had made.

"I'm so glad. I knew he would take the world by storm," Caleb said with conviction.

"I actually came here because I wanted to apologize to you, both of you." They wore matching looks of confusion on their faces so I explained. "I was raised in a pretty solitary home. As far back as I can remember it was just my grandpa and me. When he died, I was left all alone. I have my best friend, Joe, and his wife who are like family to me, but it's not the same as actually being a part of somebody's family day in and day out."

I paused to take a breath. "Then I met Carter and he became my family; he became my whole world. He invited me to be a part of your amazing family and I thought I had done that, until he left. I pushed you all away and in doing so, I know I hurt you guys as well as myself and I'm sorry for that. I went back to my old way of doing things, trying to get through the pain of missing him all on my own, but someone reminded me recently that I was wrong. That you guys love me for who I am and you were just waiting for me to get my head out of my ass and realize it too."

Caleb knelt by my chair and threw his arms around my neck. "You don't have to be sorry. We all deal with pain in our own ways. I'm just glad you're here now." I hugged him back, but pulled away when I heard Giovanni's deep chuckle.

"Don't beat yourself up. This family just has a way of helping you to see things more clearly. It was Carter who kicked my ass when *I* needed straightened out." Caleb shared a grin with him at the memory.

"Well, thank you for giving me another chance," I said solemnly.

"Oh please, do you have any idea how many chances I've given my *other* brothers?" Caleb raised his brows at me and I blushed as I caught on to the meaning behind his words. I wasn't just some guy dating his brother, I *was* one of Caleb's brothers too.

I reached down, picking up the box I had sat on the floor and handed it to Caleb. He looked at me questioningly, but then tore the paper off of it. He gasped when he saw what was inside, turning it to show Giovanni. It was a little pink dress that said, "My daddies love me" on the front. I blushed as they each took turns hugging me and then Giovanni insisted on feeding me before I left for work. I ate a heaping bowl of fettuccine Alfredo as they told me all about Sarah, the little girl who had already stolen their hearts completely. I felt like I truly fit in as they showed me pictures of my new niece.

I was still smiling when I walked into the station. It had felt good to spend time with Caleb and Giovanni. They were really incredible guys and I couldn't be happier for them that they were adopting their first child.

"Well, somebody looks like he's in a good mood. Did a visit with a certain rock star have anything to do with that?" I looked up to see Kevin sauntering down the hall towards me.

"He has a lot to do with it, but actually I was thinking about a girl this time."

His eyes grew so big his eyebrows disappeared behind his hairline. "Oh, wow! I didn't realize you were…"

I couldn't help the laugh that escaped my lips. "I'm not. I was just messing with you. I *was* thinking about a girl, but not in that way." Kevin gave me a curious look. "My brothers are adopting their first child. A beautiful little girl named Sarah. I just came from visiting them and got to see pictures of her." I shook my head. "I still can't believe I get to be an uncle."

"That's fantastic! Congratulations!" Kevin's face softened and he got a faraway look in his eyes. "I hope Toby and I are able to adopt someday," he said quietly.

I arched a brow at him. "I take it you guys are pretty serious then?"

He nodded with a shy smile. "I've been in love with Toby since we were twelve years old. He's the only guy I've ever loved." He glanced around to make sure we were alone then he leaned in to whisper in my ear. "He took me out on Saturday and asked me to marry him." When he pulled back his smile had stretched across his face and his eyes danced with happiness.

I grabbed him up in a quick brotherly hug. "I'm so excited for you. You deserve to be happy."

"Thanks. So do you." He patted my back as he stepped back.

"I'm happier than I've ever been in my entire life," I said honestly.

Just then, the alarm sounded and the door at the far end of the hallway slammed open as the other firefighters rushed passed us to get their gear. We leapt into action along with them, quickly changing into our turnout gear and climbing into our seats on the giant rig. Joe climbed in and sat beside me and within a matter of seconds we were barreling down the road to a massive warehouse fire.

When we arrived there were already five other fire divisions at the scene. The warehouse was home to a paint manufacturer and I could hear popping noises within the walls as cans of interior and exterior paints reached their pressure point and combusted. Because of the flammable substances manufactured there, the warehouse had become completely engulfed within minutes. The captain quickly briefed us on the situation, informing us that there were still many employees trapped inside the raging inferno.

I stood outside the building, surveying the trajectory of the flames. *I can't imagine anyone making it out of this alive.* I had a bad feeling that our job was going to be more of a recovery mission than a rescue. Someone bumped into my shoulder, pulling me from my thoughts and I scrambled to catch up with the others who were already securing their breathing apparatuses and helmets.

"Be safe in there, man. This is really fucked," Joe said with a grave look. He lowered the face shield on his helmet then walked away.

My heart kicked up a notch with his words. I bent to pick up my oxygen tank, swearing when I noticed the tape marked K. Collins. Kevin had somehow grabbed my tank instead of his. It was a careless rookie mistake and I was going to kick that boy's ass if he didn't start paying more attention to his gear. I glanced up, searching for him in the line of firemen, but I didn't see him. He must have already entered the building.

I hitched the tank up onto my back and adjusted the straps around my waist and over my shoulders. Adjusting the helmet on my head and securing the chin strap, I joined the formation of firemen as we walked in pairs into the burning building.

As I stepped through the doorway, I reached behind me to turn the nozzle on the tank, releasing pure oxygen into my mask. My pulse raced with anxiety and I tried to concentrate on the sounds of my breathing as I made my way through the blistering heat. Despite the fire retardant material of the suit, I could feel the heat singeing my skin and I soon had sweat dripping off of me and pooling uncomfortably in my uniform.

A chill swept through me as I heard the agonized screams of people all around me as the flames consumed their flesh. I had faced many horrific scenes in my years as a fireman, but the sheer number of lives that would be lost that day had me wanting to vomit. I pushed back my revulsion as we fanned out, determined to save as many lives as possible.

I blocked out everything else and focused on the job that I was there to do as I made my way towards the sounds of someone crying nearby. I pushed my way through fallen debris until I found a woman lying on her back under a table. There was a large piece of glass from a shattered window sticking out of her abdomen and a vast amount of blood pooled under her body. The look in her eyes told me that she knew she was going to die. Knowing that there was nothing else I could do for her, I bent down at her side and held her cold hand, speaking soothingly to her as she took her final breaths. I bowed my head and said a quick prayer that she was at peace.

"You got somebody?" I heard Joe's muffled voice through my helmet mounted communication system.

"She's gone," I answered solemnly. I started to lift her, but Joe stopped me with his hand.

"I'll take her out, you keep on looking okay? Maybe you can help the next one." I nodded to Joe. I appreciated the fact that he knew me well enough to know that after losing the woman, I would need to find someone who could be saved. It was the only way to lessen the pain; to feel like there was purpose to what we were doing.

"Thank you." I lifted the woman and gently deposited her into Joe's waiting arms then turned and began winding my way further into the building.

My ears perked up as I heard a muffled moan near me and I turned in the direction of the sound just as a blinding pain erupted across my lower back. My legs went weak and I stumbled to my knees as I was hit with another blow, that time to the back of my head, causing my helmet to fly off.

I lay on the gritty concrete, fighting back a wave of nausea. My head was pounding and the room spun around me. I blinked several times, willing my vision to clear as I tried to make sense of what had happened.

I jolted in surprise, sending pain searing through my body as someone leaned down next to me. A feeling of dread washed over me when I heard Dan's voice as he snarled through his helmet. "No hard feelings now, I just needed to rid the world of one less pervert. Oh, and don't bother with your oxygen tank, I drained it before we left the station. You only had minutes left as it was, I just couldn't pass up the opportunity to speed things along when I saw you wandering around all alone." He chuckled and it was the sound of pure evil. My head snapped to the side as his meaty fist connected with my jaw.

I heard him getting to his feet and I stretched my hand towards him, but he stepped out of my reach. A nearby explosion rocked the ground I was lying on and I squeezed my eyes shut as tiny pieces of dirt and debris rained down over me. I heard someone screaming my name, but all I could manage was a pained moan in answer.

Joe knelt over me, his eyes wide with horror as he looked at me through the mask. His hands roamed over my body, searching for injury and I cried out in pain as he touched my lower back. "It's okay, buddy, you're going to be okay. I'm going to get you out of here." His voice shook as he spoke to me.

"You've got to get Dan, he did this," I managed to get out, wincing as the hot air hit my lungs. Joe quickly slid his helmet off and held his mouthpiece to my lips. I took a grateful breath, the clean air choking me and leaving my body wracked with coughs.

"Easy, go slow. Take small breaths, not too much at once," Joe soothed. He glanced over his shoulder and his eyes were narrowed in anger as he turned back to face me. "Don't worry about him, he's not going anywhere."

I rolled my head to the side to look around my friend and saw Dan lying on the ground, his eyes closed. Paul was leaning over him, checking him for injury. I gave Joe a questioning look.

"I was on my way back to help you when I saw him go flying from the blast of the explosion. He's still breathing, just knocked out really good. Not that it wouldn't serve the asshole right if he had been seriously injured...or worse. We all heard what he said. Idiot must have forgotten about his helmet mic." I had never seen Joe so angry.

I suddenly grasped Joe's jacket in my hands. "Kevin's in trouble. You have to find Kevin." I paused to work through another coughing fit. My eyes watered from the smoke and the pain radiating throughout my body. "He doesn't have much time."

Blackness swirled around the edges of my sight and the room began to narrow into a small point of light. As I slipped out of consciousness I heard Joe answer me. "Rodrigues already went to find him. He'll make sure Kevin's alright. Now we've just got to get you out of here."

I woke to the sounds of quiet murmuring and machines beeping. I squinted my eyes against the light as I tried to make out where I was. A quick survey of the room let me know that I was in the hospital. Memories of what had happened in the fire floated back to me in bits and pieces and I did a simple inventory of myself to see what injuries I had incurred.

My head felt heavy and when I reached up carefully with my hand, I felt that it was wrapped in thick gauze. My fingers and hands worked fine, but a failed attempt at wiggling my toes had my heart racing. *Was I paralyzed?* Panic threatened to take over until I heard a familiar voice outside the door. "We need to be in there when he wakes up. He's our son and we don't want him to feel alone and scared."

The door swung open and Rick and Kathy Greene walked into the room. Rick looked more worried than I had ever seen him and Kathy had tears in her eyes when she saw me. "Oh, sweetie, we were hoping to be here when you woke up. How are you feeling? What can we do?" Kathy said as she gently kissed my cheek.

A flood of emotions swept through me. Relief at seeing them, love for them both for calling me their son, worry over what had happened to Kevin, and fear over my inability to move. Rick moved to my other side and grasped my hand in his larger paw. I clung to him like he was my safety net.

"Is Kevin alright?"

"He's fine. Your friends found him just as his oxygen ran out and were able to quickly get him out of the building," Kathy informed me. I sighed, relieved that Dan's evilness hadn't touched anyone else.

Knowing that my friends were safe, I was able to focus on my other concerns. "I can't move my legs," I said with a shaky breath.

"That's the block, son," Rick explained calmly. "When you were hit, it ruptured a disc in your lower back. They had to do surgery to repair the damage, but it will take some time for the epidural block to wear off. The surgeon said he'll be in to talk to you soon," he added with a reassuring squeeze of his hand.

"You took a pretty nasty hit to the head, but they said there's no permanent damage. Does it hurt? Do you need something for the pain?" Kathy asked. I nodded my head weakly and she raced from the room to get the nurse.

"Dear Lord, I hope she doesn't pull a scene from Terms of Endearment out there. I better go with her before she gets kicked out. There's nothing quite like a mama bear when one of her cubs is hurt." Rick hurried from the room and I couldn't help the laugh that rumbled through my chest even though it made the pain in my head worse.

A moment later the door burst open and Carter came running into the room. He skidded to a halt as he looked me over from head to toe. His lips quivered and tears swam in his eyes as he rushed to my side. His hands were shaking as he moved them gently over my face, down my nose and across my lips. "Baby," he whispered as he placed gentle kisses along my jaw and up to my ear, finally landing on my lips.

I reached up, sliding my hands around the back of his neck and held him close to me as I deepened the kiss. Pain, fear, and the realization of how close we had come to losing each other was poured into that kiss. Tears leaked from my eyes and I blinked them away as I looked into his emerald green eyes. "You're here," I whispered.

"Of course I'm here. I love you." He kissed me again, but pulled back in concern when a whimper escaped my lips.

"I'm okay," I assured him. "My head just hurts. I think more kisses will help."

Carter laughed quietly, but then his expression grew serious. "I could have lost you." His voice cracked. "I can't lose you, Ryan. We need to figure something out, because I can't lose you." I started to say something when I saw the panic in his eyes, but my words were cut off as the door opened and a nurse came in.

Carter stepped back as the young man administered medication into my I.V. "That should help with the pain. Make sure you're getting plenty of rest," he said, looking pointedly at Carter who nodded his understanding.

When the door shut behind the nurse, Carter came back to my side. He lovingly brushed his thumb over my cheek. "He's right, you need your rest. I'm going to wait outside. I think the entire Chicago Fire Department is in the waiting room." I could see the worry in his eyes as he turned to leave.

I reached out and grabbed his hand before he could go. "I don't want you to go. Will you stay with me while I sleep?"

His lips turned up in a spectacular smile. "I'll be with you for as long as you want," he promised as he crawled in and lay by my side, careful not to jostle me. His lips rubbed gently back and forth over my temple and he hummed quietly as I drifted off to sleep.

CHAPTER
Nineteen

Carter

I JOLTED AWAKE, A SCREAM THREATENING TO TEAR FROM MY throat. Nightmares had plagued me every night since Ryan's attack. They started out similar to the nightmares I had after my own fire, but soon morphed into more terrorizing images of Ryan lying trapped and helpless, flames threatening to take him from me. I turned my head to see Ryan sleeping soundly next to me and I let my mind wander over the events of the previous days as my breathing evened out.

The fire captain had come to see Ryan in the hospital and informed us that after relieving Dan of his duties, he had contacted the police to press charges against him. He would be facing attempted murder as well as multiple other charges. Ryan would probably be called to testify, but it was a weight off of our shoulders to know that

Dan wouldn't be able to hurt anyone else.

Ryan's surgeon had explained that while he had been able to re-pair the damage done to Ryan's back, the type of injury he had in-curred was considered career ending for his line of work. He would no longer be able to do the heavy lifting required to perform the du-ties of a fireman. I had tried several times to get Ryan to talk to me about how he was feeling about the stunning news, but he had re-mained pretty tight-lipped about it all and I admit it had me worried.

Landon had explained my need to be with Ryan to Lachlan Edwards who made arrangements for another singer to fill in for me in the concert line up until I was able to return. With Ryan safely at home, I was scheduled to head back to the tour in a couple of days, so I was determined to spend every minute of my time with him while I was there.

Knowing it would be impossible to return to a peaceful sleep, I decided to get up and cook breakfast for my man. I had brought him home after three days in the hospital and while he was healing quite nicely, he was still very weak.

I moved around the kitchen as quietly as I could, trying not to wake him. I scraped the pancakes free of the pan and flipped them over, wrinkling my nose at the blackened objects that resembled hockey pucks more than anything you'd want to eat for breakfast. *How the hell do Caleb's pancakes turn out so perfect all the time?* I dug through the cabinets, deciding a healthy dose of syrup would mask the burnt flavor.

I dished the food up and poured syrup over the unappetizing looking discs until they were swimming in it. I scooped some scram-bled eggs onto the plate, stopping long enough to pick out a few bits of shell that had somehow fallen in there. *Hopefully he won't notice.* I poured a glass of orange juice and placed it next to the plate of food on the tray then slowly carried it over to the bed.

Ryan was still sleeping soundly on his back so I set the tray on the bedside table then leaned over him, letting my nose run up the side of his neck. "Good morning, Sleeping Beauty," I whispered in his ear and his gray eyes fluttered open. A smile stretched his full lips when he saw me and I felt a stirring in my groin. I let my eyes wander over his smooth, tanned skin to where the white sheets pooled around his hips. *Delicious!*

"Did you cook something?" he asked, sniffing the air.

"I made you breakfast in bed," I answered proudly. He followed the smell until his eyes landed on the charred mess. He glanced at me out of the corner of his eye and I narrowed my eyes as I noticed he was trying not to laugh. "What?" I demanded, crossing my arms indignantly.

"Don't take this the wrong way, baby, because I really do appreciate the gesture, but…"

"But?" I urged.

A smile teased the side of his mouth. "But I was served better looking food in the hospital."

I huffed at him, pretending to be truly affronted. "Well that is the last time I'll ever cook for you, mister!"

"Promise?" he said with a laugh. I tried to stay serious, but my twitching lips gave me away.

"I know my cooking's terrible. That's why Giovanni banned me from ever stepping foot in his kitchen at the restaurant again."

Ryan pulled me in for a kiss, a happy smile on his face. "That's okay, baby. You have plenty of talent in other areas."

"That's right. I can play six different instruments," I said haughtily.

"True, but those weren't the talents I was referring to," he said as his tongue swept through my mouth.

Slyly, my hand crept over to the plate at the side of the bed and I dipped a finger in the thick syrup. I used it to leave a sticky trail down his neck and over his abs which I quickly lapped up with my tongue. "Sweet," I whispered, letting my hot breath fan over his straining member. His cock jerked under my supervision, bumping me in the chin.

I reached for more syrup and watched as the sugary substance dripped from my fingers onto his waiting tip. My tongue swirled around his mushroomed head, tasting the mixture of sweet syrup with Ryan's own salty goodness. He groaned as I let my teeth graze him and I looked up the length of his body to see him staring back at me intently.

He gasped loudly as I swallowed him whole and I reached up, placing his hand on the back of my head. He answered my silent request by threading his fingers through my hair and holding me to him, his trimmed pubic hair tickling my nose. When my lungs began to burn he released me and I slowly let his shaft slide from my mouth. A long strand of saliva stretched between my lips and his cock.

"That is so fucking hot," he moaned. "Come here, baby." He reached for my arms and started to pull me up, but I froze when I saw him wince in pain.

"Easy, Superman, I don't want to hurt you."

"Please don't stop. I need you, Carter," he begged.

I crawled up his body until we were aligned and looked at him sternly. "I won't stop as long as you promise to lie there and let me do all the work."

Ryan gave me a look that said he thought I was crazy. "I have a problem with that, said no man ever," he said sarcastically.

"Good. Now lie there and take it like a man."

I worked my underwear down my legs as I kissed him. Once I had kicked them free, I braced myself on one hand while my other wrapped around both of our shafts. I let my saliva drip over my fingers, using it to make the glide of my hand easier.

We both moaned at the delicious friction of our cocks as they rubbed against each other. Like a good patient, Ryan followed my orders, but he let his hands wander over my ribs and around my waist until his finger stopped at my entrance. He tapped against my hole and the nerve endings that surrounded my channel sparked to life.

"Ryan!" My voice shook. I wasn't going to be able to hold out for very long, the pleasure was too great.

"Kiss me," he demanded. I leaned down and covered his mouth with mine in a passionate kiss. His finger slipped inside me and fireworks exploded behind my closed lids as I flew over the edge.

Ryan's body jackknifed under me as he let out a loud roar. Silky ribbons of white landed on his chest as I continued to milk the two of us. Finally, he collapsed to the bed as small tremors continued to rack his body. I lowered myself next to him and licked every pearly drop from his skin. When he was all clean, I crawled back up his body.

He smiled at me as he licked a drop that lingered at the corner of my mouth. "Now *that's* breakfast in bed."

I sighed happily as I lay my head on his chest. "I hate to say it, but we need to get up and get moving. We're supposed to be at Romero's at noon."

Giovanni and Caleb had decided to host a lunch at their restaurant for the whole family so everyone could see each other since it was rare for Landon and I to both be in town at the same time. Other than the time at the hospital, I hadn't seen my family since I had left to go on tour. I missed them so badly, especially Caleb. It was torture being away from my twin for so long. I had already decided that if things worked out and I was sent out on tour again, I was going to make it a priority to spend more time with him.

After enjoying a shower together in which I took the opportunity to reacquaint myself with every single wet, soapy inch of my man, we got dressed and made it to the restaurant fashionably late.

"It's about time you boys showed up," Michelle said with a scowl.

"Yeah," Emma chimed in grumpily. "I hope you're happy. You kept two pregnant women starving with your tardiness." My eyes widened at the unusual hostility coming from my sisters.

"Girls, I have a treat for you. That's right, this way. Everything will be okay." I gave Ryan a confused look as my dad cooed at the women and led them over to a tray of appetizers. He spoke out of the side of his mouth as he walked by. "Your mother was the same way when she was pregnant. As soon as we feed the beast within, they'll return to their normal selves." We chuckled, but I was glad that I wasn't in love with a woman; that pregnancy stuff wasn't for the faint of heart.

Mom came up and gave us each a hug and I smiled as she fussed over Ryan, urging him to sit so he wouldn't wear himself out. Ryan looked flustered, but the small smile on his lips told me that he enjoyed having some maternal pampering in his life so I left him in her capable hands and wandered over to where my brothers were all gathered.

"Hey, Carter! Welcome home." Giovanni smiled at me and grabbed me in a strong hug. I laughed and patted his shoulders, waiting for him to let go so I could breathe again.

"Thanks! It's really good to be home," I said as I exchanged hugs with the other guys.

"Yeah it is!" Landon agreed. "I like seeing different places, when we actually get to stop and look around, but living out of a suitcase for months on end can really wear on you after a while."

"Try living with four other people on a bus and then we'll talk about who has it rough," I teased him.

"No thanks. I'll leave that to you rock stars," he said as he patted me on the back.

We stood around talking for a few more minutes and listened to Mark and Jason exchange their woes of living with expectant mothers. Finally, Caleb announced that lunch was ready and I quickly made my way over to Ryan and took the chair next to him.

When everyone was seated we all took hands and bowed our heads as Dad said grace. His voice was rough as he thanked God for bringing his boys home safely then praised Him for watching over Ryan and helping him heal. Ryan's hand squeezed my own and I was sure he was feeling as emotional as the rest of us at that moment. When we lifted our heads, I noticed more than one person wiping their eyes.

"Caleb, this looks incredible! I've missed your cooking so much," I exclaimed as we all began passing the rich, aromatic food that I was sure had taken my brother all morning to prepare. It looked like he had made enough food to feed an army, but knowing our group, we would manage to put a pretty large dent in it.

"Thanks," Caleb beamed at me.

"Seriously, little brother, the food on the road can't compare to yours," Landon agreed as he took a large bite of chicken parmesan, cheese dripping off of his fork.

I started to dig into my own plate of food, but suddenly felt really flushed. Startled, I glanced across the table to see Giovanni whispering something in Caleb's ear. Caleb blushed as his husband's hand disappeared under the table.

Caleb's gaze flew to mine, his eyes wide with shock when I kicked him under the table. "Knock it off," I hissed. "I'm picking up on your *strong feelings*." I gave him a pointed look and he smirked at me.

"I'm pretty sure that's just your own feelings whenever you're around Ryan," he whispered back. Giovanni chuckled and Ryan looked at me with his brow arched questioningly.

"There's no denying that," I said and leaned over to give Ryan a quick kiss.

Caleb and I exchanged happy smiles across the table. The rest of my family had probably figured I'd never meet someone that I would be serious about, but Caleb knew me better than anyone. He knew how I had longed for the kind of relationship he shared with Giovanni. Someone who I could call my own, who would not only be my lover, but my best friend as well. Now it seemed we both had found our soul mates.

I glanced around the room at my family as we laughed with one another and simply enjoyed being together. There was so much love and trust in that one room and I felt happier and more content than I ever had. No matter where my career led me or what people I met along the way, the people in that room would always be the ones who mattered most.

My phone rang as I walked out of the bank. I hated leaving Ryan when we had so little time together, but there were some necessary errands I had to run and so I had slipped out of the house while he took a nap. I grabbed my phone from my back pocket as I slid into my car.

"Hey! What's going on?"

"Are you sitting down?" Landon's voice sounded urgent and I immediately sat straighter in my seat.

"Yeah, I just got in my car. What's wrong?"

"Nothing's wrong, I promise. I just got off a video conference with Lachlan Edwards and you won't believe what he said." Landon spoke fast and I felt my heart rate speed up as I waited to hear what had him so excited.

"Spit it out, man. You're killing me."

"Sorry. Okay, you ready for this?"

"Landon," I growled, making him laugh.

"Alright, I'll quit teasing you. As you know he's been keeping a close watch on Carter's Creed. He's been very impressed with you guys and he likes what he sees. He said he doesn't need to wait until the end of this tour to know you guys have what it takes to make it."

I held my breath as Landon continued. "He's offering you guys a full recording contract and record label backing. He also wants Carter's Creed to go international. He's put me in charge of setting up a worldwide tour that will last a year. You'll begin and end in the States with shows all across Europe in between. This is it, man, you did it! Can you fucking believe it?"

"Wow! I think I'm in shock right now. Can I call you back later? I need to talk to Ryan."

"Of course, go tell your man the good news. I'll get started on this. And Carter? I'm really proud of you."

I thanked him and hung up. I lay my head back on the headrest and closed my eyes in stunned silence. Landon was right, this was everything I had ever dreamed of, everything I had worked for my whole life. Suddenly I pictured Ryan as he had looked curled up in bed, my pillow cradled against his chest like it was holding my place until I could return.

My eyes opened and I took a deep breath as I pulled the small black box I had bought that morning from my pocket. I opened the lid and smiled at the way the sunlight bounced off of the titanium band. I read the inscription inside. *The Music of My Soul.* I tucked the box back in my pocket and started the car. Ryan and I had some decisions to make about our future.

I let myself in the house and quickly climbed the stairs. Ryan was awake and in the kitchen with his back to me. He was shirtless and had a pair of gray sweats on that hung low on his hips, accentuating his pert ass. "Hey, baby, did you get everything done that you needed to do?" He smiled at me over his shoulder and I was relieved to see him looking so happy. How in the world could I walk away from this man again? *I can't. I won't.*

"Yes," I answered quietly and then slid my arms around his waist, letting my fingers trail over his smooth skin and rested my head on his shoulder as he stirred a pan of soup on the stove. I breathed in deeply, letting his masculine scent fill my lungs.

Ryan removed the pan from the heat and then turned in my arms and circled his arms around me, giving me a concerned look. "Are you okay?"

I gave him a tender smile, loving that he could read me so easily. I took his hand and led him over to the couch. "I'm fine, but I need to talk to you about something important."

Ryan turned to face me, giving me his undivided attention. He held both of my hands in his. "What is it?"

I cleared my throat as I studied our clasped hands. "Landon called me while I was out. Apparently Lachlan is very pleased with our work. He's offered us a full recording contract."

Ryan's eyes went wide and he let out a loud whoop then he pulled me against him and hugged me tightly. "I'm so proud of you, baby! You did it! I mean, I'm not surprised. Anyone with half a brain could see how talented you are and know that you were going to go far." He shook his head at me with pride. I felt his broad smile against my lips as he kissed me.

When he pulled back we were still smiling at each other. "Thank you. I appreciate your enthusiasm," I teased him with a wink before growing serious again. "But there's more I need to tell you." I swallowed hard as I delivered the rest of the news.

"As soon as this tour is over, we'll be hitting the road again. This time we'll be headlining our own concert and we'll be travelling all around the world." I watched the gamut of emotions that ran over Ryan's features. Pride, love, concern, and dread being a few.

He twined his fingers with mine and studied them as he spoke slowly. "Worldwide. Sounds like it's going to be a lot longer than three months this time."

"I'll be gone a year," I answered him and his shoulders slumped. I took his chin in my hand and lifted his face until he was looking in my eyes. "I told Landon I needed to talk to you about this first."

Ryan stood and walked over to the fireplace. His head slumped as he rested his hands on the mantle. "It's alright. I knew this was a very strong possibility when we first got together. Doesn't mean I have to like it though."

He straightened and rubbed his hands over his face then walked back over to me and sat down. "I love you, Carter. I will love you for the rest of my life and if I have to wait here while I share you with the rest of the world, I'll do that. I want you to be happy and your music makes you happy." He nodded his head as if convincing himself. "So you go out there and knock them dead and I'll be here when you get back, because you're worth waiting for."

"Thank you, but I don't want you to wait for me," I said firmly. When I saw the hurt in his eyes, I realized what my words must have sounded like. "No," I rushed on. "What I meant was, I don't want you sitting around waiting for me because I'm not going to go." I held my hand up to silence his protests.

"When Landon called to tell me the news, I was thrilled. It was everything I used to want for my life. Then I met you and my priorities changed. I no longer want to tour the world if it means leaving you again. You are my heart and my home and it nearly killed me being gone from you the last few months. I can't be away from you for a whole year, I just can't."

Ryan held my head between his strong hands and I leaned into his touch. His lips brushed over mine in a gentle kiss and then he trailed kisses over my eyelids and nose before landing one on my forehead in a tender gesture. "You are the most incredible man I have ever known and it means the world to me that you would give everything up to be with me, but I won't let you do that."

I pulled my head away from his so I could see his eyes. "But…"

"Hear me out. I have an idea of how we can compromise." He smiled when I nodded my head to let him know I was listening.

"I've had a lot of time to think since I've been laid up. I know you thought I was upset about the news that I couldn't be a fireman again, but I was surprised by just how little it bothered me. The things I've seen on the job; those kids that died…countless other tragedies and then the whole clusterfuck with Dan…I was already starting to feel like I didn't have what it took to do that job any more.

"I joined the fire department after my grandpa died because they offered a brotherhood that I desperately needed at the time. I was lost and I needed to feel like I belonged to a group of people. They became my family. I don't regret any of it because it led me to meet you and now I belong to a new family. You and the rest of the Greenes are my family."

I smiled at him, my heart surging with love. "You belong to us now." He gave me an answering kiss and then looked at me, biting his bottom lips shyly.

"So why have you been so quiet lately?" I asked.

"I've been trying to figure out what I want to do with the next chapter of my life. My grandfather left me enough money that I wouldn't ever have to work again if I didn't want to, but that's not who I am. I need to do something, feel like I'm making a difference with my life. I've been thinking about taking some online classes so I could become a firefighter instructor. If I do that, I was thinking maybe I could go with you on the tour, if that's alright with you."

I threw my arms around his neck excitedly then quickly pulled back, afraid I might have hurt him, but he laughed loudly and pulled me back into his arms. "Yes! That's more than alright. It's perfect!" I kissed him deeply, my enthusiasm and love for him pouring through. "Are you sure?" I asked when we stopped to catch our breath.

"I'm sure. I want to be with you as long as you want me there."

I smiled, knowing there was no better time for what I was about to do. "I will always want you with me, forever. In fact..." I got off of the couch and pulled the little black box out of my pocket. Ryan's eyes grew wide as I went down on one knee in front of him. "Ryan Marshall, you came into my life like Superman, saving me and literally breathing life into me. You are my best friend, my life, and my love. You are the music of my soul. I want to spend the rest of my life making you as happy as you've made me. Will you marry me?"

Ryan's eyes were swimming with tears by the time I finished and all he could do was whisper a ragged "Yes!" before I lunged for him. Our kiss was slow and deep, full of unspoken promises and hope for the future.

When we parted, I settled my back to his chest on the couch and he watched over my shoulder as I slid the ring down his finger. I let out a contented sigh as I admired the way it fit him. I liked the fact that the whole world would be able to see it and know that he was mine.

"So, you wouldn't have a problem sleeping with a college student?" he teased. My mind instantly scrambled as role playing ideas ran through my head. *There are so many possibilities: stern professor and student in need of a good grade, "straight" college roommates exploring their sexual curiosities for the first time...*

Fingers snapping in front of my face pulled me from my wandering thoughts and I found Ryan laughing at me knowingly. "No problem whatsoever," I murmured and reached down to adjust my cock which was pressed painfully against my zipper.

"Maybe we should go ahead and practice one of the kinky things that just went through that very creative mind of yours," he whispered in my ear as he reached around me and slid my zipper down.

I groaned as he freed my aching cock and began working it in his firm grasp. "Okay, but I get to be the college baseball coach and you're the player who got caught drinking and will do *anything* to not get kicked off the team."

"Fuck, baby, I love the way you think," Ryan said with a moan.

EPILOGUE

Carter

I ADJUSTED MY FAVORITE BEANIE ON MY HEAD, TRYING TO GET IT to lay just right before I had to go out in front of thousands of screaming fans. We had wrapped up the tour with Maximum Mayhem and Nathan and I promised to keep in touch. We were only given a month off in between tours to get everything ready. There had been a lot of prep work involved with putting a concert of this magnitude together, and my friends and I were thrilled when we finally got three whole days off before we had to leave again.

Ryan and I had spent most of that time with our family. We helped Dad knock off several items from the honey-do list Mom had made for him, then painted the room Caleb and Giovanni were setting up for Sarah. I smiled as I thought about how excited the two men were as the time neared for them to bring their little girl home. Any day they would get the call that the adoption could be finalized and I couldn't wait to welcome my new niece to the family.

We had been on the road for several weeks and things were

fantastic. We were playing to sold-out crowds nearly every night. The fans loved the new group, 96 Nations, who were opening for us, but they lost their minds when we took the stage. My bandmates seemed to be adjusting to the demands of being on the road long term with the exception of Rocko who still went off the rails occasionally.

I was much happier that time around. Instead of being lonely and miserable, I could focus more on the music and learning everything I could about the industry. I smiled as I looked in the mirror and caught a glimpse of the reason for my happiness, sitting only a few feet away from me.

Ryan was sitting in a comfy armchair with his feet propped up on the table in front of him. He had his laptop on his lap and his textbooks spread out beside him as he nibbled on a pencil, his brow furrowed in concentration. He took his studies seriously, but preferred to be near me as much as possible so most of the time he could be found with his nose in a book in my dressing room.

He had dealt with being thrust in the limelight rather well, considering what a private person he was. He still got flustered when complete strangers recognized him when he was out somewhere, but he was taking it all in stride. In fact, he had been amused at the magazine cover that had a photo of the two of us together. They had zoomed in on the ring I gave him and the caption read: *Hearts broken everywhere as music icon Carter Greene announces his engagement. Get the scoop on Cryan inside.* We couldn't help but laugh whenever we heard the terrible name combo Hollywood had assigned us.

I let my gaze wander over him. My fiancé was sexy as hell in his worn jeans and the tight Superman shirt I had bought for him as a joke. He ran his fingers through his hair and then glanced up, a smile spreading across his face as he caught me ogling him. "What are you thinking about over there?"

I looked at his reflection in the mirror and then lowered my lashes before bending over and spreading my hands flat on the surface of the makeup table. "Oh, nothing much. I was just thinking that you should pull my pants down and fuck me against this table so we can watch in the mirror."

I laughed as he scrambled out from under his work and came to stand behind me, his thick erection rubbing a torturous trail up and down my ass. I groaned low in my throat, cursing the layers of clothing between us. He reached forward and pinned my hands down on the table with his own. His tongue ran up my neck and then he used his teeth to nibble my ear, sending shivers of anticipation down my spine.

His eyes were a dark gray color as they found mine in the mirror. I called them his bedroom eyes. "There's only one problem with that," he growled.

"What?" I gasped as he sucked the sensitive spot below my ear.

"There are about ten thousand fans waiting for you right outside that door, not to mention your brother."

"That's what locks are for," I whined, still convinced I could get him to cave.

Ryan chuckled and kissed the back of my head. "Later, I promise."

"Fine," I grumbled then turned to poke him in the chest. "But just so you know, I'm wearing the green jock strap you love."

His eyes grew big. "The one that matches your eyes?" I nodded my head at him and let that mental image sink in. I knew my hero's weakness and sexy underwear was his Kryptonite.

A deep sound rumbled from his chest and he lunged for me, but I quickly darted to the door. "Uh-uh. You said we needed to wait and now you have to live with your decision; no matter how wrong it was." I laughed at his pitiful expression before closing the door and making my way to the stage. *God I love messing with him.*

"Thanks for coming, guys. This won't take long, but I needed to speak with you about an important matter." Landon led us into his spacious hotel room and motioned for us to have a seat on the couch. "Would either of you like a drink?"

I studied my brother carefully, wary of his strange behavior. He seemed nervous or agitated and he had a fine sheen of sweat on his brow. "I'm good, thanks," Ryan said and I noticed him looking at my brother oddly also.

"What's going on, Landon? You're acting weird. Well, weirder than usual," I joked, trying to get him to smile. It didn't work however because Landon plopped down on the chair across from us and eyed me worriedly.

"Look, there's no easy way to say this. We've received some strange letters lately and you need to be aware of what's going on."

My brow furrowed in confusion. "What kind of strange letters?"

Landon pulled a plastic bag out of his briefcase and laid it on the coffee table so we could see it. I leaned forward to get a closer look and saw that it contained a letter which had been typed neatly on a thick piece of blue stationary, much fancier than anything I had ever used. There was no signature other than a stamped picture of some sort of flowers and the words on it were shocking to say the least.

You are mine, Mr. Greene. You belong to me and no one else.

I swallowed the lump in my throat and Ryan grasped my hand tightly. He sounded angrier than I had ever heard as he stared Landon down. "What are you going to do about this? Is this the only one? We have to keep him safe, Landon." He fired off his words until Landon raised his hand to stop him.

"I know how you feel. He's my brother and I'll always do everything I can to keep him safe. This is the third letter we've received, all on the same stationary, all typed and they seem to be escalating. The first two we thought were fairly mild, just your usual fan adoration, but this one has a more sinister undertone. The person sending these letters is obviously obsessed with you and they seem to be getting more agitated." Landon looked tired as he ran his fingers through his hair.

"So what do we do now?" I asked him, reaching over to lay a comforting hand on his knee.

"Now, we increase your security. I've already contacted the studio and Lachlan Edwards is sending a personal friend of his to head up the security team. Since this threat involves you too, Ryan, you each will be assigned a security team that will be with you whenever you go anywhere until we determine there's no more threat."

Ryan and I exchanged a look. This was definitely one part of the job I could do without. Landon opened his mouth to say something, but was interrupted by a heavy knock at the door. I watched as his back straightened and his hands clenched at his side. Whoever was on the other side of that door was having quite an impact on my normally easy going brother.

Landon's jaw ticked as he made his way to the door and I stretched around Ryan so I could see who had him so riled up. As the door opened I heard a gruff voice but couldn't make out what the person said. It looked like Landon started to lean towards the person, but then he turned on his heel and made his way back into the room.

His face was flushed and he looked flustered as he walked towards me. My jaw about hit the floor when I saw the man dressed in black cargo pants and a tight black t-shirt stretched across his muscular chest following him. I had met him a few times before.

"Guys, this our new head of security, he's going to get to the bottom of our problems." The man and Landon exchanged a long look and I wondered how well they actually knew each other.

I stretched my hand out as he grasped it in a firm handshake. "Micah, it's good to see you again. Thank you for coming."

The End

ACKNOWLEDGMENTS

I want to thank the following people without whom this book would not have been possible:

My husband and children, for understanding my need to lock myself away from them for days at a time in order to meet my self-imposed deadlines and for truly being interested in and excited about my work.

Aimee, for always being patient with my never ending questions and believing in me even when I have trouble believing in myself.

Kerry, for bravely navigating your way through my book before any editing was done and for still loving me at the end. You are an awesome big sister.

Deena, for listening to my endless chatter about this new adventure in my life and for always standing by my side.

A giant thank you to my team whose knowledge, creativity and brutal honesty helped me to make this into the best book it could be. Pam Ebeler of Undivided Editing for your keen sense of my characters and for helping me stay true to who they really are. Thank you for your friendship and for your honest insights. Jay Aheer of Simply Defined Art for another beautifully designed cover and teasers. Your creativity and attention to detail never cease to amaze me. Stacey Blake of Champagne Formats for your work on the layout and formatting of my book. Thank you also for your patience in dealing with all of my little add-ons. Judy Zweifel of Judy's Proofreading for once again wading through my many flaws and making me look presentable. Jodie Temple for being willing to beta read for me a second time. Your thoughts and insights are always spot on. Thank you ladies, for your help and dedication to this project. I look forward to working with all of you again in the future.

Finally, I want to thank all of the readers who decided to take a chance on an unknown author and ended up falling in love with the characters as much as I did. Your enthusiasm, encouragement and kindness means more to me than you'll ever know.

ABOUT THE AUTHOR

I am married to my high school sweetheart who let's face it, is a saint for putting up with me all of these years. Together we have been blessed with the chance to raise two amazing human beings and so far we haven't screwed it up; I'll let you know for sure later. I am a business owner and spend more time laughing than actually working most days. I love watching movies, cooking, going to the beach and spending time with my family and best friends. I am an obsessive reader who is a complete sucker for a good love story, but loves to feel a broad range of emotions throughout a book. I think real life is hard enough and so my books offer twists and turns, but always with a happy ending.

I love to hear from my readers. You can reach me at:

Twitter – www.twitter.com/annabellamicha1

Facebook – www.facebook.com/profile.php?id=100011438515157

Blog – annabellamichaels.blogspot.com